THE
CRASH

THE
CRASH

KRYSTYNA KUHN

TRANSLATED FROM GERMAN
BY HELENA RAGG-KIRKBY

www.atombooks.net

ATOM

First published in Germany in 2010 by Arena Verlag GmbH
First published in Great Britain in 2012 by Atom

A CIP catalogue record for this book
is available from the British Library.

ISBN 978-1-907410-57-4

Typeset in Melior by M Rules
Printed and bound in Great Britain by
Clays Ltd, St Ives plc

Papers used by Atom are from well-managed forests
and other responsible sources.

 MIX
Paper from
responsible sources
FSC® C104740

Atom
An imprint of
Little, Brown Book Group
100 Victoria Embankment
London EC4Y 0DY

An Hachette UK Company
www.hachette.co.uk

www.atombooks.net

For Gisela. You are a star.
Thanks, too, to Dominic for his unstinting support.

CHAPTER 1

A stone plunged down. As it fell, it crashed several times against the cliff face, its muffled clatter still echoing around long after it had broken the smooth surface of Mirror Lake and swiftly sunk to the bottom.

Katie didn't let it distract her. She continued climbing. She was like a cat. And if she had believed in reincarnation and could have chosen what to be reincarnated as, a cat would undoubtedly have been at the top of her list. Not an ordinary pet cat, though. More like a leopard.

Some eighty feet below her, the glacial lake took up almost the whole surface of the valley. The morning sun, which was just rising behind the pale Grace College complex on the eastern shore, made the shadows on the surface of the water look like living creatures.

There wasn't a breath of wind, and Katie could sense that it was going to be another of those sunny autumn days that they had had for at least a week now. After the summer had been such a washout, the Grace students had stopped believing that the sun would ever shine again. For the past few days, though, it had been positively hot, and Katie feared that it couldn't last much longer.

It was almost seven a.m.

Katie hadn't needed an alarm clock to wrench her from

her restless sleep and the dream that had been replaying itself all night – or so it seemed to her, at any rate – as if someone had pressed a *repeat* button in her brain. She had opened her eyes just as dawn was bathing the snow-capped Ghost mountain range in an unreal light. Katie was clinging tightly to the cliff by the tips of her fingers, directly beneath the overhang that divided the ninety-eight-foot-high rock wall into two sections. This was the most difficult part of the cliff, and the chilly night had also rendered the stone cold and slippery. At least she could stand up on the ledge beneath the overhang.

It was impossible to turn back. She had already passed the point of no return. Katie had come to know this route so well that she could climb it free solo – without safety ropes and with only her chalk bag and the high-spec climbing shoes that she had bought in Fields. That was what made it so incredibly exciting: when it was just you and the cliff. Because that alone allowed you to keep looking forwards. Even if a mistake meant you would fall.

She was doing this for Sebastien. She was training her body, her spirit, her nerve. So that she could do the right thing if and when it ever came to it again.

Her right hand was searching for the first crevice in the overhang. She had two chances at most. Otherwise her strength would fail her, and without strength in her arms and fingers she would be done for here on the cliff. The hand-hold to the left worked, fortunately enough, because today of all days Katie was finding it hard to clear her mind. Maybe it was due to the fact that the college was right in the middle of preparing for a visit from the Governor General, who was

2

visiting all the top colleges in the country as part of a Canadian schools training initiative.

Most students in the lower years were expecting their parents to visit. So was it really any wonder that Katie was thinking about her own parents? You couldn't just erase the words Mom and Dad from your memory. Even if they didn't remotely deserve those names.

Katie had found the crevice, but her right index finger could feel a tiny stone inside it. It irked her, and for a moment she felt as if she were faltering. She stretched her left leg out to the side and immediately felt the ledge that she needed to use to swing herself up. She forced herself to concentrate; her body twitched, and she reached upwards with her right hand. But she could already tell that her first attempt wasn't going to work.

Beads of sweat were standing out on her forehead as she pulled her leg back in and put her right hand back in its former position. For several seconds she pressed her body against the cold cliff.

She cursed softly to herself. What on earth was wrong with her this morning? If her next attempt didn't work, she had had it. She could already feel her fingers trembling ominously.

When she had slipped out of the college a good hour ago, the apartment she shared with three other students, Debbie, Rose and Julia, had still been completely silent. Nobody would notice she'd gone – except, perhaps, for Julia. The others had got used to her doing her own thing and not giving a damn about the other students. All they ever talked about was courses, credits, grades and lecturers.

3

And anyway, nobody would guess that she might be up here in the restricted area. Not after the events of three months ago – the Night of Horror, as Debbie called it.

As if Katie were going to be put off climbing the cliff by a couple of metal warning signs. No: she, Katie West, would never accept restrictions imposed on her by other people. Not by the Dean, Mr Walden, not by her lecturers, and definitely not by her father.

She turned her head to the right where the Ghost, now bathed in the rays of the bright morning sunlight, was rising up above Mirror Lake.

Her next target.

Her heart started to beat faster with excitement and expectation.

Yes, the idea of it felt just right.

For the second time, Katie's hand felt along the cold, dew-damp stone for the tiny crevice above her. She finally found the stubborn hand-hold and clung on to it tightly. She stretched out her left leg.

Concentrate, Katie.

Just three feet. Just three small feet. And it took so much strength.

Risk everything, put all your eggs in one basket. And once she had managed to get to the end of the cliff face, she would feel free up there. Then she would be able to endure that day in the valley, just as she had already endured the past hundred days.

Giving up was not an option for Katie. She owed that much to Sebastien too.

Further up, the distances between the hand-holds

increased. She shook one arm, then the other, and reached into the chalk bag around her hips.

Her left leg seemed almost to be boring its way into the cliff as she now forced herself against it with all her might.

Take it gradually, Katie. Slowly.

Everything was resting on the next attempt. She mentally ran through the movements. It was her route. She knew every bit of it, and she herself had given it its name.

Black Dream.

She had never found any evidence to suggest that anyone before her had climbed the cliff. No hooks, no line in the rock, no trace of anyone.

And once you've managed to climb this route without ropes, once you've managed to climb up there just by the strength of your own body, you will feel good. So damned good!

In the silence she counted backwards from ten. As she reached three ... two ... one ... zero, she took a deep breath then stretched out her body until she was hanging above the ledge that she had just been standing on.

Yes!

This cliff was her cliff. This morning was her morning. This day was her day. And nobody – especially not her father – could take that away from her. Not him. Especially not him.

George West, her father, had suddenly stood before her one day, holding that letter. 'I didn't know you'd applied for this college.'

Katie had just shrugged. 'It's my decision.'

'So you want to go to Canada?'

Canada? Before, Katie would never in her wildest dreams have come up with such an idea. But the business with Sebastien had been just a few weeks earlier. He had been her first boyfriend. Her first and only, and she would have given anything for him still to be alive.

'Why not Canada? What've you got against Canada? Would you rather I stayed in DC and went to Georgetown University?'

'Absolutely not. It's bad enough seeing your picture in all the papers.'

'Too right. So why would you still need me here live and in full Technicolour?'

And her mom? She had adopted the completely emotion-less mask of the Chungs, a facial expression that had been carried down through the generations of the Chung clan, an inalienable part of the gene pool. But during the days before Katie's departure, she had been unusually agitated. She had been wandering around the huge apartment, her hands con-stantly busying themselves with moving chairs, opening and closing drawers, plumping up cushions. Almost as if her daughter's departure were panicking her. But then she hadn't even raised her hand in farewell. Nor had she come out with the typical sentence that all mothers deliver to their eighteen-year-old daughters who are about to start a new life two thousand miles away: 'Give me a call.'

An electric shock jolted Katie's heart. Well, biologically speaking, it wasn't an electric shock – but that's what it felt like. One of those briefest of moments when the most impor-tant organ in the body, the one that keeps you alive, loses its rhythm. And all because of these miserable memories.

She was dead in her parents' eyes anyway.

Other way round, Katie, you have to think the other way round. They're dead in your eyes.

For a moment, she felt utterly miserable. She was still clinging, straddled, to the cliff. She gritted her teeth and could feel her sweaty fingers slipping. Her knees were trembling.

Had her thoughts about her parents, the electric shock, broken her concentration? She knew that this could cost her her life.

But then she realised that it was something else that had startled her. And the next moment, she could hear it.

A rockfall.

Coming from directly above her.

Her fingers were clawing at the crannies in the rock. Her feet were glued to the cliff; she didn't dare move so much as a hand. A stone came whizzing past her. She instinctively moved her head forwards.

Her helmet! She had left it in her room. She'd simply forgotten it.

A quick look up the cliff. The pale light of the morning sun was painting shadows on the rock. The morning sun. For a fraction of a second, it flashed in Katie's eyes.

Her head banged against the cliff.

CHAPTER 2

Damn! She'd overslept. Even though Chris had promised to set his mobile for four a.m. If he hadn't been tossing and turning and talking in his sleep, she'd still be asleep herself.

Julia quietly pulled the door of apartment 113 behind her and took a deep breath before tiptoeing up the stairs. If anyone caught her and discovered that she'd spent the night with Chris, she'd be in trouble.

A heap of trouble.

Julia grinned to herself. In deep shit, more like. The word 'trouble' didn't actually feature in her vocabulary. 'Trouble' was a stained t-shirt or a worn-down heel; it was a little scratch on the shiny veneer of everyday life. Wow: she really was on good form this morning. She ought to remember that last sentence for Mrs Hill, who ran creative writing courses along with teaching English literature at the college.

Once on the second floor, Julia quietly opened the glass door that separated the stairwell from the long corridor that housed the fresher girls' apartments. As always, a strange smell permeated the dark, wood-panelled corridors. Something along the lines of old sweaty socks and heavy-duty cleaning products that had long since been condemned as environmental hazards.

It was almost half past five. Too early to be running around out there in a t-shirt, half naked; and too late to be certain that nobody would be awake yet. Isabel Hill, senior year student and in charge of the second floor, was among the early risers and liked to go jogging at this time of day. Julia couldn't understand why on earth the college authorities had allowed the senior students to carry on being mentors, given that they were the ones who had organised the illicit party at the lake three months ago which had led to the dreadful Angela Finder catastrophe.

Dean Walden, though, evidently didn't have a problem with it. Maybe that was partly because of Isabel's parents being lecturers at Grace.

Julia darted past the lifts, heading for her room which was right at the end of the corridor. It wasn't the first time she had spent the night with Chris, thus breaking one of the college's strict rules. Not that the violation of the sacred house rules bothered her. What did bother her was the fact that she seemed to be addicted to being around Chris. In the back of her mind was always the fear that she couldn't bear to be alone. The nights in the valley were the worst thing of all. When the darkness and the silence teamed up, opening the floodgates to terrible memories of the past and panic about the future.

Was it really Julia who went creeping down to the boys' apartment at gone midnight? Or was it her former self, Laura de Vincenz? The girl she had been before her parents had been so brutally murdered – the girl whose identity kept trying to force its way to the surface? Like a ghost from the past that goes flitting around the never-ending corridors of old buildings?

9

Nobody here at the college knew that Julia and her brother Robert had started a new life under the German witness protection programme. Not even Chris knew. Especially not Chris.

She urgently needed to talk to Katie about Chris. Not that you could really talk to Katie. It was more a case of Julia doing the talking, while her standoffish flatmate listened. And if she ever did offer any kind of comment, it never involved sympathy or understanding but, at most, a kind of dispassionate acceptance.

'Why are you always moaning about Chris?' Katie had said more than once. 'If he doesn't talk to you enough, then ask him some questions. Maybe he's one of those people who only functions in dialogue.'

'But what does he really want from me?'

'How about sex, for starters? He doesn't need to talk to have sex. Men only talk if they're trying to get women in the mood. I reckon that's the only reason they ever learn to talk at all.'

The more Katie badmouthed Chris, the more vigorously Julia defended him. 'But he says he loves me. Over and over again!'

'That's lovely. But I don't understand why it sounds so desperate when you say it.'

That was normally the point at which Julia changed the subject, since she really had no idea why Chris kept plunging her into this kind of despair. Because it had been so totally different with Kristian, perhaps? No: it's you, Julia, she thought. You were a different person then. She turned the handle of apartment 213 which, like all the four-bedroomed apartments, branched off from the long main corridor. As she quietly shut the door behind her and crossed the hallway, she heard a rustling sound coming from the kitchen.

That was all she needed. Probably Debbie in the middle of one of her binges. As if breakfast weren't going to be served in the refectory in an hour's time.

Julia stopped and listened. Somebody opened and shut the fridge door. That girl had a serious addiction – and Julia wasn't thinking about Debbie's bingeing, but about her insatiable urge to worm her way into other people's lives, suck them up, then pass on everything she knew from one student to the next. Like wildfire. Faster than any virus.

Julia could see her plump flatmate approaching the glass door. She already had her hand on the handle. All Julia could do was dart into the nearest room.

Katie's room was almost completely dark. But only almost completely. Here and there, the pale morning light was managing to find its way through the little cracks in the worm-eaten shutters. Like Julia's own, Katie's room was tiny. The left-hand wall was completely taken up by a wardrobe and a small bookcase; opposite was the bed, and to the right, was the desk. Julia slowly groped her way forwards, hoping that she wasn't going to frighten Katie to death.

As if anything could frighten Katie, she thought. At any rate, she must sleep like a log, for Julia could hear neither her bedcovers rustling nor the sound of her breathing. As though someone had pulled the plug on her.

In the hallway outside, she could hear Debbie's shuffling footsteps and her flip-flops slapping against the lino. Then she heard a door shutting.

In the darkness, Julia bumped against something that suddenly moved. The shadow of the old rocking chair swayed to and fro. Katie had bought the hideous piece on eBay, and spent more time in it than she did in bed. Sometimes when Julia was passing Katie's room, she could hear the chair creaking to and fro, to and fro. Another thing that didn't seem to go with her uncommunicative flatmate, just like the photos and pictures that she'd plastered all over the walls of her room.

Katie was the only one who had rearranged her unwelcoming college room with its wooden ceiling, shapeless utilitarian furniture and grey walls.

Julia sidestepped the chair, which was still rocking to and fro, and groped her way forwards towards the bed. There was still not a sound to be heard.

She wondered briefly whether she ought perhaps to let Katie carry on sleeping, but she was too wide awake and too overwrought to sit on her bed twiddling her thumbs. After all, Chris had said those three words again last night: *I love you*. And Julia didn't know whether to be glad about it. She absolutely had to talk to someone.

'Hey, Katie,' she whispered.

No reaction.

Julia cleared her throat, audibly this time. 'Katie!'

Nothing.

God, it was going to take shock treatment. Julia fumbled for the bedside light, and the next moment the room was filled with a glaring light that dazzled her.

But nobody gave an angry exclamation – and Julia could now see why.

Katie's bed was empty. The covers had been smoothed down, and the pillow looked untouched.

Julia put her hand beneath the covers. It was icy cold.

Katie seemed not to have slept at all – or, at any rate, not in her own bed.

And although Julia's brain was telling her that there had to be a completely harmless explanation – after all, her own bed had lain untouched that night – she couldn't stop herself from thinking about that dreadful night three months ago.

The night that had ended with Angela Finder, one of the senior students, going missing from her room. Julia and the others had found her – in the lake. She would never forget the sight of the corpse, its long hair drawing through the water like fine threads.

CHAPTER 3

Don't lose consciousness.

Don't lose consciousness.

DO NOT lose consciousness!

Katie murmured the words to herself like a mantra as she clung helplessly to the rock.

Beneath her gaped a sixty-six-foot drop. If she fell from the cliff, she was done for. Something wet was running down Katie's forehead where she had banged her head against the rock.

Forget it. Forget the blood. All you have to do is cling on. Press yourself against the cliff. That will keep you safe. Come on: you've spent weeks training for this.

She could hear a noise from above. A scraping, then a rustling. It finally brought Katie to her senses.

'Is anyone there?' Only after a moment did she realise that it was her voice that sounded so thin and hesitant in the morning air. She tried again, more firmly this time. 'Here! I'm here!'

No reply. Just the gentle breeze wafting over the cliffs, and the roaring of her voice in her ears.

No one was there. Of course they weren't. Nobody went roaming around in the restricted area – especially not at this time of day. It must have been some animal. An animal, Katie? When was the last time you saw an animal here?

Anyway. The main thing was that no more stones were falling away.

Secure yourself.

The procedures, the climbing movements that Katie had memorised, always the same pattern that made the difference between life and death, emerged from the depths of her subconscious and took control once more. Katie tightened her grip in the crevices whose sharp edges were cutting her hands, and breathed deeply in and out.

If only her toes didn't feel so numb and lifeless, as if they were made of plastic. When Katie moved to check whether they might in fact have dropped off, she could feel her whole foot slipping.

Damn it! Hold tight and keep your balance. You're not a beginner.

Her heart was pounding in her chest and she could feel her entire body trembling. Katie knew she had to calm down and regain her concentration before she could climb any further.

Breathe in. Breathe out. Find your own rhythm. As regular as clockwork.

That's what Sebastien had taught her.

No, don't think about him. Not here, not now.

Katie moved her head slowly so she could look up the cliff. She could see nothing but grey rock above her.

There was serious risk of a further rockfall.

Her father had called it an addiction, an obsession, a form of madness. Whatever. She didn't have any choice. Being up high was something that helped her keep things in perspective. And heights had always been Katie's only escape.

'You're toying with your life, Katie!' the bald psychiatrist had said to her. Her father had insisted that she see him.

'Oh yeah? I thought I was toying with death. You know. Like hide and seek. I'm challenging death, you see? I'm saying to him: here I am, bet you can't catch me.'

'Are you afraid of life?'

'No. I'm just afraid of being bored.'

'So you need the kick to make you feel something?'

'Just in the way that you're using my problems as a way of hiding your own.'

'Right,' he'd said. 'That's what you're doing, Katie. You're running away.'

Crap, Katie was thinking now. All that drivel was just a pile of crap. What did he or anyone else know about why she did what she did? She just loved heights and hated the depths. End of story.

But on this cliff she still hadn't moved. She couldn't feel her fingers any more either.

Come on, Katie, she told herself. Don't give up. Don't prove them right.

She could taste the metallic tang of blood on her lips. She took another deep breath, shut her eyes, opened them again, let the air stream through her lungs, and then removed her right hand from the crevice. Her arm swung upwards and almost simultaneously her fingers felt for the cliff above her.

Not every cliff face had a hole, a crack, a gap that you could cling on to. But there was one there, she knew it. She just had to find it.

There. It was more a crack than a hole, but no matter.

Okay. Stick with it. Now for her left foot. Almost immediately, Katie saw the ledge out of the corner of her eye, even though it was inconspicuous. Almost as if glued to the cliff, she pushed herself upwards, her knee bent. Just a bit further – would it be enough?

Yes.

Her leg finally found its support, and she pulled herself up. One final heave, and it was done.

Done – and by her alone.

She, Katie West, had conquered this overhang. Rockfall or no rockfall, head wound or no head wound.

Nothing and nobody could stop her.

Katie could feel the adrenaline whizzing around her entire body. It felt heavenly. And she suddenly remembered why she was doing all this. Why she was alive at all. Now no more than sixteen feet to go. Child's play. A moment later, she had done it. She had reached the top ... As Katie dropped down to the damp ground and stared at the mirror-like lake below her, she could have cried with triumph and happiness.

It was like being intoxicated.

A feeling of power and freedom that you couldn't help but find addictive.

No, Sebastien wouldn't have wanted her to give up.

Barely two hours later, Katie found herself staring through the huge panoramic windows of the foyer at a group of workmen on the meticulously mown lawn. They were busily setting up folding chairs in front of the temporary stage that faced the lake.

The college was making such a fuss about the Governor

General's flying visit that anyone would think the Queen of England herself were coming, rather than her proxy. The Governor was visiting five specially chosen colleges. Her tour had something to do with new education laws that had been passed six months ago. Katie had already forgotten exactly what it was all about. How weird that Canada was still a monarchy. And hadn't anyone noticed how absurd it was that the *Grace Chronicle*, the student rag, was actually saying that the visit of The Honourable Michaëlle Jean and her viceregal husband was a great honour for the college. Katie still couldn't understand it.

There would be a couple of speeches, clever lectures by the professors, the Governor General would presumably nod wisely and do a lot of hand-shaking. Then it would be time for the press – a couple of interviews and photos – and then the nightmare would be over. Katie knew all about these phoney events. Her childhood had been full of them, and she loathed them more than anything else in the world.

Politicians. They were just like this college – or its facade. Everything – entrance foyer, refectory, sports centres, seminar rooms – so splendid, so immaculate, so beautiful. But behind all this, where real, grey everyday life happened, it looked completely different. The college consisted of a historic main building with several lower and longer annexes and bunga-lows behind it, all connected by underground tunnels. The whitewashed complex, arranged in three wings, looked invit-ing at first glance. But although the campus had been renovated not all that long ago – when the college had been re-opened – entire blocks of the older part had been left out, as if they had run out of money.

The paintwork in the long corridors of the side wings, for instance, which housed the student apartments, still bore the cracks of the last decade, and the stairwell walls were covered in ancient graffiti.

The Governor ought to look at that bit, thought Katie. That would give her a very different impression. But the Dean, Mr Walden, would be bound to know how to avoid that.

When Katie had returned to her apartment, she had been relieved not to bump into any of her flatmates. It meant she was spared the concerned looks and persistent questions.

Debbie in particular couldn't get her mind around the fact that Katie invariably ignored her. Rose, for her part, kept trying in her low-key way to get Katie on side and gain her trust. But Katie normally rebuffed her too. The only one who had remotely gained her confidence was Julia. That might be due to the fact that they shared a secret: together, they had sunk Angela Finder's secret files in Mirror Lake. They hadn't needed to swear each other to secrecy. Katie was quite sure – as sure as you could be, where another person was concerned – that Julia was never going to breathe a word about it.

'Hey Katie, you're late!' A voice jerked her back to reality. Standing in front of her was David Freeman, one of the boys in their gang, as Debbie called it. Katie had never felt like part of any gang. She didn't mind David, though, simply because his life strategy was based on dogged patience and what Katie could only call naive optimism. Everyone liked David. Hardly anyone liked Katie – but the feeling was pretty much mutual.

David, clad in black as usual, was carrying a couple of books.

'If I'd known what was going on here, I wouldn't have

bothered getting up at all!' She pointed to the workmen who were installing one row of chairs after another. 'Have you seen the crowds out there?'

'The college wants to show the Governor and all the parents its best side.'

'Well, they need to after Angela's death. Students dying isn't exactly a great advert for the college.'

Katie noticed David looking at her. 'What's that on your forehead?'

She shrugged and turned away. 'Bumped into a tree.'

David shook his head. 'Has anyone had a look at it?'

'Nobody needs to look at it, okay?'

Then she turned on her heel and ran up the stairs to the refectory on the first floor, where most of the students were clearing away their crockery and leaving the room. Her hand touched the plaster on her forehead. A look in the mirror had shown her that the wound was quite deep.

She automatically pushed a strand of black hair across her forehead in the vain hope of hiding the plaster. Though the others could think whatever they liked. Nothing and no one could spoil the elation she had felt that morning.

When she left the serving counter, her tray was fully laden with a double helping of scrambled egg, granola, wholemeal bread, yoghurt and fruit.

'So what's up with you, then?' came a mocking voice behind her. Katie turned and saw Chris standing there. 'It must have been a hard night for you to be that starving. You normally only eat fruit and vegetables.'

'Dreams can be exhausting too,' she replied as cheerfully as possible, and turned her back to him.

20

'And dangerous. What happened to your head?'

Katie rolled her eyes. So much for being cheerful. Oh well, she'd tried.

'I cut myself shaving,' she retorted sharply.

Chris laughed.

'And, by the way, it wouldn't hurt you to shave either.' Katie picked up her tray. 'I'm not sure Julia's that keen on three-day stubble.'

As he always did when the conversation turned to Julia, Chris went weird. As if she belonged entirely to him. 'Don't you start telling me what Julia likes!' There was a smug undertone to Chris's words. Katie was sure that Julia had spent the night with him again.

She had no idea what Julia actually thought of Chris – but that really wasn't her problem. She pushed past him with her tray and thrust her way through the crowd of people streaming towards the door.

The sun was shining through the high glass doors that led out to the balcony. Most of the tables there were occupied.

This part of the college had been built at around the turn of the last century. The main building always reminded Katie of one of those gigantic manor houses in pseudo-historic romantic movies. It consisted of one central building and two side wings, all dripping with chimneys, bays and balconies. At the heart of the building was the huge entrance foyer with the refectory stretching above it.

As she always did when she was up there, Katie found herself looking across the broad surface of Mirror Lake at the massive rocky face of the Ghost with its two lower neighbouring peaks and the glacial area behind it. So far away and yet so monumental, as if they had been put there by human hands as a memorial to God's almighty power. Which Katie, by the way, didn't believe in. And yet the mountains exerted an irresistible pull on her.

Why the fascination?

Katie thought once more about what she had undertaken. The Ghost was her next target. But if she wanted to reach the summit that year, she couldn't wait much longer. There wasn't any snow on the cliffs yet. She had analysed the weather reports for recent decades and had made detailed enquiries. There was almost always a period of calm before the autumn storms. And the forecast for the next few days was good; the forecasters were up to eighty-five per cent certain.

But you could never be entirely sure in the mountains. The weather could change, and then ...

'Hey, Katie, is that, like, blood under your plaster?' Debbie's shrill voice penetrated her thoughts.

Katie turned her head. She was standing right next to the table where her flatmates were sitting: Debbie, or Deborah Wilder, Rose Gardner and Julia. Julia's brother Robert was there too, but he had his nose buried in a book as usual and didn't look up as Katie put her tray down.

Katie liked Robert, even though lots of people at the college thought he was some kind of psycho. But Robert could see things that others couldn't even guess at. He had even predicted Angela's death. And he asked different questions from everyone else.

If Katie had learnt one thing over the last few months in the valley, it was that up here in isolation, shut inside the cliffs, the answers weren't always as clear and straightforward as everywhere else in the world.

This both excited and horrified her. And if her parents knew how she felt they would immediately come and fetch their daughter and put her in a psychiatric ward.

But the really thrilling thing was that everyone had to find the answers for themselves. And Robert was the only other person who could see that.

Even Julia, his sister, was different in that respect. That evening in May when Katie and Julia had thrown the memory stick into the lake and the water had swallowed up their secrets, Katie had been sure that she understood too. But since then there had been several instances when she'd had her doubts about Julia. She hadn't doubted that Julia had good reason to destroy the information that Angela Finder had gathered about them all – but she had doubted whether Julia had a strong enough personality to do battle with the valley.

Do battle with the valley? she thought. God, Katie, are you going mad?

She sat down next to Julia, who gave her a concerned look. 'Where were you this morning?' she whispered to Katie. 'I looked in your room, but you'd disappeared without trace. I was going to send out a search party after breakfast!'

'Later,' Katie replied, glancing at Debbie. Debbie was scrutinising them curiously and was evidently just about to repeat her question about the injury. In order to draw attention away from herself, Katie raised her hand and said: 'Not a word, no questions, and absolutely no dumb comments about my plaster! Just shut up and let me get on with my breakfast in peace. Unlike you lot, I've still got time before that bastard Mr Forster drives me nuts with his never-ending sentences.'

'If you hate the subject that much, why did you choose to major in French?' asked Rose. Beautiful Rose who seemed so gentle but who specialised in trying to prove to others how inadequate they were. Or that's how it seemed to Katie, at any rate.

'And why are you bald?' Katie snapped at Rose. 'Didn't I say no questions?'

For a moment, an icy silence reigned at the table. Even Robert looked up from his quantum physics book.

Katie could feel Julia giving her a sidelong glance. Yes, she knew that as soon as she appeared in any cosy little group, the mood plummeted to sub-zero – even if she was on good form, as she was today.

Rose stood up, stood there for a few seconds undecided, then finally turned to Julia. 'Coming, Julia? Isabel's looking for volunteers for the information stall about all the societies at Grace.'

Julia looked hesitantly from Katie to Rose.

Katie found herself suddenly desperate for Julia to stay.

The commotion in the college and the sight of the triple peaks in the beaming sunlight had strengthened her resolve. She simply couldn't get the idea out of her head, and she urgently had to talk to Julia about it.

But you could never be sure with Julia. Sometimes she had the feeling that Julia was two different people. Julia often just went along with everything without asking any questions; she would take the easiest route simply to avoid rubbing anyone up the wrong way. At other times, though, she'd act all cool and aloof. If Julia went with Rose, there was no way Katie was telling her flatmate about her plan. But like hell was she going to give Julia even the tiniest pleading look, never mind say anything. She could go with Rose and show off the country's future elite to the Governor and all the others. She could sell Grace to all the proud parents as some kind of paradise. Katie didn't care.

Oddly enough it was Debbie who decided the situation in Katie's favour. She suddenly jumped up and before Rose knew what was going on, Debbie was blazing at her. 'Why don't you ever ask me, Rose? Why's it always Julia? As if all the boys don't fancy her anyway!'

As so often when Debbie got worked up, she generously sprayed her saliva around the assorted company. Katie herself managed to avoid the spray, but she saw Robert taking off his round glasses and wiping them, a disgusted look on his face, as Debbie continued her poisonous tirade. 'Do you think I don't know what you get up to at night, Julia? Hopping from one bed to another ...'

'You shut up now, Debbie, or ...' David was suddenly standing by the table with the angry expression on his face that always made Katie think that she wouldn't like to have him as her enemy. He was forever suppressing his aggression. Katie was quite sure that if he ever let it out there would be a massive explosion. And that would put paid to his nice-guy reputation.

'Or?' Debbie's face was the colour of a tomato. 'Or? Or what? Trust you to defend her. Maybe it's your bed she was creeping out of this morning ...'

'Debbie, that's enough!' Rose grabbed her arm. 'And I don't mind you coming in the slightest. But let's get a move on. I have no desire to end up on the politics stall.' She dragged Debbie away with her.

'My God,' Julia burst out. 'I'll really go for her one of these days.'

'Watch what you say,' David replied sombrely. 'Don't forget what happened to Angela.'

'Why do people have to keep on bringing that up?' Katie demanded. 'Did they print it in the prospectus for the Governor? The particular highlight of Grace: murder included. And I bet there's some detailed information sheet somewhere about the other students up here in the seventies ... '

It was Robert who interrupted Katie. Julia's younger brother snapped his book shut, stood up and turned to Katie. 'You keep Julia out of it!'

Then he left the table.

Baffled, Julia watched him go. Several seconds later she turned to Katie and asked: 'Keep me out of what? What did he mean? Have I missed something?' And then, more quietly, 'Where were you this morning? Have you got a secret lover or something?'

But Katie's only thought was: I have to find out whose side she's on.

CHAPTER 4

Katie was sitting abstractedly in her Proust class, amazed that a writer could need seven books to tell one story – and one story that he'd called *Remembrance of Things Past*.

Proust was Mr Forster's specialist subject, and this particular work was his hobby-horse. And given its length, he would have no trouble occupying his students with it until he took retirement. The author's slow pace had evidently rubbed off on the lecturer – he had the annoying habit of swallowing after practically every word, with the result that his lectures seemed to go on for ever.

But while Forster's reputation among the students might have been debatable, Proust scholars around the world were in complete agreement that Forster was the best in the field.

Katie didn't give a damn about that. Yawning, she stared at the map that she had doodled on her notepad. Studying meant so little to Katie that she had spent the last few weeks as if in a trance – not that it mattered so long as her grades remained high. So while Mr Forster delivered his lecture, she busied herself with writing an alphabetical list of all the equipment she would need for her expedition, and mentally ran through her trip once more.

It seemed to her that there was in fact only one suitable way to reach the main summit of the Ghost.

The steep face was ruled out, much to Katie's dismay. Even from here, she could see that she would need to be with a whole team of experienced climbers. She had asked around several times, but had had to put the idea out of her mind – for the time being.

Climbing across the lower neighbouring peak was the second possibility. But that would take too long, and would require total surefootedness; she would need to be at least a Grade 7 climber. Or at least that's what she had worked out from the countless photos that she had taken. Such a nuisance that you couldn't get hold of any decent maps of the valley. Robert had discovered months ago that even Google Earth blocked access when you tried to zoom in on the area – but there weren't any ordinary maps of the valley either, whereas it had been easy enough in Fields to buy a map of the glacier region.

My God, how often had she stared at the mountains? And she had always arrived at the same conclusion.

They would first have to skirt around the sheer face and climb up via the back and the southern flank to the summit, even if that meant having to cross the glacier.

The only question was whether the others would have the strength and skill to do it. Quite apart from the fact that Katie still had to convince them to go along with her plan. Without a decent map, what she was proposing was sheer madness. But that wasn't going to put her off.

For a while, she had hoped to learn something from the newspaper cuttings about the disaster in the seventies. Nothing. Nada.

That's not true, Katie: you found out a name. Without that, you'd have to forget about your plans completely.

My God, how Katie hated sitting in that windowless seminar room with its concrete walls. She felt as if she were in a bunker as Mr Forster carried on bombarding his sleepy students with his terrible French pronunciation. How the hell could someone like that be an international authority on anything? Fortunately this full-frontal attack on Katie's well-developed linguistic sensibilities ended before the stuffy air in the room could render her unconscious and make her fall off her chair.

As she was packing her things away at the end of the lecture with a good degree of relief, she asked herself for the hundredth time why she was spending her life sitting there and why she had ever chosen to major in French. Why, Katie?

Because hearing and speaking French brings you close to Sebastien.

At any rate she hated Mr Forster, with his black suit, his neatly tied tie and his handkerchief in his breast pocket, even more that morning than she normally did. And it would have to be today of all days that he accosted her as she was passing him. 'Miss West? I see you haven't signed the French Department list of volunteers for the Governor's visit. May I ask why?'

Katie wanted to say in French, 'No, you may not.' Instead, she said, 'I wasn't aware that volunteering was compulsory.'

Mr Forster knew who Katie's father was. He had a very high regard for her father as a politician and diplomat. And he presumably wanted to show Katie off to the Governor General – to prove that only the very best students were accepted at Grace.

'Katie, I'm warning you. I was the one who recommended

that they accept you at Grace,' said Mr Forster. His eyes looked tiny behind his thick horn-rimmed glasses.

'Oh, really? Unfortunately nobody asked me whether I accepted you as a lecturer.'

Unperturbed by this comment, Mr Forster carried on. 'I am sad to see that I was mistaken about you. However brilliant your work may be, I'm not the only one who has detected a flagrant lack of responsibility and team spirit.'

Katie shrugged and turned to go. Mr Forster, though, had evidently not finished. She could see the rage in his face and – if she wasn't mistaken – even a threat. 'That business that you were tangled up in did after all create significant political waves.'

'I don't know what you're talking about.'

'That young man, the son ... '

No, he wouldn't talk about Sebastien. Not him. And neither would anybody else.

'And what about the business that you were tangled up in, Mr Forster?' she retorted.

He was disconcerted, that was for sure. The question had clearly thrown him off balance. She could tell by the nervous twitching of his left eyelid. It almost made Katie laugh. The very idea that people believed that they could hide their weaknesses just by dressing themselves in the right sort of clothes. It simply didn't work. They always let slip some little tic. Like Mr Forster who, as now, succumbed to his compulsive swallowing, and simply couldn't stop doing it.

'I mean the business back then,' Katie continued. 'Eight college students – they can't have just vanished.'

He was silent for several seconds.

Students walked past them, glancing at them. Katie saw Julia coming through the glass door at the end of the corridor. Her flatmate waved at her, but then suddenly vanished from Katie's line of sight as Mr Forster actually had the nerve to stand right in front of her. She could smell his pungent after-shave, which presumably burnt off any remaining traces of stubble, as he murmured, 'I've got my eye on you, Miss West. You're a risk to the college.'

Katie shrugged. 'And I've got my eye on you.'

Then she turned and walked off.

She could feel him watching her from behind, and her heart was pounding. But not because she feared the lecturer's threats. It was something else that was upsetting her. The black suit. The meticulous side parting. The face that was so cleanly shaven that the skin on it must be like parchment. The expensive horn-rimmed glasses. And then those leather shoes. Presumably custom made.

But they were the blot on the perfect image. Because they were dirty. Not just ordinarily dust-marked. On the contrary, great lumps of muck were stuck to the soles and uppers, as if Mr Forster had been for a long walk before work that morning. A walk across rough terrain. A walk in the restricted area where Katie had been climbing, perhaps.

'What did Forster want with you?' Julia had appeared at her side.

'Oh, nothing much.'

'It didn't look like nothing much.'

'Sorry, I've got to get to my next class.'

Julia still looked suspicious as she asked, 'So where were you this morning? I was waiting for you in your room.'

31

Katie looked up, irritated. Julia of all people was spying on her? She suddenly regretted not locking her door, as Debbie tended to do.

'Have you been snooping around in my room?'

'Oh, don't be silly. I was hiding from Debbie. She was in the kitchen and I didn't want her to see me. I spent the night with Chris and overslept.'

Katie heaved a sigh of relief at the sight of Julia's embarrassed grin. She didn't want any kind of stress with her.

'Tell you later,' she said, looking at the clock that hung above every glass door. 'We've got Math, remember?'

But Julia didn't give up. 'Why do I have a vague feeling that you're hiding something from me?'

Katie glanced around. Should she tell Julia her plan? This soon? She had an idea as to how she could convince her. The only question was whether it would work.

Gangly Benjamin, year clown and self-styled video artist, strolled past and took off his lens cap. 'Hey, you'll both be late for Math. I wonder why?' His camera was whirring away. 'Anything important that I should know?'

'You of all people are asking that? You're the king of lateness,' said Julia, pushing the camera away.

'But that's precisely the secret. Being late all the time. Then the lecturers come to expect it.'

'Shove off, Benjamin,' said Katie.

'Come on, I've got a director's eye for it. I can tell by your face, Katie, that something's going on. And I'm longing for something new.'

Katie turned her back on Benjamin and dragged Julia along with her.

'Hey, folks, have pity on me! Since the Angela Finder business, nothing interesting's happened up here,' Benjamin called after them.

Julia and Katie ignored him. They had almost reached the seminar room when Julia pulled her flatmate into a corner by the washroom. 'Okay,' she said, looking around. 'The coast's clear. Are you going to tell me or not?'

Katie gave her a long look before deciding. 'You know the students who disappeared, and the memorial stone in the forest above the lake?' she finally asked.

Julia stared at her. 'What's that got to do with where you were?'

'In a minute.' She leaned over to Julia. 'But first I need to know why you always take flowers there.'

'How about: because I think what happened out there was terrible?' Julia frowned. 'Katie – what's this all about? What are you getting at?'

Katie glanced over her shoulder into the corridor, where Benjamin and his camera were once again approaching them.

'I'm quite certain that the explanation for the students' disappearance is up on the summit of the Ghost. Something happened back then. And I've decided to go up and find out what it was.'

'You're going up the Ghost? Because of those students?'

'Aren't you curious? If it was just an accident in the mountains, the college wouldn't shroud it in silence.'

'They just don't want to damage Grace's reputation.'

Katie shook her head. 'No, that's not it. But regardless of that, I'm going up there anyway.'

'You're crazy.'

'That's nothing new. But what about you? Are you coming too?'

'I don't even have proper shoes.' Julia shook her head. 'Shit, Katie, it's ten thousand feet high. I bet you haven't even got a decent map of the route.'

'Don't worry about that. I know what I'm doing, believe me.'

'Hey, girls, glad I've seen you!' Isabel Hill was coming along the corridor. Their senior-year mentor was holding yet another one of the lists that she'd been brandishing non-stop for the last few days. 'Have you signed up for any events yet? I still need someone for the podium discussion with the Governor General. How about it, Julia?'

CHAPTER 5

The weather had been simply blissful that whole day. A high summer heat lay across the valley, not even cooling off by late afternoon.

Katie followed the crush of people making their way outside.

'Are you coming down to the lake?' A hand reached for her elbow and pulled her away. It was Rose. 'We might get a last dip today. You can't do much actual swimming because of that stupid safety net that the security guys have put up. But I prefer the water in the lake to that chlorinated muck in the sports centre. Whenever you've been in that, you have to spend an hour in the shower, just to smell human again.'

And that was Rose of all people, who was a walking advert for mega-expensive body lotions and deodorants. Even now, although she was spending the entire day going from one lecture to another, from one stuffy lecture theatre to the next, she was floating around in a cloud of scent. And you could tell from a mile away that she was from one of those prim, snobby, wealthy East Coast families.

Katie pushed her sunglasses down over her eyes. Her fingers touched the plaster on her left temple. 'I'll see.'

'The boys were going to sort out the drinks. And Julia and

I said that we were going to the supermarket to get a few nice bits for the picnic.'

'I hate big groups.'

'Big groups? There are eight of us, just our gang.'

'My God, I hate the word "gang".' Katie sighed – although she had already decided that she was going to go. It would be a good opportunity for her to talk to the others in peace and quiet. 'Go on, then, I'll come. So long as I don't have to go supermarket shopping.'

'Any particular requests?'

'Red wine – and make it French.'

Rose grinned. 'You're so funny. See you later!' She set off, heading for the main building.

Katie set off in the opposite direction, particularly avoiding the big area outside the entrance foyer, where most of the students were watching the marquee being set up for the numerous guests.

My God, how she hated all this. Constantly being among people. All the pomposity. All the talk about the great honour of being at Grace.

If she didn't get out soon, she would go mad. Her gaze automatically turned to the rounded summit of the Ghost. She felt as if the mountain and she – Katie West from Washington, DC – were standing there face to face, and at that very moment she made a pact with it.

The reply was a big black cloud that pushed its way from the glacier and up towards the summit. She looked away and pulled her list out of her back trouser pocket. On it she had made a note in her tiny, squiggly, inscrutable handwriting of everything that she would need. Shoes, ropes, crampons.

She remembered the old rusty crampons that she had pulled out of Mirror Lake. She had spent ages searching for that particular model on the internet. They were still made nowadays, by a small, traditional firm in Switzerland. Katie hadn't been able to find out precisely how long the crampons had been at the bottom of the lake.

However, the question wasn't just 'how long'. More to the point was 'why'. What were the crampons doing in the water? Why had someone thrown them in the lake?

She was again reminded of the eight students who had set off on their fateful expedition and had never returned. All that remained of them was an inscription. Just their names – not even 'missing' after them. No stories or legends, just a couple of rumours whispered by one student to another. And the college officials' huge silence about the whole thing.

Katie pulled Sebastien's photo out of her trouser pocket and looked at it. It was a portrait which his mother had had taken on his sixteenth birthday. She'd stolen it the first and last time she'd visited his gigantic villa in Georgetown. It was on a chest of drawers in the hallway, and Katie had just taken it.

She couldn't remember when she'd started having conversations with Sebastien. Of course it was just a photo, but it made her feel less horribly lonely. She didn't have to make decisions on her own.

Katie looked around and took out her phone.

She dialled a number. It rang three times before it was answered.

'You're right,' Katie said. 'This weekend will be perfect.'

*

When she arrived half an hour later at the one part of the lake where swimming was permitted, the only other person there was Chris. He was lying on a blanket, his sunglasses covering his eyes. He was plugged into the latest iPod, which was lying on his naked torso. Chris was good looking – *too* good looking for Katie's taste – and he knew it. That was the only reason why he wore those jeans with their machine-made rips and holes. Undoubtedly a designer piece from some massively expensive online shop. Katie, though, wasn't sure whether Chris could actually afford stuff like that. She couldn't say why, she could just sense it.

'Hey, Chris.' She nodded briefly and looked around.

The beach was the length of two football fields, though not quite as wide. Beyond the strip of sand was the asphalted lakeside path, which many of the students used as a jogging track. Not surprisingly, they weren't the only ones who had thought of having a picnic. Groups of students were milling around everywhere, lighting barbecues. Katie spotted a couple of girls from their year playing volleyball in skimpy bikinis.

'Where are the others?' Katie asked, turning back to Chris.

'David and Robert are putting the drinks coolbox in the lake, Benjamin's around somewhere with his camera, and the girls are still at the supermarket.' He pushed his sunglasses up onto his forehead and looked at her. 'Julia said you had an argument with Mr Forster.'

'Julia ought to keep her mouth shut.'

'She tells me everything.'

Katie dropped down onto the sand. 'Are you sure about that?'

He gave her a tired look with his grey eyes. 'Don't you go trying to drive a wedge between us.'

He was desperately trying to sound cool, but Katie could tell that he was irked.

'Don't worry, she still believes in you.'

She watched as Robert and David appeared at the lakeside followed by Benjamin who, as ever, was hiding his face behind his camera.

David came over and flopped down in the sand beside Katie. He passed her a litre-bottle of Seven Up.

'That's not really lemonade in there, is it?' she asked suspiciously.

David grinned. 'Not if you believe O'Connor in the third year. Top-notch Pinot Grigot, Napa Valley.'

Katie groaned. 'Sounds to me as if a headache's on the way. Is it cold at least?'

'As cold as our fridge is today.' David looked across at Robert. 'What do you reckon, Rob, how cold is that water?'

They had come to accept that the water in the lake bore no relationship to the outside temperature. The glacial lake seemed to abide by its own set of rules. Sometimes it was so warm that it seemed more like Florida than Canada. 'Fifteen degrees. At most.'

'Obvious,' murmured Chris. 'Makes complete sense, given how hot it's been these last few weeks.'

Robert shrugged as if to say: whatever. Then he pulled a copy of *Science* magazine out of his rucksack and buried himself in it.

'We've got another bottle as well. Otherwise, it's just Coke and water,' David said with a grimace. 'No beer. O'Connor's supplies have run out.'

'Does the college really think we're going to do without alcohol just because they don't sell it in the campus supermarket?' murmured Chris. 'It just provokes us into getting it for ourselves. I mean, come on, we're all eighteen or nineteen.'

Katie shut her eyes. She'd heard this conversation once too often. And she was fed up with talking about it. Katie didn't need alcohol to give her a kick. 'Oi!' A shrill voice floated across to them. 'David! Chris!'

Debbie was bright red and sweating profusely as she flung herself down beside Chris.

Moments later, she was giving Katie the evil eye. 'Ah, so Madam has deigned to join us? Waited on hand and foot, as usual.'

Katie didn't reply. Debbie was always whingeing about something.

Julia, who was close behind her, put the shopping bags down and put her hands on her hips. 'Hey, you've started without us,' she said indignantly.

Chris patted the blanket next to him. 'Come on, sit down with me.'

Julia shook her head. 'Work first, then ...'

'What?' Chris grinned smugly.

'Food,' Julia replied. 'We've bought some great stuff. Pineapple, papaya, salmon, real shrimps. It'll be like being in paradise.'

'We *are* in paradise,' Debbie cried. 'I heard someone back there saying they were going to like go, like, skinny dipping once it's dark.' She stretched out her arms, with the result that everyone could see and smell the huge sweaty patches on her orange t-shirt. When, Katie wondered, was someone going to tell her that orange together with her fluffy egg-yolk hair made her complexion look as if she'd just thrown up?

'What's the point,' Chris murmured, 'of skinny dipping in the dark?'

They all laughed. Even Robert managed a grin.

'Maybe because it's just, like, really brilliant and natural, being naked?' Debbie was using her squeaky tone now. As if to cover up her annoyance, she adopted an exaggeratedly cheerful manner. 'So, did you get the Seven Up?'

David pointed to the blanket in front of him, while Rose and Julia unpacked the food from the paper bags.

'Let's tuck in – and about time too,' Chris sighed, reaching for a slice of Canadian wild smoked salmon. 'I need this after all that refectory muck.'

'Tuck in'! Katie thought. My God, are these stupid clichés all they've got to offer? Was that what she wanted from life? To become a well-functioning adult? With the perfect life that meant nothing but working all day then spending Happy Hour at some buffet party with champagne and nibbles?

Julia lay down on the blanket next to Chris, put her head on his bare chest, and popped a shrimp into her mouth. 'God, I could stay like this for ever.'

The peaceful silence lasted no more than ten seconds. Then a pretty girl in a red bikini suddenly ran towards the lake and plunged in, disappeared beneath the water, and didn't reappear for ages. She was invisible for so long that they all fell silent. A sense of menace hung in the air. Then

Benjamin started to laugh, and said, 'Do you remember how shit-scared we were three months ago? All those horror stories about the valley? The stories about something being wrong here?'

The others laughed hesitantly.

'It was basically all because of you, Robert,' Ben continued. 'You infected us all with your "this place is evil" stuff. But your brain has presumably gone quiet now. No evil premonitions, eh? No spooky visions of the future?' Robert looked up from his magazine. Benjamin trained the camera on him. 'This is a live report from the brain of Robert Frost who, by the way, isn't to be confused with the poet of the same name who wrote: "I have stood still and stopped the sound of feet / When far away an interrupted cry / Came over houses from another street".'

'Wow,' Rose laughed. 'I had no idea you were so cultured.'

Robert, however, was sitting unperturbed and cross-legged on the ground. He reached for the bottle, took a swig, and then said quite calmly, 'I know what I know. You all just want to forget everything.'

Chris also sat up at this point. 'Robert might be right. Three months of peace and quiet don't necessarily mean anything.'

'Oh yeah? So what's going to happen next?' Benjamin grinned. 'A Loch Ness Monster lookalike, perhaps? Or a snowman, a yeti like in the Himalayas. That'd be fine by me. I'd get millions of hits on YouTube with that one.'

The others laughed again.

'But don't you ever wonder about the eight students who vanished?' Julia said. 'And about that memorial stone that we found over by the boat house?'

'Maybe they were, like, abducted by aliens,' Debbie giggled.

Robert put the bottle down on the blanket and looked calmly at Katie through his round spectacles. 'Ask Katie.'

They all stared at her.

Katie jumped. How the hell did Robert know about her plan? Or was he just guessing, shooting in the dark, just to see if he scored a direct hit? Then she pulled herself together. He'd presumably just been talking to Julia about it.

But what was the purpose of his allusion? She couldn't imagine him being particularly enthusiastic about her plan. But on the other hand, he was offering her the perfect opportunity to tell the others what she was intending to do.

The sun was already casting long shadows on the turquoise surface, a harbinger of dusk. The sky, though, was still blue, and there was a clear view of the mountains which seemed to go on for ever behind the Ghost, interrupted only by the glacier's snowfields. It was the kind of day that hid nothing.

The next moment, Katie was standing up and starting to speak. They all stared at her, baffled, and she knew what they were thinking. What's got into her? She never normally opens her mouth.

But they would soon find out.

'What do you reckon?' She looked around at them all. 'Who wants to challenge the valley? Who wants to solve the mystery of the students? Who's going to climb the Ghost with me this weekend?'

CHAPTER 6

'Brilliant idea!'

'Yeah, let's do it!'

'Let's challenge the valley!'

'Hey, Ghost, here we come!'

Julia couldn't believe what she was hearing. She couldn't understand the enthusiasm. But they all – apart from Robert – seemed to find Katie's idea infectious. That really was unusual. Even Debbie looked as if she actually believed that she could manage to climb a ten-thousand-foot mountain. For Julia, though, it wasn't just a ten-thousand-foot mountain. That mountain held a far greater significance for her.

A cloud seemed to appear from nowhere, pushing its way in front of the sun. In the same way, a name forced itself from the depths of Julia's memory to the surface.

Mark de Vincenz.

The last name on the memorial stone.

She hadn't found out how her father's name, of all names, came to be on the stone. Indeed, it might be pure coincidence; someone else might just have happened to have had the same name. But all the same, she kept on taking flowers, using the place as a graveyard and the stone as a gravestone. For her father was dead. The victim of a crime. Fact. Fact. Fact.

Or was it?

She shut her eyes.

Why did Katie have to go raking all this stuff up with her idea of climbing the Ghost? Why did she have to go opening up old wounds?

Julia wished she could jump up and run away.

'When?' she heard Chris asking.

Don't ask, thought Julia.

'This weekend,' Katie replied. 'The forecast is good. And it's the perfect time for it. The Governor's visit is going to cause such bedlam that nobody will notice if we disappear.'

The clouds were casting long shadows on the water. Its glassy surface was disturbed only by the waves that gently lapped against the shore.

'What exactly do you have in mind?' David was asking.

'I want to find proof. I want to know whether those students were really up there or not,' Katie replied.

She's lying, Julia thought. She's got some other reason. She doesn't give a toss about the missing students. Why would Katie, who wasn't interested in living people, be interested in dead ones?

Julia hadn't seen her father's dead body, and had often wondered how she could be so sure that he was really dead. The police had said he was. But what if he wasn't? What if he'd actually gone into hiding, like she had? She imagined him living somewhere – in Florida, perhaps – with a new family. Why Florida of all places? Julia had no idea. Or maybe, like her, he had been living under an assumed identity. Maybe he had been no more Mark de Vincenz than she was Julia Frost. While the real Mark de Vincenz was lying up there at the top of the Ghost.

Rose was asking something, but Julia had simply shut out the noises around her. The light of the low-lying sun was blinding her even though her eyes were shut. The kind of brightness that you get when the sun shines on snow. She imagined herself tramping through a freezing fastness – completely alone. The wind biting into her limbs, icy cold. Don't stop.

Don't turn round.

If she didn't carry on, if she ignored that voice, she would freeze solid.

If only it weren't for that black shadow that was awaiting her over there. The closer she came to it, the further away it moved.

Mark de Vincenz?

What made her think that it was him?

She didn't know. She simply didn't know.

She had only one chance to find out whether it was a stranger or whether her father was this black shadow.

She had to follow him, put her hand on his shoulder until he turned round and she could see his face.

The thought of it made her feel dizzy. She started to feel sick. Her entire being was screaming *no*, but still she kept on walking. It even seemed as if the shadow were waving to her.

For a fraction of a second, her brain sprang into action and told her that it was all just a dream. But she wanted to carry on dreaming, just as she wanted to carry on walking.

It took all her strength to put one foot in front of the other on the white surface. She might have given up if she hadn't felt as if she were getting closer to the figure in front of her. She would soon reach it. She just had to keep going.

Voices in her ear.

Robert's voice coming from reality. 'Julia?' Once again. 'Julia?'

It would have been a chance to wake up from this weird dream, but Julia couldn't do it. Not least because her heart was pounding.

Not yet, she wanted to reply, but she couldn't say anything. Instead, she was panicking inside. Soon. I'll know soon.

She ran off. Towards the white surface. The shadow was waiting for her at the end of it. Just a few yards to go. She felt so sick, she could hardly walk. Then she fell to her knees.

A black cloud was blowing across the sky. The shadow was dissolving. The white surface became the dark blue sky above Mirror Lake, where Julia found herself kneeling and vomiting into the dark green water.

'Oh my god', she heard a voice say close by.

Someone was pressing a tissue into her hand.

There was a shrill squeal, then someone said, 'Ugh, something we bought must have been, like, off. What did she eat? Oh, God, Chris, what did she eat?'

'Shrimps,' Julia said weakly. 'It was just the shrimps.'

There was a kind of squeaking sound. 'Oh my God, oh my God, oh my God. Me too! I had at least, like, ten of them. I think I feel sick too.'

'Sweet Jesus, Debbie, just shut your mouth for a change.'

Was it Chris who said that, or was it David?

CHAPTER 7

'Are you okay now?'

Katie watched impatiently as Rose jumped up, ran down to the lake, and returned with a bottle of water. Trust Julia to choose that particular moment to throw up. But Katie wasn't going to give up that easily. She had been labelled stubborn ever since she was a child; she was surprised it didn't appear in her passport under 'particular characteristics'.

She tried to sound as cool as possible. 'So, what do you reckon? Are we going on a trip to the Ghost?'

The others stared at her.

'You actually, like, mean it?' Debbie asked.

'Unlike you, I mean everything I say.'

'Why do you want to take the risk?' David asked calmly.

'She's bored,' murmured Chris.

Katie looked at him. 'Aren't you?'

Chris shrugged.

'Just think about it. All hell's going to break loose here this weekend. We're going to be shown off like dressage ponies. That in itself is a good enough reason to be elsewhere. And – I mean, just look at that mountain. Just imagine yourself being up there and ...'

'Assuming, that is, that you actually manage to get that far,' David interrupted her.

She ignored him. 'The view must be amazing. The whole world at our feet. The college would look so tiny that we'd never take it seriously again.'

'I don't take it seriously anyway,' laughed Benjamin. His camera had been trained on Katie the whole time.

'Just use your imaginations! It could be the ultimate adventure. All this landscape here. Shouldn't it be more than just a backdrop? A lake we're not allowed to swim in; a forest that's forbidden territory; mountains we're not allowed to climb. I can't go along with that. Can you? It just makes me want to do the opposite.'

She had said what she had to say, and even she couldn't think of anything further to add. Nobody else said anything until Julia, of all people, broke the silence.

'I'll come with you.'

They all stared at her. Julia was still scarily pale and Katie felt a brief pang of fear that Julia wouldn't be able to make it to the top. Then she remembered how fit her flatmate was. She went jogging for an hour pretty much every morning, and had been selected for the college athletics team.

'You shouldn't,' Chris murmured.

'Don't tell me what to do,' his girlfriend replied firmly. She turned to Katie. 'But let's just get this clear. I'm not doing it for the good view or anything. I want to know what happened to those students. They were the same age as us, and now there's nothing left of them but rumours. If you ask about them, all you get is silence. The yearbooks from back then have disappeared; I know, because I tried to find them. Apparently they decided against keeping stuff when the college was shut down.' Julia shook her head. 'There's nothing left but names on a stone, and that seems wrong to me.'

'You've obviously thought about this a lot.' Rose shook her head. 'And that's why I don't get why you're so desperate to go up there. The fact that the students disappeared must mean it's really dangerous.' She shook her head again. 'So far as I'm concerned, you're welcome to break every bone in your body – but you can count me out. In any case, I'm already signed up for stuff this weekend.'

Katie shrugged. 'Suit yourself. But I've got no desire to spend the weekend sucking up to her honourable eminence the Governor General.'

She saw Robert staring at his sister and Julia returning his look. He then got up and packed his things away without a word. Benjamin pointed his camera at him as Robert stopped in front of Katie and said, 'It's an insane plan and whatever it is you're looking for up there, you won't find it. The answers you're looking for aren't on the summit of the Ghost: they're inside you.'

'Wow!' Benjamin moved his camera back to Katie.

'All I'm doing is climbing a mountain. That's no reason to start acting all Sigmund Freud,' Katie retorted – although Robert's words had hit home. 'And Julia has her own reasons for doing it.'

Robert and Julia exchanged glances again. 'Don't do it,' Robert said quietly. But instead of replying, Julia merely shrugged.

'If Julia's going, then I'm going too,' said Chris, taking his sunglasses off. 'In any case, Katie's right. We shouldn't just accept the boundaries that other people impose on us. Boundaries are there to be crossed.'

'Oh my God, you're serious. You're really, like, serious!' Debbie had been quiet for a surprisingly long time, but now she had found her voice again.

'You can't go off just like that.' David stared across at the summit of the Ghost. 'It's not like going for a walk.' The low sun was bathing the mountain range on the opposite shore in an orangey light. 'You need some decent kit, maps and stuff. And, more importantly, you won't manage it in one day. You'll have to spend the night somewhere.'

'There's supposed to be a hut somewhere on the other side of the Ghost,' Katie replied. 'And so far as equipment's concerned, don't worry – I know where we can get stuff. Ropes, helmets, crampons ...'

'Crampons? You're surely not planning to cross the glacier?' David's eyes, intensely blue against his brown hair, stared at her angrily.

Katie bit her lip. Damn! David had guessed what she was planning to do. And she definitely needed him. He was the most reliable of all of them. Someone who wouldn't get flustered.

'And who's going to be team leader, Katie? Who's going to make decisions? You?' asked Chris. 'Do you suppose we all trust you that much?'

They all fell silent for a moment. Katie, though, had anticipated this.

'No. There's someone who can take us across the glacier.'

The others looked at her, puzzled. They hadn't counted on that one.

'Her name is Ana Cree. She works as a ski instructor in winter; in summer, she has a part-time job in a sports shop in

Fields, and runs occasional mountain tours. For years, her grandfather Nanuk Cree was head of the Mounties, who have a station in Fields. She's up for it no matter what. So you see,' Katie turned to David, 'I'm well prepared. Crossing the glacier without a guide – now that really would be irresponsible.'

She said this as if it were completely self-evident – and yet it was Ana Cree who had actually said this. And it was also Ana Cree who had insisted that there be a group of at least six of them when Katie had suggested going as a twosome.

'How long have you known her?' David asked.

'Long enough.'

'Cree?' Chris propped himself up on his elbow. 'Does that mean she's Native American?'

Katie nodded.

'And you say she knows her way around up here?'

'Her grandfather was in the team who went looking for the eight students. So, where are we? Who's coming apart from Julia and Chris?'

Nobody said anything.

Katie stood up. 'Suit yourselves. I'm going anyway.'

She turned to head off in the direction of the college. 'Listen up. If anyone changes their mind, we're meeting at nine p.m. in the equipment room of the sports hall. We'll find all the equipment we need there. So if you want to come, then come.'

Katie was sitting in a deckchair on the balcony. She had put her feet up on the rail and was staring down at the black lake beneath her. It was still warm, although the sun had long since set. The campus and the grass leading to the lake were full of people. Laughter and shouts floated up to her.

She had been sitting there for an hour, mulling over everything.

Ana, Chris, Julia and her.

Would that be enough people for what she'd planned? Ana had insisted on six. The more people the better, she had said, and Katie knew this was sensible. What if there were an emergency? What if they had to split up to try different routes to the summit? But on the other hand ... two groups of two. Wouldn't that be enough?

She could feel Sebastien gazing at her. His photo was on her lap. *He'd* even have gone on his own. That had always been the difference between them. Sebastien had always taken everything right to the limit. Katie, however, had hesitated at the last minute more than once.

She looked at the time. Quarter to nine. She stood up, put on her hoodie, slipped on her Converse trainers, and opened her bedroom door. The apartment was dead silent, as was the second-floor corridor. All the students had evidently chosen to spend the unusually mild evening outside, rather than hanging out in their stuffy apartments.

Katie stopped by the lift and pressed the button. A tunnel led from the second basement floor to the sports hall and rear campus buildings. She could have made her way round outside, but she didn't want to bump into Debbie or anyone else who would annoy her by making comments or asking questions.

The lift stopped on her floor with a loud clang. Just like the wood-panelled corridors and their tatty carpets, it was past its prime. It was one of those lifts with an old-fashioned concertina arrangement behind its glass door. Not exactly confidence-inspiring.

Katie got in, and as the lift doors slowly closed she immediately felt the anxiety that always seized hold of her in confined spaces.

She hadn't always felt that way. Her fear had developed bit by bit. It hadn't been that bad at first: nothing more than an unpleasant sensation. Katie couldn't really have given it a name. It was only after the business with Sebastien that she had been hit by full-blown panic.

She had taken the lift up to the psychiatrist's office, on the ninth floor of a tower block in Belmont Road, and it was as if a thousand black spiders had been crawling over her body. Everything was prickling; she was trembling from head to toe, and she desperately wanted to lash out in all directions.

That's how she felt now, too. The psychiatrist had cost her parents a small fortune, but he hadn't been able to help her.

As the lift set off now, Katie shut her eyes. Just don't think about it. Just cast aside your fear that the walls, the ceiling, the floor of the lift are going to start moving in and crushing you. And she did indeed manage to picture herself standing on the summit of the Ghost, seeing everything going on below her for what it really was: a pitiful pageant.

So who might be at the meeting place? Definitely Julia: she'd sounded so certain. Well, certain might not be quite the right word; more like 'desperately resolute'. For whatever reason. And if Julia was coming, then Chris would too. But even if he said he was just going because of Julia, he had another reason for going too.

Adventure? Fun? Adrenaline? He wasn't the type. He was

a gamester. He challenged other people. And he knew quite a lot about the valley. An astonishing amount, if you thought about it.

The lift jerked and Katie was thrown against the wall. Then came a squealing sound. The lift jerked violently again. Katie involuntarily stretched out her arms and pressed them against the walls, as if she might be able to stop them from closing in on her.

The lift had stopped. It was hanging in its shaft, somewhere between the first and second basement floors. The light flickered, went out, came back on, and then everything went completely dark.

Katie's most hideous nightmare had become reality.

Just wait a few minutes, and the lift will start up again, she thought, trying to calm herself. This can't last long. She found herself counting the seconds.

At a hundred and eighty, she stopped and reached for her rucksack. The flashlight she hadn't unpacked that morning had to be in it. Her fingers trembled as she opened the zip. No, it wasn't there. Try the side pocket. Now she remembered. She had put it in the side pocket.

Her fingers felt their way along the nylon rucksack. There it was – she could feel it. She flicked it on, and a weak beam of light lit up the lift.

What a mistake. What a terrible mistake.

It wasn't a lift, it was a prison. A dingy box with room for no more than two people. Its walls were made of plastic panels, tarnished and stained.

The cage was hanging from wires. Katie could hear them squeaking. Maybe they were frayed. Maybe they were going to snap at any moment. Maybe someone was at that moment cutting through one of them.

Fear was whispering countless possibilities in her ear. She could die a thousand deaths here. She, who wasn't afraid of climbing a hundred-foot-high cliff free solo. She whose next goal was to cross the glacier and climb the ten-thousand-foot-high Ghost. She was afraid of four plastic-coated walls? Of a power cut, which was always happening in the college? Of a lift that had been working perfectly well for more than thirty years?

Beads of cold sweat were standing out on her forehead.

Keep cool, she told herself, just keep cool, Katie, and think.

Suddenly, she could have groaned with relief. How could she be so dumb? There must be an intercom somewhere. The security men spent all day sitting in their office, staring at their screens. They were presumably killing themselves with laughter, watching her sitting there like a frightened rabbit instead of pressing the red emergency button and saying to them: get your asses over here and get this thing working again.

The beam of torchlight illuminated the control panel to the left of the lift door. She pressed the red button and immediately heard a comforting hiss.

'Hello? Can you hear me? I'm stuck in the lift.'

More hissing.

'Hello?'

Silence.

Then a whispering.

No, not a whispering. More like a monotonous murmuring, words in the same quiet, unchanging tone.

56

'Forget ...'

Had she heard rightly?

'What? I don't understand. I'm stuck in this crappy lift, and I need help.'

'Forget the plan.'

Okay. Katie was scared witless of getting into a lift. Fact. She had the feeling that the oxygen was running out and, yes, she could already see herself lying unconscious on the floor. Another fact. But she wasn't yet at the stage where she was hearing voices. No way. That meant that the whole crappy radio communication system, or whatever she was supposed to call this damned technology, must have crashed.

'Can you hear me? Who's that? Are you from Security?'

'Someone will die up there. Do you hear me? Katie? Katie? And it will be your fault, Katie. Your fault ...'

Dripping with sweat and trembling from head to toe, Katie slid to the floor. Her heart was pounding. And with every beat, the final words rang in her ears: *your fault, your fault, your fault.*

She didn't come round until the light came back on and a deep, powerful voice came through the intercom. 'You pressed the emergency button. Please wait a few seconds – we're remedying the problem now.'

And before the sentence had even ended, the lift jolted again. Barely a second later, it stopped on the second basement floor and the doors opened. Katie stumbled out and bumped into someone waiting by the lift door.

It was Mr Forster. His lips were twisted into an odd smile. 'Is something the matter?' he asked.

Katie ran. She ran through the tunnel that stretched out

deep underground. Her footsteps bounced off the concrete walls, as did her panting breath. Only once she reached the glass door which led to the neon-lit swimming pool did she slow down and try to calm herself.

If you want to convince people to follow your plan, you need to demonstrate exactly what you have to offer. A firm will. You know how to persuade people, how to convince them. You've watched your father do it thousands of times. And Katie had also perfected the emotionless facial expression that her mother used to demonstrate her distance from and superiority over others.

So when Katie went into the sports centre, nobody could ever have guessed that she had just been through a nightmare. Exaggeratedly slowly, her rucksack slung casually over her left shoulder, she sauntered into the equipment room.

They were already waiting for her. She suddenly didn't have to fake her enthusiasm, for there were more people there than she had anticipated. Julia and Chris were leaning against a fitness machine by the door, but David and Benjamin were there too. Benjamin hailed her cheerfully. 'Here she comes, the leader of our reckless expedition, Katie West.'

And there was someone else. A boy whom she'd never seen before. Katie was sure of it. She wouldn't have forgotten his face. Not his combed-back sandy hair. Not his neatly trimmed beard, not the lines on his forehead, and definitely not the scar on his left cheek.

'Hi,' he said, going up to her. 'I'm Paul. Paul Forster. I'd like to join your team.'

CHAPTER 8

Paul Forster?

As Katie registered the astonishment and curiosity in the others' eyes, her mind was turning somersaults.

How did he know about her plan? Which of the others had told him? Who had been blabbing? Benjamin, hiding behind his camera? Chris, leaning against the fitness machine with his arm around Julia? David? They all looked baffled, tense, nervous – yes; guilty – no.

Katie turned back to the boy. 'No idea what you're talking about.'

'Oh yeah? So what's this?' He pushed past Katie, his arm brushing her shoulder, and went to the low cupboard at the far end of the equipment store. Unlike the brand new ultra-modern fitness equipment, the cupboard was old and scratched and looked as if nobody had bothered with it in years. Almost as if it had come from a different age altogether.

Katie suddenly felt her heart pounding in her throat. This Paul guy knew about the cupboard! Had he seen her there two days ago, when she'd broken the lock?

Yes he had. As calmly as anything, he reached for the padlock that Katie had put on the locker doors so that nobody would notice anything amiss, and opened it up.

Before them was all the equipment that Katie had found:

ropes, chest straps, hooks, crampons. Carabiners and ice-picks. Paul Forster pulled out one of the latter, held it in one hand and then the other, seemed to think for a moment, and then said with an indefinable smile, 'You need me.'

'Oh yes? Why's that, then?' Katie replied mockingly, simultaneously wondering how she could get rid of him without anyone else finding out what they were up to.

His hand reached into his back jeans pocket. 'I'm the only one with a map.'

Katie started. She saw the others looking at him, fascinated. Paul was evidently enjoying unfolding the map slowly, very slowly. The paper was old and tattered, falling apart along its folds. Paul carefully spread it out on the dusty floor of the equipment room, and Katie couldn't ignore the heading.

Solomon National Forest.

She felt hot.

This guy had the map. The map she'd spent so long searching for in vain. And as she now stared at him in astonishment, he returned her gaze with amusement. The colour of his eyes was highly annoying. They gleamed such a pale brown that they looked almost yellow. And, damn it, she couldn't look away. For although she didn't have the faintest idea what Paul wanted, she also had the feeling that she had found an ally.

'Where did you get that?' she heard herself asking.

'It doesn't matter where I got it. All that matters is that you can forget your plan without it.'

Oh yes it does matter, Katie thought. But she ignored the host of warning bells that were screaming inside her, and let her curiosity get the better of her. Before she knew it, she was kneeling on the floor, bending over the map.

She immediately recognised the Ghost towering over Mirror Lake, and the glacier behind it. For the first time, she saw that the glacier had a name: *Never Summer Fields.*

Moreover, the Ghost wasn't the only mountain named on the map; the two neighbouring peaks bore names as well: *White Soul* and *Black Spirit.*

'How on earth did you find out what we're up to?' Until now, Chris had been standing by the door with David, Julia and Benjamin, watching the events unfold. Now he went over to them.

'You hear stuff,' Paul replied. 'And I always keep my eyes open.'

Katie found herself staring at his shoes. He was wearing battered Adidas trainers. Some ancient design.

She suddenly remembered something. That morning at the cliff, just before the rockfall, she had seen a shadow above her. And for a moment, she'd had the overwhelming sense that she wasn't alone. Could it have been Paul standing there? And even if it was, how could that have told him about their plan?

She shook her head and bent over the map again.

Her finger traced the path that she had planned out. Oh my God, she'd known it. She'd been spot on.

She looked up and said as coolly as possible, 'The map doesn't tell me anything I didn't already know.' But before she knew it, Paul was kneeling directly in front of her. His arm brushed hers and he reached out and traced his index finger along the red dotted line that marked the way up the mountain on the fragile paper.

'Along the shore first, until about here. Then we turn right to the foot of the cliff. I reckon we should be able to bypass it to the east and climb up the back of it to the glacier. Then we can cross the glacier that's in the wind gap and climb the south ridge to the summit.'

His hands – slender and somehow sensitive – didn't go with the rest of his appearance.

She stood up abruptly and took a step backwards.

Chris took her place. He knelt down by Paul and studied the map. 'If I'm not mistaken, Katie, it will take us a day even to reach the glacier.'

'That's why we're going to spend the night in the cabin.'

Chris shook his head and looked up at her. 'There's no cabin on this map.'

'Ana says there's one. You can get into the glacier from it.'

'So where's this Ana now? I'd love to know who I'm dealing with.'

'You'll meet her soon enough. Her family has a log cabin in the woods. We'll meet her somewhere around here.' Katie pointed to the map. 'She'll be waiting for us at the lakeside, where the path from the lake branches off towards the Ghost.'

'And where's the mountain cabin?'

Katie's index finger pointed to the smaller summit in front of the Ghost. 'Up here. From there, we can get down into the wind gap and ... '

At that point, Paul interrupted her. She could hear the same excitement in his voice that she felt herself. '... And that's where the glacier starts – and so does our real adventure.'

Silence filled the room. Julia, Benjamin and David seemed

unsure of what to make of it all. The tension was tangible, and Katie knew that her next words would be crucial. She took a deep breath, stood up, and reached for her rucksack.

'I've printed out an alphabetical list of all the equipment we need. If anyone's missing anything, we can get hold of it. The shoes are the most important thing. But you need warm clothes, waterproofs, a strong rucksack and a sleeping bag. Crampons, ropes and safety equipment are in this cupboard here. Make sure you bring enough provisions. Water, ideally in plastic bottles. We can throw them away when they're empty. The less baggage, the better. Only bring what you really ...'

The door to the equipment room opened with a creak. Katie started and whirled round. And then she groaned loudly.

Debbie! What on earth was she doing here? She wasn't seriously planning to climb the Ghost with them, was she? Debbie was the very last person on her list. Though Paul, she thought suddenly, wasn't on her list either.

'What's going on?' she asked irritably.

Rose appeared in the doorway behind Debbie. She gestured apologetically. 'I couldn't talk her out of it,' she sighed. 'She wants to come. You can tell her yourself that she won't manage it.'

'I *will* manage it,' Debbie declared. She gave them all a challenging look. 'I'll manage it.'

'You run out of breath going upstairs in a lift!' Benjamin panted exaggeratedly. He turned to Katie and grinned. 'Or are you hiding an oxygen mask in that locker over there?'

'You never do any sport either,' Debbie hissed.

'I don't need to do sport. The gods gave me special powers. But your legs are like blancmange. And you'd have to heave all your flab up the mountain as well as all your gear.'

'If you don't let me come, I'll tell on you.' Debbie folded her arms, a venomous expression spreading across her face. 'I'm telling the Dean. Either we all go, or nobody does.'

It was Chris who reacted. 'No you won't. It's not in your own interests.'

'I'll have to go to the Dean,' Debbie declared. She raised her hands apologetically. 'I've got no choice. What if something happens to you? I'll simply have to report it.'

'Oh yeah?' Julia glanced at David, who was shrugging, then took a step forward. 'Then let me tell you something, Debbie. So far as I'm concerned, you can kiss the Dean's ass.'

'And when you've finished kissing his ass,' Chris continued, 'you'd be finished at the college. Nobody would ever speak to you again – we'd make sure of that. That's what happens when one student rats on another. Get it?'

Debbie burst into tears – as she always did when she couldn't have her own way.

Katie only just managed to suppress another groan. Everything was going wrong, badly wrong. She'd thought of everything – except for that pest Debbie screwing up the entire plan by seriously imagining she could manage this kind of expedition.

Surprisingly, it was Paul who was the first to stir himself. He went over to Debbie and put a comforting arm round her shoulder. 'Hey, calm down,' he said. 'You're Deborah, aren't you?'

Debbie nodded through her tears. 'Who are you?'

'Paul Forster.'

Debbie was going to say something but he didn't let her speak. An achievement in itself.

'Deborah, they don't mean it that way,' he continued. 'Didn't they tell you why they wanted you to stay here?'

Debbie's tears immediately dried up. She looked at him suspiciously as he turned to the others and continued. 'You should have told her.'

'What? What should they have told me?'

Nothing, Katie wanted to reply, but she kept her mouth shut, intrigued to see how Paul was going to get out of this one. 'Of course you're one of the team,' he carried on, his expression deadly serious. 'We're absolutely counting on you. We need someone down here who can cover for us if anyone notices we're missing. What's more, the college is our base camp, and we have to have someone who's in contact with us – in case we have to split up once we're up the mountain. Someone has to be able to co-ordinate the groups by mobile.'

Debbie hesitated. Katie held her breath. Paul's ruse was pretty transparent, and Debbie wasn't as dumb as she made out. But on the other hand, her performance was presumably all put on. Like hell did she really want to come. Benjamin had been spot on when it came to Debbie's feelings about sport. She'd never choose to lift a finger, never mind seriously consider any kind of strenuous expedition. All she was interested in was not being left out. That being the case, Paul's suggestion was the perfect way for her to slide out of it without losing face.

And indeed, Debbie sniffed and wiped her face. Then she screwed her eyes up and looked more closely at Paul. 'Paul Forster?' she asked. 'Is Mr Forster your father? And hasn't he got a son who's on probation?'

'Precisely,' Paul replied, turning and looking hard at Katie. '"Probation" is what this is all about: proving yourself.'

CHAPTER 9

Katie barely slept that night. At four a.m. she got up and went to the window to stare at the Ghost for the hundredth time. In the darkness, all she could see was its silhouette. Nothing but the jagged lines of the two neighbouring peaks and the oval of the main summit which, as almost always, was shrouded in mist, as if the mountain were hiding its true face behind it.

Now it was five a.m. and although the horizon was still pitch black in the east, she could already feel the new day. The air smelled different and one by one the stars disappeared from a clear sky that promised a cloudless day.

Katie was the first to slip out of the apartment. There was still no sound from Julia's room and Katie herself wasn't sure why she didn't wait for her flatmate. Maybe because she wanted to be first at the meeting place. Maybe because she wanted a last half-hour to herself before it all kicked off.

That's how Sebastien had always done it.

Katie looked around. The formidable main college building lay behind her. The long picture windows behind the balconies had an air of menace, as they always did when the building was in darkness. In any one of those rooms, someone could be secretly watching her set off.

To do what, exactly?

She didn't know.

Katie turned round resolutely and headed off quickly into the forest which bordered the road to Fields. Here, the trees weren't as dense as they were on the other side of Mirror Lake, and the tall spruces kept being interspersed with deciduous trees. Gnarled old oak trees and tall, slender beeches broke up the impenetrability of the forest. Moreover, it seemed almost as if a cleaning crew carried out their meticulous business on a weekly basis. Wood was piled up neatly at the edge of the path; there wasn't a pine needle, leaf or fallen branch to be seen. Katie knew that this was a particularly popular place with college couples.

She stopped abruptly. A good sixty feet away, a figure was sitting on one of the benches. She could clearly make out a light-coloured jacket in the darkness. And she immediately knew who it was. Paul Forster, who had simply elbowed his way into their team. She had lost any hope of getting him out once he'd said that he had the only map. Which, incidentally, he still had.

If only she didn't feel so flustered at the sight of him. If only she weren't so dumbstruck in his presence. It was a feeling she couldn't resist. Paul Forster had perfectly mastered the art of persuasion – as he had clearly demonstrated by getting Debbie on his side and convincing her to abandon the idea of taking part in the expedition. So watch out, Katie, don't let yourself be manipulated by him!

She took a deep breath and walked quickly up to him. He absolutely mustn't see how unsure she felt.

Paul was sitting, completely relaxed, on the bench. His arms were propped against the backrest and his eyes were shut.

Next to him was a loaded rucksack; an ice-pick handle was sticking out of the side. Katie stopped three feet away from him, slipped her rucksack off, and without any form of greeting asked him, 'Won't Daddy miss you this weekend? After all, he doesn't often get the opportunity to introduce his own son to the Governor General.'

Had he felt, sensed, her presence? At any rate he didn't seem surprised but replied, without opening his eyes, 'He won't miss me. Any more than I'll miss him. I'm the black sheep of the family.'

Then he suddenly opened his eyes and stared straight at her. His yellowy-brown eyes were glowing even in the darkness and his gaze was like a punch in the stomach. He knows, she thought. And at the same time she wondered what exactly it was that he knew.

'By the way, we can't be doing with losers up the Ghost,' she said in an exaggeratedly snappy tone. 'I can only hope that this isn't your first expedition. We're talking about life and death here.'

She had managed to insert maximum arrogance into her voice – but at the same time she could hear herself sounding laughably dramatic.

'Every expedition is a first,' he retorted, matching her arrogant tone. 'And don't worry – I know the risks. I knew them at the Victoria Glacier and the Snow Dome. That's what gets me going.' He paused a second. 'You too.'

He stood up with an elegant movement and came towards

her. Katie had no time to back off, and found herself standing face to face with him.

'Have you thought about whether we actually need the others?' he murmured. Even in the darkness, she could see his eyes; it almost seemed as if they were glowing with some kind of internal fire. 'How about going on our own? The others will just hold us back.'

It wasn't fear that Katie was feeling. It was surprise. Surprise, because she wanted to say: *You're right. Let's do it on our own.*

But that was of course completely ridiculous. She'd never say that, and in any case it was too late. She could already hear voices and a second later the others were coming around the bend: Julia, Chris, David and Benjamin, who was dashing towards her with his camera. His loud voice broke the silence. 'Take one. First scene. The team about to set off. How are you, guys? How do you feel? Ready for an adventure?' He panned slowly round. 'Here we are at the starting point for the legendary climb up the Ghost. At first sight, a mountain just like all the others in the Rocky Mountains. But the name says it all. It holds a dark secret. For, thirty years ago, eight students apparently went missing en route to the summit. Truth or legend? We're setting off to solve the mystery. But what are we going to find ten thousand feet up?'

Benjamin lowered his camera, switched it off, and laughed happily. 'Yeah, the first scene's in the can.'

In the dawn that was gradually breaking, they could hardly make out one another's faces, but the excitement and expectation in Benjamin's voice transmitted itself to all of them. Katie could finally feel the long awaited surge of adrenalin, and savoured the feeling of energy. Your plan won't fail, she thought, not if you can help it. Anything is possible. You just have to fight for it.

'Okay, here we go,' she said firmly, reaching for her rucksack as Julia's voice came through the darkness.

'What about that girl? What was her name? Ana? When are we meeting her? Is she actually coming?'

'Yes, I already told you, didn't I? She'll be waiting for us at the fork in the path,' Katie replied. 'We're in good hands with Ana Cree. Nobody knows this area better than her; I asked around in Fields. Her grandfather lived in a log cabin in the forest until he became too ill to take care of himself. Ana sometimes uses it when she goes on expeditions on the glacier.'

'So has she ever climbed the Ghost?' David asked.

Katie hesitated. 'Listen, the whole thing is an experiment,' she said. 'Each of us has our own reasons for doing it. And though to be honest we're all go-it-alone types, none of us could make it to the summit on our own. So we've got to trust one another whether we want to or not, okay? Ana said she'll meet us, and I'm sure she'll be there. I trust her.'

Katie had no idea whether the silence that met her meant agreement or doubt. She didn't care either.

It was Paul who defused the tension. 'Hey, guys, why all the fuss? We've all chosen to be here. If you've changed your mind, no problem. Go back to your warm beds and look forward to the Governor arriving in six hours' time.' He looked at them all. 'But if you want to see it through, let's get started and not waste time standing here talking.'

Katie heaved her rucksack onto her back. It felt heavy, but

exactly right. Without looking again at the others, she turned and set off at a brisk pace.

Everyone has to make their own decision.

She didn't get far. A slender figure emerged from the darkness of the path. Despite the early hour, Robert was wearing jeans and a scruffy white t-shirt, as if he'd thrown some clothes on very quickly. He was pale and his expression behind his round glasses was one of embarrassment. But his voice had its customary firmness as he said, 'I'm warning you. Don't do it.'

Benjamin removed his lens cap and pointed the camera straight at Robert.

'Why not, Rob? Tell us. Why not? What are you feeling? What can you see in the future?'

Robert, however, ignored him and went over to Julia, who was standing close to Chris. 'He isn't up there. Not any more.'

'Who?' Katie heard Benjamin exclaim. 'Who's he talking about, Julia? Who isn't up there?'

'Leave me alone, Robert.' Julia turned away and stomped off.

Chris followed her.

Robert stared helplessly after them. 'I know something terrible is going to happen.'

Before Katie could reply, she could already hear Paul answering. 'Maybe. Maybe not. That's just the way fate is, Robert. Whatever is going to happen, happens, and we can't do anything about it. And you, Rob, may be able to see disaster coming. But have you ever thought that you can't stop it? That you might only be able to see it – and that's that? You can't stop fate. No matter how hard you try.'

Robert was silent. He looked once more at Julia's retreating figure, then turned wordlessly and disappeared between the trees, heading back to the college.

Katie followed Julia. But she couldn't stop the voice in her head. It was the voice from the lift.

Someone will die up there, Katie.

CHAPTER 10

The path that led along the edge of Mirror Lake had long since turned into a rough track. To the right, it was soon bordered by deciduous woods, dense undergrowth, thickets and then, again, cliffs. It would take more and more time and energy even to make out the path at all, but Katie was becoming increasingly impatient and agitated.

To their left was the lake. As there wasn't a breath of wind, the surface lay before them immobile, almost unreal.

Katie was desperate to exert herself, desperate to plunge at last into the adventure that she had been planning in her head for so long.

Instead, their only obstacles to overcome were a few stones, boulders and uprooted trees.

They had long since seen the boat house on the opposite side of the lake, and Solomon Cliff, which had caused such a commotion several months ago, was becoming ever more visible. But Katie had no eyes for it. Instead, she kept seeking out the massive steep face of the Ghost which rose up to their right. The peaks behind it were mirrored in the surface of the lake – a fantastic sight. Yet Katie couldn't shake off the strange feeling that the rounded summit of the Ghost was moving further away, the closer they got to it.

Katie sighed. She had to take care not to become too impatient yet. But she was feeling increasingly annoyed by the way that Paul had taken over as leader. As if the whole thing had been his idea, Katie thought irritably, and she felt especially incensed by his habit of stopping, pulling out the map, and examining it with Chris and David. It felt as if he were deliberately setting out to provoke her, to show her that she was dependent on him.

She was walking alongside Julia. They barely exchanged a word. Julia was lost in her own thoughts. The only one who seemed cheerful and contented was Benjamin. Too jittery to keep up a steady pace, he kept changing direction. He would sometimes walk backwards in front of them, his camera trained on them, prattling on about secrets, legends, risks and other such nonsense; then he would fall behind or disappear somewhere into the undergrowth, only to reappear again in front of them.

Katie found the others' silence just as annoying as Paul's behaviour. She remembered how she and Sebastien could be silent – but that had been something different. They had never had to talk much; they had understood one another without words. It had been like that right from the start.

Katie had first met Sebastien at one of those receptions that her parents were always dragging her along to. A charity event of some sort, where politicians and celebrities donated a tiny fraction of their fortune to the starving millions in Africa, some current catastrophe, or children with terminal cancer. At any rate, it was an evening when Katie had wished that all the people there would themselves get terminal cancer and spare her from having to endure the kinds of remarks that people made to suck up to her parents – about how very clever and pretty their daughter was. Yeah, right. Katie sometimes actually believed that everyone at these receptions had had some kind of microchip implanted into their language control centre, which made them spout this fake party drivel.

Anyway, Katie had been horribly bored. Then, suddenly, she had felt someone watching her. A boy was staring at her; his parents were talking to hers. She had returned his gaze – and it was like a revelation.

If someone had told Katie beforehand that there was such a thing as thought transference, she would have laughed at them. Telepathy, like romance, was completely outside her radar. But what happened between Sebastien and her in a matter of seconds had as much to do with romance as climbing had to do with walking upstairs.

They had exchanged looks, and it was as if their eyes were sending SOS signals across the room.

Sebastien was incredibly good looking – one of those types that Katie immediately steered clear of. Boys who were interested in their looks were, in her experience, either gay or womanising idiots. Real boys, whom you could talk to, who understood you, weren't good looking.

Sebastien, though, was the exception. His dark blond hair was a touch too long for him to have come straight from the hairdresser. His skin was almost perfectly evenly brown – but only almost. Even from a distance, Katie could see the white line of a cap at his hairline. He wasn't wearing a white shirt and black tie like the others, but a black shirt and a white tie. And when he smiled, his smile would have been perfect – if he hadn't put his head slightly to one side, giving him an almost mocking air.

Their parents talked and talked. Katie couldn't remember what they were talking about. The world economic crisis, perhaps, or the climate summit, or the mission in Afghanistan – or maybe the best hotels and restaurants in DC.

At any rate, Sebastien was suddenly standing beside her. He looked at his watch and said, 'Eleven. That's how long I promised to stay. Shall we go?' He jerked his head towards the exit, and together they left the party. However, they didn't go to a club, as she'd expected; instead, he took her to Theodore Roosevelt Bridge. That's how it all started.

'How long have we been walking?' Julia's voice interrupted Katie's thoughts.

Katie pulled her mobile out of her pocket. 'It's really weird, the way you still don't have a mobile.'

Julia, however, merely shrugged. 'I don't need a mobile to tell me the time.'

'How about a watch, then?'

Julia laughed.

Katie looked at the screen. They had been walking for a good three and a half hours, and she estimated that they must have done over half of the path around the lake. But there was still no sign of the fork that would take them round the cliff wall, and no sign of Ana Cree.

'What do you make of that Paul?' asked Julia.

'He's a smart-arse and I don't trust him.'

'Why did you let him come?'

'He could have blown the whistle on us.'

They were silent for a while until Julia said, 'I just wonder where he got that map.'

Katie kicked a stone aside. 'Don't worry – I'll find out.'

Julia slowed down and sounded slightly anxious now. 'What do you think Debbie meant when she said he was on probation?'

'No idea.'

'But we ought to know,' said Julia.

Katie glanced at her. 'Are you getting cold feet? If so, you should have stayed in the college.'

Julia shook her head silently. She was about to reply when the boys, a good third of a mile ahead of them, stopped and turned round.

'What's up?' called Katie.

'Come here! You have to see this!' Benjamin was waving excitedly at them.

Katie and Julia hurried over to them, and saw what they meant.

The forest to their right suddenly gave way to a vast swathe of treeless land that looked as though it had been devastated by an almighty storm or stripped bare in some wanton clearance project. Instead of trees, they saw ahead of them a shimmering green expanse well over a mile in length, and so broad that Katie couldn't see where it ended.

The wasteland was covered in dense grass, reeds and scrub – but although the sight of the dead branches and trunks poking up from the swamp made Katie feel sick, she only had eyes for the rock face arising from the swamp to her right, still some distance away but surprisingly clear. All of a sudden, at one stroke, the Ghost seemed to be within reach.

'What's that?' Julia asked.

'Swamp,' Chris replied. He picked up a boulder and flung it in the direction of the greenish sludge. It sank within seconds.

'What a revolting smell.' David shuddered.

Katie nodded. The stench was overpowering. She looked around. 'Where are we?' she asked.

Paul pulled out the map. It fluttered gently in the wind as he spread it out on a stone. They all gathered around him. Paul put his finger on the map. 'The path to the Ghost must fork off somewhere around here.' He looked in the direction of the mountain. 'If we carry on along the lakeside path, we'll end up going away from the mountains.'

Chris shook his head. 'There's no swamp on that map.'

'Maybe we should have turned off earlier? What if we missed the fork in the path?' said David.

'The shore and the forest have barely changed the whole time. There are barely any clues.'

'Fork in the path?' retorted Chris. 'A fork in a path that's not there?'

'Hey, guys!' Benjamin appeared on their left from the reeds that bordered the lake, waving excitedly. 'You absolutely have to see this. It's really weird!'

Julia was first to react. Katie followed her through the three-foot-high reeds whose sharp edges whipped her in the face. Her shoes kept sinking into the damp ground, and the smell was getting worse. When she finally reached the lakeside minutes later, she found Julia looking distraught.

'What's wrong?' asked Katie.

Julia pointed behind her.

Katie came closer, and saw what Julia meant. A dead fish was floating belly up on the grey water. The longer she stared at it, the more uneasy she felt. There wasn't just one dead fish. There were hundreds of them entangled in the tall brown grass. As if the plants were reaching for the fish corpses, digging themselves into the silvery scales, pulling them out of the safe depths of Mirror Lake to die miserable deaths.

Katie felt sick, and a strange fear overcame her. Oh come on, she told herself, they're just fish. But then she suddenly realised what was causing the smell: layer upon countless layer of rotting fish.

Death and decay.

The fish corpses that were quietly rotting away here were anything but normal. Something had stopped them from reaching the lake.

And there was something else. There was no greedy buzzing of insects. None of the bluebottles that pounce on rotting corpses. Instead, they too were lying dead in the brown slop – millions of tiny black dots.

'What on earth had happened here?' Julia asked, horrified.

'I'd love to know too.' Paul appeared next to Katie as if from nowhere. He pulled a knife out of his pocket, cut down a reed with one swift movement, went over to the swamp and pulled a fish corpse towards him.

'One day, maybe two,' he said. 'It's been dead for no longer than that. But there might be more that have been lying here since for ever. It's disgusting.'

'But,' Julia's voice was trembling, 'how's that possible?'

'Maybe something's wrong with the water,' David mused.

'We should take a sample back to the college with us on our way home.'

'No, no, that's not what I mean. What I'm wondering is where all the fish came from in the first place. Robert's tried to go fishing a couple of times, but he's never caught anything. He says the lake is dead. And you said something similar, Chris.'

'I was evidently mistaken,' Chris said drily. 'These fish must have come from somewhere.'

Katie stared to her left, at the swampy landscape with its brown grass and thick undergrowth. Then she looked to her right, at the dense band of reeds that bordered the lake and between which mouldy, almost black, water was lapping.

'Whatever. The dead fish aren't our problem. Our problem is the swamp. It's definitely too wide for us to cross,' Paul said, stuffing the map back into his bag. He took a tentative step forwards. His shoes immediately sank into the morass.

Katie's attention was caught by a loud screech above their heads. She looked up and saw a black dot in the sky, heading straight towards her. She watched anxiously as the jackdaw, its neck outstretched, passed above her, its wings flapping heavily, before curving off to the right. A swamp, she thought. It's just a swamp. Nothing more.

'What do you suggest?' Paul turned to Katie.

'We need to find another place and ...'

She broke off as the bird suddenly stopped mid-flight. It hung in the air for no more than a second, then plunged headfirst to earth. Katie's initial assumption that it was hunting for fish was shattered as it shot like an arrow straight into the swampy mud and sank within a fraction of a second.

They all held their breaths, staring at that bit of the swamp, their hopes diminishing by the second. The bird didn't reappear.

'Oh my God. Something pulled it under,' Benjamin whispered.

'The current,' a voice said behind them. 'The current pulled it under.'

Katie turned round and breathed out again.

Before them stood a tall, slender girl. She was wearing a poncho on top of her black trousers, and a wide-brimmed hat protected her face from the sun. She took it off, and her sparkling dark-brown eyes glanced mockingly around the group.

'Hi,' the girl said, setting down her rucksack. 'I'm Ana. You haven't made much progress, have you? I've been waiting for more than an hour.'

'What current?' David asked without introducing himself.

'An underground river. My ancestors called it Black River. It's the reason why this valley was never settled. They say it brings death.'

CHAPTER 11

Julia listened hard, but she could barely hear a sound beyond the gurgling of the swampy ground beneath her feet. They were all silent, lost in their own thoughts. The only thing that broke the silence was the sound of Katie's breathing. Or was it her own?

Nobody had used this path in a long time – if it could be called a path.

The grass and undergrowth stood several feet high along the narrow gap between the forest and the swamp. That summer's bad weather seemed to have left its mark. The rain and the nocturnal storms that had swept through the valley several times seemed to have left behind a track through the undergrowth, which they were now walking along in a curious zig-zag fashion. And when they couldn't go any further, they beat the thorny branches aside with boughs that they picked up as they walked. It took an enormous amount of energy – energy that they really needed to save for tomorrow's climb.

Only Paul seemed to derive pleasure from hacking down the stubborn branches. He kept on holding the knife that he had pulled out of his rucksack, acting as if he were slashing his way through the jungle.

And a jungle was what it reminded Julia of.

Whilst the stink diminished as they moved further away from the lake, the air became ever warmer and muggier, all the more so because Ana – who, with David, had taken the lead – was taking them further and further away from the edge of the forest, so that there was no longer any shade. Bushes and three-foot-high reeds alternated with one another, the reeds hiding muddy puddles or even small pools. And the worst thing wasn't the mouldy smell which the swamp was now giving off in the morning sunshine, but the colour of the water that was lapping between the green blades of grass. Muddy, dark green, brown like sewage, yellow like pus.

Julia was still thinking about the bird. About how quickly it had been swallowed up by the mire. As if there were creatures in the depths of this swamp, disguised by the grasses, stretching out their fingers to capture anything that was alive. A shiver ran down her spine despite the heat. A picture appeared in her mind of faces emerging from the green slime. Human faces peeling out of the depths, frozen into muddy masks.

She heard the others' voices as if from a long way away. Someone was calling her name.

The swamp seemed to hold a magical attraction for Benjamin. He kept darting off and disappearing into the tall reeds. All they could hear of him then were his squelching footsteps. Then he would reappear and content himself with poking around with a long stick in the soft mud.

Chris, who was walking along silently in front of her, hadn't turned round to her for quite some time now. He had spent the whole of the previous evening hassling her, trying to find out why she wanted to climb the Ghost. But she didn't want to tell him – and even if she had wanted to, how could she have explained it to him? Now he seemed to be punishing her by giving her the cold shoulder. He had attached himself instead to Paul, who had appeared as if out of nowhere.

She tried to catch a glimpse of the steep face of the mountain. There would have been a good view from the shore, but the tall grass here tended to block everything out.

She was making a mistake, Julia suddenly thought. It just didn't feel right; in fact, it felt like something she ought to have been avoiding at all costs. Something inescapable that she couldn't quite put her finger on. They were heading straight for it. And her heart felt heavier with every step. It seemed a mockery for the sky to be so unusually blue, the sun so incredibly bright.

Julia stopped and wiped the sweat off her brow. The terrain was becoming increasingly rough and difficult to negotiate. Ana and David just kept on tramping their way through the tall grass. Sighing, she set off again and rejoined the others. She could hear Ana talking to the boys about the underground river, as if there really could be such a thing; a river that brought death. Julia wished Robert were there to quash such fantasies.

Katie came up from behind and overtook Julia. Her flatmate, who had walked alongside her for most of the way, had set a rhythm that Julia found truly exhausting. One moment she would be walking very slowly, as if she were hesitating – and the next moment, quite out of the blue, she would strike up a strict pace which Julia struggled to keep up with. Once she had more or less caught up with the boys, she stopped and slowed down again, hesitant once more.

'Have you ever seen that Paul around the college before?' Katie was asking.

'I've never noticed him, and I didn't even know that Forster had a son,' Julia replied. 'And then there's that probation business.'

'Debbie!' Katie snapped contemptuously. 'Who believes a single word that Debbie says?'

'He didn't contradict her, which suggests to me that there's some truth in it,' Julia mused. She scrutinised Paul's back carefully, as if it would tell her what type of person he was. There was something too self-important about him for her taste – but was Chris really any different?

Yes, he was. Chris kept upsetting her with his mood swings. Paul, however, seemed to know exactly what he wanted.

'You don't trust him either,' she continued.

Katie didn't reply at first, and Julia was starting to think she hadn't heard when she burst out, 'He's got the map.'

'But Ana's the one who knows the way, isn't she?' Julia said. She groaned. 'And on that subject, I'd be mightily glad if she could lead us out of these stupid reeds. I'm afraid of sinking every time I take a step. I can't bear to think of what's rotting all around us. I really hope that we're going to be out of this swamp soon.' She paused briefly. 'Just imagine if Debbie were here. Can you imagine the moaning and groaning?'

Katie gave a snort of laughter. 'I can't believe she even

thought of it. I sometimes think her brain has been infected by some kind of virus. I've never met anyone with so little self-awareness. Doesn't she ever look in the mirror?'

Benjamin suddenly appeared behind them. 'Hey. Stop. Just stop for a second!'

Julia turned round. Benjamin's face bore an expression of triumph and excitement and in his outstretched hand he was holding a branch with mouldy reeds hanging off it like the remains of an old cloth.

And something else.

Something brown and rectangular.

'Hey, guys. Come and see this! The swamp's giving up its secrets.'

The four ahead of him stopped. David said something to Chris and they came back together while Ana and Paul waited uncertainly.

Benjamin detached the brown object from the branch, and came over to them holding it in his hand.

'Are you playing at Indiana Jones or something?' Chris called.

Benjamin wiped the object with his hands, turned it around several times, opened it up and exclaimed, 'Oh my God! It's a wallet or something.'

He opened it and gave a low whistle. Then he pulled something out. There was a tense silence that lasted several seconds until Benjamin thrust his find into the air like a trophy.

Julia immediately realised what it was. She turned to look at the swamp that stretched out to the foot of the Ghost, looking like a broad green path. But if you concentrated and looked at the details, you could see the soft ground dotted with almost black pools of water. They had to beware of them: they were dangerous and could drag a human down into their murky depths.

What Benjamin had discovered seemed at first sight to be harmless. It was a photo.

CHAPTER 12

When Benjamin dragged out the filthy article and they all started getting excited, Katie initially felt merely impatient. Shit. That's all I needed, she thought. They'd been walking for ages and had basically got nowhere. That didn't seem to bother the others. They were clustering round Benjamin, full of curiosity, while Katie was desperate to move on.

What Benjamin had pulled out of the stagnant water wasn't a wallet but a nylon neck purse. It had once been orange, but this became evident only when Benjamin opened the zip. The nylon fabric had kept almost all the water out so that the contents – albeit somewhat crumpled and foxed – had been well preserved.

'A load of money,' exclaimed Benjamin.

Well, a hundred Canadian dollars wasn't exactly a fortune, but it wasn't to be sneezed at either.

The next thing he pulled out was a note which he passed to Katie.

'A list like yours.'

'Mine?' Katie had no idea what he was talking about.

David glanced over her shoulder. 'An alphabetical list of the stuff you need to climb a mountain.'

Katie was only half listening as he read aloud. 'Batteries,

cutlery, down jacket ...' Instead, she was watching Paul, who was staring at the photo.

She went over to him and looked at the yellowed print. A girl with long blonde hair, smiling for the camera. Behind her, water. Nothing else.

The photo was from a different era. An era when girls wore flares and multi-coloured blouses and were photographed making peace signs. But that wasn't all. What was most disconcerting was that someone had cut the photo in two. The girl hadn't originally been on her own.

'Hey, she doesn't look too bad,' said Benjamin. 'But there was obviously someone else in the photo who broke her heart. What do you reckon?'

He turned the photo over and whistled loudly. 'I can't read the whole date, but I can read 1974. Is that when the disaster was?'

'We need to report it,' she heard David replying after a pause of several seconds. 'And hand the stuff in to the Dean.'

'You're surely not saying we have to turn back?' Katie retorted, shocked. 'Just because we've found an ancient photo? Listen, guys, it's just this place that's getting to us. The stink and all this decay – it gets to your nerves. What we need to do is get moving right away.'

Paul joined in at this point. 'Katie's right. It's just a load of ancient junk.' He took his rucksack off, opened up one of the side pockets and pulled out a plastic bag.

'What are you doing?' Julia asked anxiously.

'Nothing. I'm putting that thing in this bag – just like our friends the police do it.' He grinned broadly. 'I know all about evidence.'

'Paul?' It was the first time Ana had spoken since they had found the money bag. She had watched the whole thing uninterestedly, just waiting for them to move on. 'You're called Paul?'

'Ah yes, we haven't been formally introduced. I'm Paul. Paul Forster.' He raised his hand.

'Isn't there a professor called Forster at Grace? My grandfather knows him.'

Paul froze, just briefly. Nobody except Katie seemed to notice. He heaved his rucksack back on and turned round. 'So?' His voice was suddenly hard. 'Are we going or not? We've already spent too much time here.'

The others hesitated, and it was Julia who said, 'So where do we go from here, Ana? If you ask me, this isn't a path – it's a sodding nightmare.'

Benjamin laughed. 'Which would explain why it isn't shown on Paul's map.'

Ana pushed back her hat. 'You could use that map as toilet paper,' she said. 'That's all it's good for. The valley is unpredictable. You can only rely on two things here.'

'And those are?' Chris asked mockingly.

'Instinct and yourself. We have to carry on following the swamp.'

With these words, she turned and set off. Paul followed her with a black expression. And although Katie knew it was weird and crazy, she derived surreptitious pleasure from Ana's rubbishing of Paul and his map – though a map was precisely what she could have done with now. Although she had been able to see the rounded summit of the Ghost so clearly earlier on, it seemed impossible that a swamp was going to lead them to the mountain. In fact, nothing was as she'd expected it to be. But no matter what surprises lay in store for her, Katie was determined to face them all down.

'Didn't you think he turned really aggressive all of a sudden?' Katie heard Julia's voice behind her. And although Katie knew whom Julia meant, she still said, 'Who?'

'Paul.'

'Dunno.'

'Do you think it was because Ana mentioned Professor Forster?'

'Why don't you ask him?' Damn it: she'd stepped in yet another pool of water. Her trousers were already wet up to the knees, and she was wondering whether they would dry overnight in the cabin.

'I'd rather not.' Julia laughed. 'He'd probably stab me with his pocket knife or something.'

'Chris wouldn't let him. How are things going with him, anyway?'

'Don't know. They're going. Kind of.'

'Doesn't sound exactly like the love story of the century.'

'No.'

'No intimate girly gossip?' Katie said mockingly. 'No confessions? No exciting details of your sex life?'

Instead of a reply, she heard a yelp. Julia had stopped and was staring at her hand. 'Oh damn. These reeds are sharper than a knife. It's bleeding.'

Before she knew it, David was by her side. 'That needs disinfecting.' He produced the red nylon pouch that he was carrying around his neck, unzipped it, and pulled out a little bottle and a cotton wool pad, onto which he dripped an orange-coloured fluid. Then he carefully took Julia's hand and dabbed the wound slowly and carefully. 'I'll stick a plaster on it. I hope you've had a tetanus jab.'

Katie noticed Julia turning pale. 'I've no idea.'

'You must know.' David sounded worried. 'You can't just go running around here without being vaccinated. What if the mosquitos get you?'

'Mosquitos? Have you ever seen so much as a single fly in the valley?' Katie said acidly.

'And what if she encounters a snake? My God, I should have checked before we ...'

Chris's voice suddenly came from behind him. 'Hey, stop that. You're not our self-appointed medic.' He pushed David aside. 'I'll take care of Julia.'

'If you really cared about her, you wouldn't have let her come in the first place.' David's voice was trembling.

Wow, thought Katie. Something's brewing up here. Something they could do without. 'Oh, stop acting up, both of you,' she said briskly. 'Julia isn't a little girl. She knows what she's doing. And there aren't any snakes here.'

'I wouldn't be so sure about that,' replied Ana. 'But don't worry. My grandfather taught me how to suck out a snake bite.' She laughed. 'Old witch-doctor trick. I've always wanted to do it.'

'You're all crazy,' David burst out. He turned and set off at a fast pace.

He's right, thought Katie. We're crazy. And that's just as it should be.

*

The further they walked, the higher the reeds became. Katie could only see what was immediately in front of her and the sky directly above her. She felt as if she were in a jungle. They had completely lost sight of the mountain. Ana, however, remained completely composed. She carried on ahead of them unperturbed, as if she had an internal compass pointing her in the right direction. She never turned round, never said a word, never hesitated. She walked quickly, with long strides across the almost impassable terrain, and Katie had to increase her own speed in order to keep up. She could feel herself breathing more quickly. Definitely not a Sunday stroll, she thought with satisfaction. It's just the challenge I wanted.

Julia, on the other hand, looked exhausted. However, one look at Ana told Katie that their mountain guide wasn't going to stop until she'd reached the cabin.

Katie gradually got used to battling her way through the stubborn reeds, past feeble juniper branches and uprooted trees. And as she walked, she began to recognise from the colour of the grass when she was about to encounter one of those sneaky criss-crossing pools of water into which you could sink up to your knees. If she got too close to the swamp, if she saw pools with water glistening darkly in them, she automatically kept her distance.

Apart from the bird they had seen before, they didn't disturb a single creature. It was as if they were the only living things in this horrible wasteland.

But swamp or no swamp, Katie was moving. She was in her element.

As a child, Katie had felt that her entire life was determined by silence and stagnation. The atmosphere had been just as desolate as the landscape she was walking through now.

Katie hated immobility and stagnation. It reminded her of her mother, a woman who was even afraid of moving her facial muscles in case it caused a crease in her face. Her mother had been desperate for a daughter in her own image. Instead, she had had Katie, the polar opposite. It wasn't just that Katie, at almost five foot nine inches, was much too tall even for a *half*-Korean, and also lacked her mother's svelte manner. No, it was that she showed her irrepressible drive even as a three-year-old – much to her mother's disappointment. She had been an almost uncontrollable child, and had stayed that way. No matter where they had lived while her father made his way up the political ladder, she had always remained restless.

And that's why she always had to stay on the move, today as always.

She glanced ahead of her. David, Chris, Ana, then Julia and Benjamin, who was filming yet again. But where was Paul? She involuntarily quickened her pace and overtook the others until she reached Ana.

'Where is he?'

'Paul? No idea. Gone for a pee?' There was a short pause before she said, 'He's going to cause us problems.'

'How can you tell?'

'I can just smell it ...' It seemed as if Ana were going to add something, then she thought better of it. 'When we met in Fields, I never imagined you'd take me at my word and rustle up so many people for the expedition.'

'They're my friends.'

'I thought you were more of a loner.' She leapt nimbly across a wide rivulet. 'Oh, whatever. I just hope you've chosen the right friends for the expedition. As for me, I've guided so many people through the mountains just because they fancied an adventure – and quite a few of them I'd sooner have left at the top ... '

Ana broke off and Katie didn't pursue it.

She looked around for Paul once more, but couldn't see him anywhere. She let the others gradually overtake her until she was at the rear of the group.

Friends? Why had she said that?

Up until now, she'd only had one real friend.

It was Sebastien who had come up with the bridge idea. She had stared down, fascinated, at the Potomac River, at the place where an empty plastic bottle was bobbing about on the current. The evening had been very windy, almost stormy, and they had clung to one another in order not to be blown away. If only you could liquidate yourself, Katie had thought then. If only you could liquidate yourself and disappear into that bottle which would take you to the Atlantic. Or just let yourself be blown away in the wind.

'We ought to jump,' Sebastien had said, interrupting her daydream.

'Jump?'

'Yes, jump off the bridge.'

Katie could still remember suddenly realising how high it was, and feeling as if she were actually going to climb onto the railings and stand up there. It was the coolest feeling of all time. The abyss. The depths. Assessing the danger. And then: jumping.

The Theodore Roosevelt Bridge was bristling with safety precautions, including a six-foot-wide mesh to deter desperados bent on ending their lives, particularly at Christmas, New Year, Thanksgiving or some other gloomy national holiday.

'That would be suicide.'

'Only if you want to die,' Sebastien had replied.

'Do you?'

'Not today.' He had laughed.

'But it's forbidden.' *Forbidden* was the boundary that Katie was particularly intent on crossing. Precisely because her superdaddy was pulling all the strings in the State Department.

Sod prohibitions, she thought, as she returned to reality, suddenly aware that it was hours since she had last seen one of the countless *Danger!* signs that festooned the valley.

Katie demonstrates a clear and persistent lack of responsibility, and contempt for social norms, rules and obligations.

That was what the psychologist Professor Lebkowski – a diminutive man (compared to Katie) sporting a travesty of a beard – had written in his report about her. Of course, she had never been given the report. Katie had found the envelope in her father's desk drawer and when she had seen that the return address was Professor Lebkowski's, she had decided that the report actually belonged to her. But she would have learned just as much from reading her horoscope.

Inability to sustain long-term relationships.

She was walking as if in a trance now, which was not good for memories. Sebastien on the bridge railings, standing high above her. That wind. It had felt to Katie as if the railings were swaying and Sebastien were swaying with them.

'Come down! I have absolutely no desire for the cops to appear and slam our heads on the hood of their car while searching us for weapons.'

'Oh, you Americans. Supporters of the death penalty. No balancing on the Theodore Roosevelt Bridge. No smoking. No alcohol in public. No kissing in public places.'

And then he had jumped down and was standing in front of her, then he was grabbing her shoulders, then his mouth was on hers – for a long time, and Katie realised that she had never been kissed in her life before. Not by anyone. And the longer it went on, the more she liked it. And . . .

'Hey guys! Looks like we've reached the end of the line.'

She was wrenched from her thoughts – and she realised that she had taken her eyes off the ground for a moment. Damn. It was even darker and muddier than before. Her right leg was stuck fast.

Benjamin must have overtaken everyone without her noticing. He was now standing in front of them, his hands raised.

'Dead end. We can't go any further.'

Katie looked up. Ahead of them were cliffs. Nothing but cliffs. They cut through the swamp to Katie's left and the impenetrable undergrowth to her right.

'We've made it,' said Ana. She pulled off her rucksack, put it on the ground, and dropped down next to it.

CHAPTER 13

The sun was positively unbearable. There wasn't a cloud in the radiantly blue sky. Katie wiped the sweat off her forehead, put her rucksack down, and looked around. Then she put her head back and stared upwards.

The rock face was gigantic and seemed to arise from the nothingness of the green marshland. Katie had never seen anything like it. 'Steep' didn't begin to cover it. The stone was as smoothly polished as a mirror, so far as Katie could make out at any rate. And then, a hundred and sixty-four feet up, came the overhang – and God knows what came after that.

This must be the wall that you could see from Solomon Cliff, the one that led ten thousand feet directly up to the summit of the Ghost. Katie had studied it from a distance for weeks now, always coming to the same conclusion: climbing up here was completely unthinkable. Crazy. Suicidal.

But now that she was standing right in front of it all of a sudden, she could barely contain herself. What if she were to try? True, the others lacked the necessary experience. But just with Ana – yes, they could do it. Katie estimated that they had to be standing directly beneath the main summit, which would mean that the entry point to the wind gap had to be on their right.

Katie's vision blurred, and her eyes were watering in the

glaring sunlight. She pulled her sunglasses from the side pocket of her trousers and turned to Ana. 'Where exactly are we?'

Ana pushed her leather hat back, opened her rucksack, and pulled out a bottle of water. It wasn't made of plastic; nor was it aluminium. Instead, it was a round water bottle of the type that Katie had seen in Westerns. It even had leather fringes dangling off it. Should she take that as a cliché, or as a spur to carry on?

Ana pointed to the wall. 'You're exactly where you wanted to be. You're right underneath the Ghost.'

'Thank God for that. I was convinced we were never going to get there,' Julia groaned, dropping down onto the ground. 'I thought it couldn't possibly be worse than being on the athletics team. Why on earth do I bother going jogging so much if I then immediately collapse in a heap? That swamp was a complete nightmare.'

'The nightmare's only just beginning.' Ana grinned. She could have been in a toothpaste advert: her white teeth were gleaming in her smooth, olive face.

Katie interrupted her. 'Where do we start climbing?' she asked irritably.

'Start climbing? Give us a break, Katie!' Benjamin leaned his hand against the rock face – and quickly withdrew it. 'Christ, that's hot. You could burn your fingers on it.'

'Yeah, course you could,' Chris grinned. 'But only if you're a wimp like you.'

'No, honestly, it's not normal.'

David took a step forwards, put his hand on the stone and immediately took it off. 'Wow, you're right. That's weird.'

Julia pulled her water bottle out of her rucksack, did up

the straps again, and put her head back. 'Why's it weird? The sun's been shining like crazy the whole time. It must be at least eighty-five degrees.'

Chris leaned forward. 'Stay there, gorgeous,' he murmured, and gave her a long kiss.

He's only doing that to stake his claim on her, Katie thought.

David was pacing nervously up and down, looking down the path that they had come along. 'Paul still hasn't turned up, damn it. Where on earth has he got to?'

'Not my problem,' Chris murmured. He took his lips off Julia's and shut his eyes.

'We were supposed to stay together so that nobody gets lost,' David said.

'Paul won't get lost. He's the keeper of the sacred map that's led us through a swamp that isn't even marked.' Chris blinked slowly. 'Honestly, I really can be doing without that guy.'

'I'll take a look to see where we go next.' Like David, Benjamin couldn't settle. Holding his camera, he turned right and then vanished into the bushes at the edge of the wall.

Katie was still staring up at the cliff. Her whole body was tingling. Her need for the ultimate high had gradually become an addiction. She'd been told never to jump off a bridge again, and she had promised not to. That's over, she'd said again and again. But it wasn't over, even if she was now doing precisely the opposite.

It was her addiction to ever greater risk that kept driving her on; the desire to conquer increasingly dangerous routes without safety precautions, in the full knowledge that one single mistake could be fatal. She needed the euphoria, the feeling of delirium, hanging off the middle of a cliff face and – she needed the sense of mortal danger.

Crazy.

Yes, it was crazy. She was crazy.

But the fact was, Katie couldn't understand the others. She couldn't bear the way they were so calm. Was there any better sensation than defying gravity?

'Up there?'

Katie whirled round, shocked, and saw Paul standing directly behind her. His breath brushed her right cheek as he laughed quietly. 'Forget it. You'll never manage it.'

She took several steps back and looked up. Yes, it was a murderous rock face. But all the same.

'No cliff is too difficult if you're properly prepared,' she said.

He pointed upwards. 'But you're not prepared.'

'And how would you know that?'

'I know it.'

'So what exactly do you know?'

'That you're inviting disaster.' He paused briefly. 'And not for the first time.'

Katie froze. 'I have no idea what you're talking about.'

'Oh no?' He raised an eyebrow.

Katie would never be able to flee far enough. Sebastien's shadow would follow her everywhere. And how could it be any different? He was the only person who had ever touched her soul, who had seen her for what she was, who had understood her. The only one who had managed to bring tears to her eyes – until now.

She turned away, suddenly glad to find Ben appearing at

the side of her, saying in his silly CNN reporter voice, 'Katie West and Paul Forster – the new Grace dream team?' He raised his camera, but Paul had already disappeared back into the undergrowth.

The episode did at least give Katie time to regain her composure. She squared her shoulders and walked away from Ben and back to the others, who were sitting on the ground unpacking their provisions.

Katie wasn't hungry.

'Where's Ana gone?' she asked, looking around.

'Dunno.' Julia shrugged and held out a bar of chocolate. 'Do you want some, Katie?'

'No! And don't you all go thinking that you can lounge around here for eternity,' she added irritably. 'If we still want to make it to the cabin, we need to get going again.'

'You're a born slave-driver,' Chris growled. 'We've been walking for five hours. We've more than earned a break.'

'Earned?' Katie shook her head. 'We haven't even climbed three feet yet.'

'That's not true,' said David. He was sitting on the ground, leaning against the rock face as he pulled out his pocket knife. 'We've already done more than three hundred.'

'Yeah, and we've still got three thousand to go until we get to the glacier tongue. And that's a big ask.'

Loud shouts interrupted her. It was clearly Benjamin's voice. The next moment he came thrusting his way through the undergrowth and stopped before them. 'Guys, you won't believe this!'

David, who had meanwhile sat down on the ground, looked up tiredly. 'What won't we believe now?'

But instead of answering, Benjamin threw himself down on the ground and burst out laughing. 'Oh my God, that girl's awesome. Honestly, guys, I saw it with my own eyes. Ana can walk through walls!'

Over the past few months, they had all got used to Benjamin. They shrugged and accepted his bad jokes, his mood swings, his nerviness. They put up with him constantly following them around with his camera, doing his *Big Brother* number. At some point they had made him promise that he wouldn't put any footage on YouTube or anywhere else on the internet, although Katie doubted whether he had kept his word.

But all the same, Benjamin had seemed equally unreliable and harmless to Katie up until now. Quite unlike Chris, whom she couldn't work out at all, Benjamin wasn't a real mystery. He presumably took drugs every now and then; that would explain his mood swings and why he seemed so psyched up. Katie didn't have a problem with that. But if he was going completely crazy, that was a different matter entirely. The very fact that he was claiming that Ana could walk through walls was absurd enough in itself – but his laugh was so hysterical and shrill that a shiver ran down her spine. She ought to have known it: Benjamin was a safety hazard.

'Oh, come on, Ben,' she heard Chris saying. 'Give it a rest with your stories.'

'No, honestly, see for yourselves. I'll show you where she did it. One minute she was standing right there in front of me, and the next she'd vanished.'

They all looked at him, annoyed.

'She's presumably just gone to look for the path,' David said, looking nervously around him.

'Ana knows the way,' Paul replied, pushing the sandy hair off his forehead. 'She's not like you lot. She doesn't go blundering into an adventure without having the faintest idea what to expect.'

'So you know what to expect up there?' Chris raised an eyebrow and pointed to the rock face.

'Of course I do. Why else would I be here?'

'I don't care where she is, so long as she doesn't just leave us sitting here,' growled Chris. 'I wouldn't put it past her. She doesn't give a shit about us.'

'Oh yeah?' Katie retorted. 'And I suppose you're here because if need be you'd put your life on the line for us?'

'Don't worry, I wouldn't go that far.' He grinned. 'Not for you, at any rate.'

'Exactly. All you're out for is a dirty weekend.'

'Oh, stop bickering, you two,' David interrupted.

'And you stop your holier-than-thou peace and harmony stuff. We're all egotists, David. Including you. It's high time you admitted it.' Even Katie didn't know where her aggression had come from. It was presumably the sun's fault. Its rays must contain something that humans hadn't yet investigated, something that made them aggressive, herself in particular.

She jumped up. 'I'm going to look for Ana,' she said. 'You can all calm down in the meantime.'

Julia laughed softly. 'Who needs to calm down, Katie?' she asked gently.

Without replying, Katie turned to the right and forced her way through the undergrowth.

More juniper. At least the scent got the stink of the swamp out of her nostrils.

Why on earth had she asked the others whether they wanted to come? Was she really dependent on them? Why had she listened to Ana?

You know full well, Katie. Because Ana wouldn't have agreed to be your guide otherwise.

Katie pushed a branch aside, and just as suddenly as bushes and shrubs had appeared, so too they now disappeared. She found herself face to face with the cliff face once again. But instead of the rock face looming up at a ninety-degree angle as it did further on, what confronted her here was a smooth, shimmering outcrop jutting from the cliff.

She was just trying to estimate the height and width of the outcrop when she was startled by a noise coming from the mountain.

Nonsense.

But there it came again.

Something was resounding behind the cliff, almost as if it were hollow.

Footsteps?

Yeah, right, Katie.

She shook her head and continued walking. But the noise followed her. It was directly behind her. An echo?

She stopped and glanced behind her. Then she stared at the cliff, irritated. The outcrop was just like the cliff face itself. No gaps, no holes. Even the tiniest crack was smoothed off, almost as if the stone were stuck on.

Only once before had Katie seen anything like this, and that was in Brittany. There, the primal force of the Atlantic Ocean had abraded the cliffs to such an extent that they had looked completely smooth and immaculate. But here they were in the mountains. Could rain and wind do the same as wind and waves?

Katie pressed her hands on the cliff, but immediately pulled them back again. Damn it – she'd forgotten Benjamin's warning. You really could burn your fingers on those stones.

Katie didn't know much about architecture, but she did know the cliffs around the college pretty well. She hadn't climbed them all, it was true, but she had vast numbers of photos. She'd looked at them over and over again. And this outcrop didn't just *look* unnatural to her: it *was* unnatural.

She hadn't noticed it at first simply because it was over-grown with juniper bushes and scrawny pine trees.

Katie fought her way once more through the undergrowth until she could see that section of the cliff from further away.

The outcrop was some twelve feet wide and stuck out from the cliff about six feet. Her common sense told her that what she was seeing was impossible. But there it was none the less: a semi-circular column that looked as if it had been designed on a drawing board and rose into the air for what seemed like for ever.

Oh come on, Katie. A freak of nature. Nothing more.

No, it wasn't that simple. There were columns like that in churches or museums.

Was it possible?

Could it really be the case that humans had carved a column of these dimensions out of the mountain?

Katie plunged back into the bushes and paced to the end of the protuberance. At least everything had gone quiet. No more noises were coming from the mountain. Instead, though, she noticed something else in the play of light and shadows.

Then she bounded forwards. The others' voices were audible in the far distance. They were calling Ana and her. She could hear the concern in their voices. But she didn't reply.

Light and shade.

A broad black line.

That could mean only one thing.

And indeed, at the point where the semi-circular column met the cliff face, Katie could see an opening, a deep crevice. Katie moved closer and stared inside. The crevice was no more than twenty inches wide.

Without a moment's thought Katie climbed up and forced herself feet first into the crevice. And just as she was thinking that she would be stuck there for ever, she suddenly managed to free herself.

CHAPTER 14

Katie found herself in complete darkness.

But that wasn't the worst thing. No: the worst thing was that Katie was surrounded by bare, cold cliffs. She could touch them on either side of her when she stretched out her hands. Dampness permeated her clothes. The walls and floor were slippery; the air freezing cold and foul.

It took only seconds for Katie's body to react. Her heart was pounding in her chest – just as it had when she'd been stuck in the lift the day before. It was becoming harder to breathe. Her mind was telling her: you're shut in. You're going to be here for ever.

She took a step backwards and banged her elbow against a wall. For a moment, the pain lessened her anxiety, but then panic hit her with full force once more.

Scream. Katie wanted to scream, but something was stopping her. Her voice would never have been loud enough to drown out the noise that was overwhelming her, seemingly from the core of the mountain. A thundering and roaring that echoed off the cliffs. Like a high-speed train racing through a tunnel. The walls were clamouring around her.

There was no point screaming for help. Nobody would hear her.

She could hear something else, close by. A rattling; her

own breath. She groped forwards. The way out. It must be here somewhere. Damn. Where the hell was that gap that she'd got through? There was no light to be seen. Not a single ray of sunlight made its way in, and she knew why. Because the crevice that she'd squeezed through was only six feet high and unbelievably narrow.

All around her was nothing but total darkness. All that seemed to exist was the roaring sound and her own rattling breath.

Water. She suddenly realised. Water was pouring in somewhere. With full force.

But where? How far away?

It didn't matter. She had to get out of there as quickly as possible. But without her headlamp, she was completely at the mercy of the darkness.

Instinct.

That's what Ana had talked about.

Katie, rely on your instinct.

The crevice she had squeezed through must be somewhere to her left. But where was her left? She ran her hands along the walls around her. Cracks, gaps, stones.

A pain shot through her hand, meeting up with the pain in her elbow. Nothing. Absolutely nothing there. Involuntarily, she pressed her back against the wall behind her, sliding her way along. That was how she had squeezed through the crevice; that was how she had to get out again. It simply couldn't be the case that there wasn't any way out. There was always a way out. Always.

And then she felt it. Felt the wall changing behind her. It was suddenly smooth. As if polished. She turned, put her face against the icy cold bare stone, and let it rest there for a moment as she gradually started to feel calmer.

People, Katie thought. People have worked on this cliff at some point. Why? She didn't know. All that mattered now was that these people had created a way in and, more importantly, a way out.

She spread out her arms. To her left, she felt bumps and cracks once more – but to her right, it was completely smooth. Slowly, she edged her way in that direction, carefully, cautiously, her mind set only on noting every little change.

And then at last her hand reached into emptiness. That had to be it, the narrow passageway between the mountain and the column that she had squeezed through. She clung to the stone edge and pulled herself forwards until her body slid through the crevice as if of its own accord. Then, after a horribly long moment of complete constriction, she felt the breeze on her hand, which was still hurting.

She screwed up her eyes. After the darkness of the cavern, she was completely blinded. All she could see were flashes of light. But she could hear a mocking giggle.

'You found it. You found the way all on your own.'

Katie blinked. Her eyes were gradually becoming re-accustomed to the light, and she saw Ana sitting on a stone, holding her water bottle and grinning broadly at her.

'What are you talking about?'

'That's it – the way to the Ghost.'

Katie stared at her. 'The way to the Ghost?'

'Yes. The tunnel you just found.'

Katie held her breath. 'You can't be serious!'

Ana shrugged. 'There isn't a safer way. Or a faster one. The mine behind this wall leads right under the wind gap between the two summits and through the mountain. Once we're on the other side, we can climb straight up to the cabin.'

No way, was Katie's gut reaction. No way am I ever going back in there.

'Forget it,' she said loudly. 'I'm taking the direct route over the wall.'

Ana gave a snort of laughter. 'It might look possible from down here. But you'll be done for if you try it. Guaranteed.' Ana stood up and stowed the bottle away in her rucksack. 'That's precisely the problem with this mountain. The stone is so smooth that you can forget about pitons and wedges. You need a drill. The tunnel is the only feasible way from here to the Ghost. You're the one who wanted to start from the valley, remember. It would have been much easier to get to the glacier from Fields.'

'A tunnel? Sounds pretty easy to me. At least we'll stay dry if the weather changes.' Chris and the others emerged from the undergrowth. They all had their rucksacks with them. David was carrying Katie's bag, which he threw across to her.

The others were looking at Ana. None of them seemed to be questioning her authority. Why would they, Katie thought. She's the one who grew up in these mountains.

'Is this passageway marked on your map?' Katie asked Paul. He was standing slightly apart from everyone else watching events with scorn in his eyes.

'Nobody knows about this tunnel,' Ana replied for Paul. 'But it's the only way, believe me.'

'Why didn't you tell me that before?' Katie said angrily. 'I kept telling you which route I was planning, and you never said a word about tunnels.'

'Why would I?' Ana shrugged. 'We're basically going your way. Just under the wind gap rather than over the mountain.'

'This is supposed to be a climbing trip, not a potholing expedition.'

'Don't worry. We'll start climbing soon enough. And the way through the mountain saves time and energy, something we'll need if we're to climb across the glacier and up the Ghost tomorrow.'

Katie looked round at the others. David and Chris were clearly on Ana's side. She couldn't see Benjamin's face as it was, as always, hidden behind the camera. Julia was the only one who seemed to notice that her friend was scared. 'Come on.' Her lips formed the words, and her smile wasn't mocking like Paul's but, rather, encouraging.

It was Chris who finally broke the silence. He unstrapped his rucksack, put it down, and looked around. 'Ana's right. Why are we still standing here? Off we go!'

'Okay, Chris, you go first,' Ana said firmly, pointing to the gap. 'Then we'll push the rucksacks through and you can grab them. Then we'll come one after another.'

Chris nodded and headed towards the crevice. You really could only see it if you knew it was there. He took a deep breath, turned his head to the left, and squeezed himself sideways between the cliff and the wall.

For a moment there was silence, then his voice came from within the mountain, strangely muffled. 'Okay, here we go. Shove the bags in. And you'd better get your headlamps out beforehand. You can't see a thing in here.'

113

Katie shut her eyes. She felt so helpless that she found it hard to breathe. This was her trip, her plan. But nobody seemed to care about that. The whole thing had taken on a life of its own and, worse still, it was heading off in the one direction that Katie feared more than anything else in the world. But they were all rummaging around in their rucksacks, finding their lights, and Katie automatically pulled her light out of her rucksack side pocket and put it on her head.

Did she have any choice?

'I hope they work,' Benjamin said, laughing nervously. 'But I'm keeping my camera with me.'

'Do you reckon you can film in there?'

'I'll be sending live images from my coffin.' The nervous laugh came again, almost as if he feared that he might be heading for his coffin any minute now.

'Julia, do you want to give me your rucksack?' David was standing close to the cliff, holding out his hand. One after another, they passed him their rucksacks, and he carefully squeezed them through the gap. Katie hoped it would take for ever. Her mind was spinning. Might she still be able to persuade the others to abandon their plan?

'What about the water?' she burst out.

The others stared at her, baffled.

'What water?' asked Julia.

'There's water breaking in somewhere in there. I heard it as clearly as anything.'

'That's the subterranean river which flows out further down into the lake,' Ana replied. She grabbed her rucksack and shoved it through the gap. 'But the river bed is a third of a mile away behind the tunnel wall. It just sounds as if it's

114

nearby. There's presumably a waterfall somewhere around there.'

The others unquestioningly accepted this explanation.

Katie bit her lip. She had to watch helplessly as Julia, Benjamin and David disappeared into the gap one after the other, leaving just Katie, Ana and Paul behind.

'Who's next?'

When neither Katie nor Paul replied, Ana squeezed through the gap. It did look as if she were disappearing through the wall.

There was silence, then Paul shrugged and said, 'I asked you if you wanted to do it on our own. You were the one who insisted on the others coming.'

Katie hastily ran through the possibilities. She had no idea exactly where they were. That's why she had been depending on Ana. Ana, who knew the way through the tunnel. Wasn't that proof enough that she knew what she was doing?

'No,' she said between clenched teeth. 'I'm not leaving the others in the lurch.'

'Have you ever thought,' Paul replied, heading for the gap, 'that *they* might leave *you* in the lurch?'

The next moment, Katie found herself alone.

Should she follow the others?

Turn round?

That was out of the question, no matter what.

She ignored the gap and felt her way along the cliff. The stone was still hot. She could barely touch it. But she didn't let go. Her fingers searched for a crack that she could cling on to. There – a bumpy bit. Barely noticeable. Katie used it to pull herself up, drew her legs up after her – then slipped and fell back down. It was impossible. The wall was too smooth and so hot that she couldn't stand it for long.

Climbing up there alone wasn't only dangerous; it was a complete non-starter.

She took a deep breath and stared at the gap.

Come on, Katie. You can do it.

This is a cinch compared to what you've already done. You jumped off a hundred-foot bridge. You do free solo climbing. You can make it through that gap.

She went for it. Almost at once, she felt her pulse speeding up as she pushed herself into the gap and everything became dark around her. Her hand reached up to her forehead. She switched her headlamp on and squeezed her body through the narrow rock.

She promptly felt sick.

You could have told them, the thought occurred to her. You could simply have admitted that you suffered from claustrophobia.

But what would that have achieved? She would just have shown weakness. She had given in to her fear once already. She'd sworn then that it would never happen again.

The rushing sound filled her ears once more, but this time she wasn't sure whether it was really the water or the blood pounding in her veins.

She suddenly felt someone touch her.

Someone was shouting loudly to her. 'Hold my hand!' It was Paul. She could barely hear him above the crashing sound. 'And watch your step. The walls and ground are seriously slippery.'

Katie clung to Paul's hand, her heart thumping. She could feel the sweat running down her spine.

'You're trembling.' Paul's voice was now directly above her. 'Are you cold, or are you afraid?'

This time, though, he sounded concerned rather than mocking. Or was she imagining it?

She cleared her throat. She absolutely mustn't let it show. 'I'm cold. What do you think I am?'

'Isn't it weird, the noise of the river, even though it's so far away?'

Yes, it was weird. It was weird that Katie was stuck down here in this dark tunnel instead of hanging from a rock in the airy heights. But she knew that she had only one chance if she wasn't going to surrender to this weirdness.

She opened her eyes and blinked in the brightness. All of them apart from Benjamin had switched their headlamps on. But although the light wasn't sufficient to illuminate even part of the space they found themselves in, Katie could see that they must be in a natural underground cave. It turned into a long, low tunnel, its side walls dotted with cracks. The roof was supported by timber beams.

Another wave of nausea swept over her.

Katie shut her eyes again. Think about something else. Anything else.

No, not about Korea. Not about her grandmother's garden. Not about her parents, and definitely not about Sebastien. Don't think about the past at all. Think about the future. Picture yourself standing in the sunshine on the summit of the Ghost tomorrow instead.

CHAPTER 15

Katie didn't know how much time passed before she dared to open her eyes again. It felt to her like hours, but it had presumably been only seconds.

'God, it's cold in here,' she heard Julia complaining.

'You'd best put your climbing gear on,' Ana advised them all.

By the light of their headlamps, they all rooted around in their rucksacks for their thick Gore-Tex jackets and pulled them on.

'And make sure you've not left anything behind.'

Katie took a deep breath. Okay, she could do it. At least she wasn't alone down here.

She concentrated on pulling on her jacket. Then she devoted her attention to closing her rucksack properly.

'When you're all ready, quick march!' Ana was gradually adopting a tone rather like that of an army general.

Katie snorted peevishly, feeling something like life returning to her.

It's okay, she thought, relieved.

Slowly, she set off. Her right hand pressed against the wall of the tunnel, Katie felt her way forwards, the whole time fighting off the desire to simply turn and run back out into the fresh air.

The floor of the underground passageway was covered

with debris and broken stones. They couldn't stand up, so had to proceed at a stoop. Ahead of Katie was Paul's head-lamp. Despite the damp on the walls, every step cast up a cloud of dust which hung in the air and which swallowed up the beam of light within a matter of seconds.

They had gone only a few yards when the group ahead of Katie stopped.

'What's wrong?' she called.

'Dunno.' That was Paul.

The next moment, Benjamin was pushing his way past them, heading for where they had come in.

'What's wrong?' she cried impatiently.

'The lens cap must have fallen off my camera when I took my jacket out,' he called over his shoulder.

'Oh, forget the lens cap,' she replied.

He stopped. 'If I do that, I can forget about the entire camera. The damp and dust will wreck it.'

Katie sighed. 'Just put the damn thing in your rucksack. Benjamin. You can't film in the dark anyway.'

'No, I'm not going any further without my lens cap. This camera's my third eye – I could barely exist without it. Just wait here – I won't be a minute.'

Wait? Was he crazy? Pressing on was Katie's sole means of escape.

'Suit yourself,' she yelled at him. 'But I'm carrying on. We've already wasted too much time as it is. I want to get to that cabin today.'

'I'd never have thought you were so selfish.' In the weak light of her headlamp, she saw David turning and shaking his head in disbelief.

'I'm not selfish. I just want to get out of here!'

She should never have come down into the tunnel.

She should never have listened to Ana.

She should have forgotten about the others.

She should have taken up Paul's offer.

But now it was too late for any of that.

Katie didn't hesitate for another second. She pushed her way past the others and felt her way forwards, step by step.

Julia called after her, 'Wait, Katie! It's better if we don't split up. Ben won't be a minute.'

But she didn't stop. Instead, she stared fixedly at the weak beam of light that flickered around with every movement. Damp glistened on the walls, and the timber beams above her gave off a foul smell. They were old. Ancient. And presumably rotten from the damp down below.

At the same time, the flakes of dust tumbling down from the damp, rotten walls took her breath away. As if the stone were disintegrating. The flakes had already got everywhere. Into their hair, onto their clothes, onto their skin. It was revolting.

Katie started to come to her senses after she had walked what must be a good third of a mile. And at that moment she thought of something that might be even worse than being shut in this tunnel.

Being shut in this tunnel *alone*.

What an idiot she was. How could she have allowed her panic to get the better of her and make her run off like that?

She stopped and listened.

Nothing.

By the light of her headlamp, she could see barely thirty feet.

Could it really take that long to look for a stupid lens cap?
'Where are you guys?'

No reply.

Just the constant roaring sound.

She retraced her last few steps, then noticed that she was standing in a pool of water. Had the water been that high beforehand? She remembered something. Something that Julia's brother Robert kept saying. He said that the water in the lake rose and fell again for some unaccountable reason. Was that what was happening now? Was the underground river taking additional water to Mirror Lake?

Get a grip, Katie. There are no tides in here. And anyway, Ana said the course of the river was way back behind the tunnel.

Katie took off her headlamp and shone it around.

'Hello? Where are you?' she called once more.

She suddenly slipped on the wet ground. The water was now a good two inches high. She just managed to hold on to the wall. A stone came loose as she propped herself up. Her heart was pounding. Was the tunnel even safe? If she didn't find the others soon, she'd never get out again. She'd go mad. Her heart was pounding, and she could feel panic threatening to overwhelm her.

She was almost running now, although running was practically impossible on the slippery ground. Her rucksack was chafing against her back and seemed to be getting heavier with every step.

Katie pushed aside the thought that it might be more sensible just to stand still and wait for the others to find her. Fear had invaded every corner of her brain, making her hasten on

121

through the darkness until she suddenly tripped over something and fell to her knees. The headlamp that she had been carrying flew to the ground and went out – leaving Katie in total darkness.

Katie's breathing was quick and jerky and her heart was banging against her chest as she felt along the ground for the lamp. In vain. She squatted down, her hands on the floor. She span round. Nothing. Where was the damn thing? She stood up, and then realised that she was completely disorientated. She now had no idea which was left and right. Which direction had she come from?

Katie had sometimes had this sensation before, but only in dreams. And on that day two years ago, the twenty-third of December.

It was this desire, this urge, this need to scream – along with a feeling of being petrified, unable to make a single sound. She stretched her arms out, hoping to feel a wall somewhere that she could lean against. Her hand finally found rock. She stumbled towards it and pressed herself against it, trembling.

Later on she would realise that her ordeal could only have lasted a matter of minutes – but now it felt like an eternity. And she was stricken by the sense of loneliness that had seemed normal to her until she met Sebastien, and had returned again. For Sebastien was dead.

Now, in the darkness, it really hit her. She, Katie West, was the loneliest person she knew on this whole planet.

Katie had once heard Sebastien's mother chatting to a friend about what being a mother meant to her. 'Once you have children,' she'd said, 'the world suddenly seems so threatening, don't you find? Every branch, every stone, every car, every animal, yes, every person, suddenly seems like a terrible danger. I don't know about you, but I'd do anything for Sebastien: steal, lie, kill. Anything.'

Katie had listened as if frozen to the spot. Sebastien's mother hadn't noticed her come into the room. And Katie had suddenly felt deep within her that her mother would never say that kind of thing about her. She would never kill or steal for her. She wouldn't even lie for her.

A noise made Katie jump at first – then she exhaled, relieved. Her foot was touching something on the ground that was rolling slightly forwards. She bent down and picked up the headlamp. Her cold fingers grasped the elastic band and she looped it round her wrist, then felt for the switch with her index finger.

Let it work. Please let it work.

Light!

Her sigh of relief shook her whole body. Slowly, cautiously, she looked around.

She was still in the same long corridor, but right in front of her was an opening that led into a cave.

She held up the lamp and flashed it around her. She must have stormed past here before without noticing the hole in the rock.

She went through the opening and looked around. The space was about twice as big as her college room and so far as she could see, this was the only entrance.

A wooden vault stretched out above her, like the vault of a church. Its cross braces were evidently meant to stop it from collapsing. More panic, more nausea.

Step by step she retreated, her hands outstretched, until she found the opening to the tunnel once more. Until her fingers touched the cold rock. Relieved, she leaned against it.

Okay, she said to herself. The others have to come this way too eventually. She hadn't left the tunnel. She simply had to wait there.

For minutes she stood there until she could feel her heart rate gradually slowing down and she could think more clearly. Only then did she realise that she could no longer hear the roaring of the river. As if she were in a soundproof room.

She reached up and used her headlamp to inspect the cliffs to her left and right.

Pictures.

Pictures everywhere.

Incredible. Plain incredible.

Cave paintings, like the ones she'd seen in history books.

No – more like graffiti in subways. Or was it like both?

On the walls were animals. Herds of buffalo. Rattlesnakes. Gigantic birds flapping enormous wings. Strange human figures. And then a heart with an arrow, like the ones that lovers carve on tree trunks.

Initials. And in a great big sun, the carved words *We were here*. Then a smiley, a huge grin on its face. *Don't worry, be happy*.

And a peace sign.

Katie felt a waft of cold air, and shivered. It was as if a dark cloud were passing over her.

Her lamp flickered, came back on, and then she read a name.

Katie was here.

The sentence was carved above a silhouette of a life-sized figure. As if someone had stood against the wall, and someone else had drawn round them.

She swung the lamp to the right.

Another human shape, just taller and broader, and another one next to it – and next to that, one, two, three ... five more silhouettes. Eight life-sized human outlines.

Eight.

Eight students who disappeared.

Coincidence? Katie didn't think so.

Had the students come this way? Had they come the same way and stopped here, discovered the cave paintings, and immortalised themselves on the cliff walls before they disappeared?

Instinctively she felt her way back to the tunnel opening. It gave her at least a vague hint of security.

Katie was here?

Katie was here?

What did that mean?

Katie?

Katie?

Had someone called her name, or was she hearing voices coming from the cliffs once more?

No, someone was definitely calling her name.

'Katie?'

'Over here.'

My God, she sounded so quiet. So unlike herself.

'Here!' Katie shouted at the top of her voice.

Another silence. Katie couldn't bear it. 'Where the hell are you all? Do you want to spend the whole night in this goddamn cave?'

And then someone was standing in front of her, flashing a light straight into her eyes. Dazzled, she gathered her wits about her and said as coolly as possible, 'The whole place is under water. I only hope we don't all drown. Where are the others?'

'They'll be here in a minute. I only came on ahead because I thought you might start feeling lonely in this darkness.'

It was Paul who was flashing his headlamp in her face. His grin was starting to get on her nerves. If there was one thing Katie hated, it was people making fun of her.

'Don't worry about me,' she snapped. 'You just worry about our trip. We need to get a move on if we want to get to the cabin today. I have no desire to go running around in the dark.'

Which is precisely what you're spending your whole time doing, she thought furiously. You're groping around in the darkness big time.

Paul put his rucksack down and stretched. 'The others will be here any moment, but my offer still stands. We could carry on alone. The more people, the greater the risk.'

Katie stared at him. 'What do you really want?'

'The same thing as you. To climb the mountain. Don't you feel it too? We're kindred spirits.'

'Kindred spirits?'

'Precisely.'

'What gives you that idea?'

There was a long silence, and Katie had already given up

expecting a reply when Paul moved closer to her. She hated this kind of physical closeness. She had only ever tolerated it with Sebastien – indeed with him she had positively yearned for it.

'We're guilty,' breathed Paul. 'Guilty as charged.'

Her heart stopped for a second, then she pulled herself together and summoned up the super-cool tone of voice that she was so good at.

'So Debbie was right that you're only out on probation?'

'They let me out a week ago.' There was no hesitation, no apology in his tone.

'Why?'

'For good conduct.' Paul laughed. 'Or do you want to know why the cops nabbed me and then had to let me go again?'

Yes, Katie was dying to know – but she decided not to ask. She wasn't going to make him feel important just because he'd been in prison. Or make him think that it was going to impress her. Instead, she said, 'Your father must be really proud of you.'

'My father's one giant asshole.'

Okay, so maybe they were somehow kindred spirits after all. Katie's father was also a giant asshole, but, unlike Paul, she had never said so. Maybe that's where she'd gone wrong.

And then she heard the others' voices and was unspeakably relieved to see them all arrive.

Maybe they're not my friends, she thought. But at the moment, they're the only people I have in the world. The only ones whom I even remotely trust. However hard she had found it, she had evidently manoeuvred herself into a situation that required a degree of trust.

'God, Katie,' Julia was saying, 'I thought you'd gone. We really do have to stick together from now on. First Paul, then Ana, and now you. People keep on disappearing – I can't stand it.'

It was Chris who interrupted her. He had lifted up his lamp, and the incredulity in his voice was plain for all to hear. 'Guys, look at this!'

CHAPTER 16

'Stone age graffiti. Awesome. God, they must *so* old.' Benjamin was standing next to Chris, examining the pictures on the walls.

Katie groaned in horror at the thought of what was coming next. And, yes, Benjamin had cast off his rucksack and was already getting out his camera.

'What do you reckon?' Paul flashed his lamp across the walls. 'What do these pictures mean?'

'No idea,' Chris replied.

'Maybe it was the cave dwellers' holy of holies,' Paul speculated.

'I'm not sure they knew about smileys.' Benjamin laughed. 'No, someone's just scribbled on the old pictures. Hey, Katie, was it you? Your name's on it.'

Even in the semi darkness, Katie could feel the others staring at her.

'Do I look like a three-year-old who goes around scribbling on walls? Don't you get it? Take a closer look and you might work out who got here before us, wrecking the pictures with their stupid scribbles.'

There was silence for a while.

Julia was the first to realise. Her voice was completely

toneless as she counted. 'One, two, three ... there are *eight* little stick figures.'

Benjamin laughed again. 'Okay, so we finally know what happened to our missing students. They presumably followed the same route as us. And as this is some reeeeeally ancient Native American shrine, all their peace signs and scribbles incurred the wrath of the gods who cursed them for all eternity.' He put his head back and let out a howl that echoed off the opposite wall.

A shiver ran down Katie's spine.

'Hey—' Katie was about to speak, but Julia was quicker off the mark.

'You stop that crap at once!' she said, glancing at Ana, whose expression was stony.

Benjamin held up both hands. 'Sorry, babe,' he said. 'I didn't realise you were so super-sensitive.'

Chris went over to the wall, paused for several seconds, then stood with his back to the rock. 'Julia, come on. I bet that's a girl on my right. Maybe those are her initials in the heart.'

But Julia didn't move a muscle. Katie could tell that her friend was agitated for some reason or other – which Chris didn't seem to realise. Either that or he was just ignoring it.

He moved his body into exactly the same position as one of the silhouettes and pulled Julia towards him. He touched the silhouette next to him. 'I think they were holding hands. Everything was still okay then. Hey, Ben, you ought to film this.'

Benjamin didn't need telling twice. 'Cool idea. Julia, just get a bit closer to Chris.'

'Yes, come on, gorgeous.' Chris pulled Julia towards him again. 'I always wanted to kiss you in front of a native American cult site. Who knows what the gods would have to say about it?'

Katie couldn't tell whether Chris's behaviour was deliberately unkind or just thoughtless. But she was in no doubt about Julia's reaction. Her face twisted into a mixture of horror and disgust. At that moment, David took a step towards her – and then something happened that took Katie completely by surprise. Her flatmate, whom she had always known to be quiet and reserved and who had only just insisted that they all stay together come what may, simply ran off. Without a word, she headed for the dark tunnel – and disappeared into the darkness.

Horrified, they all stared after Julia.

'Julia,' David shouted anxiously, 'come back!'

But nothing happened. Julia didn't reappear.

'You think this is all just kids' stuff,' they heard Ana saying. She emerged from the half shadows from where she had been silently watching the whole scene. 'A plain joke. But it isn't. This mountain here above us – conquering it means putting yourself on the line. And yes – you're right.'

'Right? In what way, right?' David asked, an equal mix of anxiety and concern in his voice. 'What do you mean?'

'Whoever destroyed these cave paintings with their idiot slogans and scribbles *did* bring a curse upon themselves. Not because the ghosts of stone-age chieftains wanted to wreak vengeance on them, but for a very simple reason: they didn't take any of it seriously.'

Ana calmly undid her helmet from the straps that held it

131

to her rucksack and put it on. 'You're just the same as them.'
She turned away.

'What didn't they take seriously?'

Ana looked back over her shoulder. 'It obviously never
crossed their minds for a moment that these scrawled mani-
kins might one day be the only remaining vestige of them.'

A cold shiver ran down Katie's spine. The roaring of the
underground river had still not resumed, and the silence suddenly weighed her down like the stones themselves.

Ana raised her hand. 'Right, let's get back to business. We
have to find Julia. Put your helmets on. The tunnel gets pretty
uncomfortable in a couple of hundred yards. Be prepared for
it to get narrow. And be careful. One false move and you'll
create a rockfall. And, what's more, the tunnel gets so low in
places that anyone over five foot three needs to watch their
precious heads. It's said in Fields that only geniuses go to
Grace. I know footballers insure their legs for millions. Have
you done that with your heads?'

Nobody attempted to reply. Ana had left them all lost for
words.

Ana handed Katie the end of a rope and wrapped the other
end around her. 'We all need to hold on to the rope, one after
another. I'll go first and Katie will bring up the rear. I'm the
only one who needs to put their headlamp on. It evidently
hasn't occurred to any of you that we need to save batteries.
There isn't a supermarket up there to buy replacements.'

'But what about Julia?' came David's voice. 'She didn't
even put her helmet on.'

'So it's all the more important that we catch her up as
quickly as possible. If you'd all put your fabulous intelligence

to good use for once instead of fooling around down here, you'd have realised what you've let yourselves in for.'

'Julia!' There was blind panic in David's voice now. 'Julia, come back!'

'Shut your mouth,' Ana interrupted impatiently. 'Down here a loud noise can start a rockfall. Ever heard of sound waves?'

'But Julia doesn't know anything about it,' David persisted. 'She hasn't got a clue . . . ' He whirled round and faced Chris. 'How could you? Didn't you say you'd look after her? If anything happens to her, I'll kill you.'

'Oh yeah?' Chris was unmoved. 'You think I'm scared of you? I've never met such a wimp in my life. Do you think I haven't noticed that you fancy her? But you take it from me: Julia would never want a loser like you.'

Katie stepped between them. 'What's got in to you two?' she hissed. 'This isn't the time or the place for macho performances. Let's just hope that Julia's waiting for us round the next corner.'

Silently they put their helmets on and switched off their headlamps one by one.

Before Katie switched off her headlamp, she leaned over to Ana. 'Why the hell didn't you tell me about this tunnel beforehand?'

'You didn't ask me.'

Ana hadn't been exaggerating. The route through the first part of the tunnel had been a breeze. What followed it was sheer hell. Or it was for Katie, at any rate, who felt as if she were being tortured and desperately wanted to thrust the suffocating walls away from her. In her panic she even thought for a brief moment that she could do it. But as her hand reached out to her right and slid over the rock, she found herself touching something soft and immediately jerked her hand away again. It wasn't cold stone that her fingers had touched, but something else. It had felt as if the wall were covered in creepers – an impossibility, of course, for no light could find its way into this tunnel. But moss and algae could presumably grow there.

They progressed only very slowly, partly because of the darkness and partly because the ceiling above them was getting lower and lower. It was no longer enough to draw their heads in; no, it was soon impossible to proceed at anything other than a crawl, which used up an incredible amount of energy. On top of that they had to take care, for their rucksacks kept banging against the ceiling and more and more bits of broken stone came tumbling down on their heads. And they felt as if they were still going uphill.

One or other of the boys had at first kept on swearing loudly, but Ana's warning 'Shhhhhh' and a strange growling sound had soon put a stop to that.

Katie's only option was to count her steps and stop herself thinking. That was the only way she could stick it out. Simply switch off her thoughts. But the more Katie tried, the harder she found it. She kept picturing Julia storming off into this black tunnel without knowing what awaited her, without being warned about the risk she was running.

And soon Katie wasn't counting her steps any more but was focused on one thing alone: where the hell had Julia got to?

'Where is she?' she heard David whispering at that precise moment. He was directly in front of her. 'We should have caught her up by now.'

'I have no idea,' she replied quietly.

'Chris is such a dumb-ass.' David added something that Katie couldn't hear.

'You're both complete dumb-asses,' she hissed back. 'Keep your trench warfare for when we're lounging around at Grace with nothing better to do!'

Trench warfare. That's exactly what the noise sounded like that suddenly stopped her in her tracks. A booming sound was rolling through the tunnel, heading straight for them. But it was no longer the roaring of the water; that had become ever fainter the further away they crept from the cave with all the paintings.

Katie bumped into David, who had also stopped. 'What's up?'

'No idea.'

Katie flicked on her headlamp.

Ana raised her hand and motioned them to be quiet. Then she undid the rope around her waist and dropped to her knees. Paul, immediately behind her, was about to follow suit, but Ana shook head and crept on all fours further along the tunnel. The darkness swallowed her up faster than Katie would have thought possible.

At the same moment, she could feel her breathing becoming more laboured. Then she understood. It wasn't only the darkness. The air was nothing but a grey mist.

She held up her lamp and then saw the cloud of dust moving towards her. It was coming from right in front of her.

'Rockfall!'

Katie had no idea who had said the word. Had anyone actually said it? But what it meant was clear within a fraction of a second. Just as she'd immediately understood what it meant when the rope that Sebastien had been hanging from suddenly went slack. Somewhere ahead of them, a stone had come loose and somewhere up ahead was ...

'Julia!'

Just a name. Just a word.

Said at the wrong time. In the wrong place.

Just a word.

A word that could shatter a relationship – and an entire world. One single name that David was calling loudly, shrilly.

Katie acted without thinking. She put out her hand, held it tightly over David's mouth, and his desperate scream turned into a strangled gasp. Then she pulled him down onto the ground before the stones came raining down on them and buried them for ever.

Katie's earliest memory was of a wall. A high wall made of grey stone. A garden. Flowers so sweet-smelling that they made you feel sick. And voices. Women's voices. If she hadn't known better she'd have remembered them as singing, as she'd felt sick in just the same way when she heard sopranos in the operas her parents dragged her along to.

Katie had never been afraid of walls. Walls were just boundaries behind which lay adventure or, rather, a whole world of promise. Quite what this promise consisted of, she couldn't have said; but even as a child, she had worked out for herself that it didn't matter either. The only thing that mattered was that walls formed a boundary. A boundary to the river, which she wasn't allowed to go to, and, later on, a boundary to streets leading to places she wasn't allowed to visit.

But she had always sensed that roads and rivers led to somewhere important and offered possibilities that she found irresistible.

On that day in Korea – she must have been three or four years old – she had been standing for ages gazing at a wall. Then a cat appeared. Without a second's hesitation, it jumped effortlessly onto the wall. It balanced on the top for a long while before leaping off the other side and disappearing without trace. Katie had never seen the cat again, but she had realised that walls always meant that there was something on the other side to be discovered.

And she could still clearly remember what she had thought at that moment. Well, maybe it had been a feeling more than a thought. She had simply tried to follow the cat's example. And – she could still remember this clearly too – she had already climbed a fair way when the sing-song in the garden behind her had suddenly stopped. Hands had grabbed her and pulled her down, voices had scolded her – and the adventure was over.

She had screamed for all she was worth. To this day, she didn't know what had been behind that wall. But one thing was clear: walls were a prison. She had realised this as a three-year-old.

And that wasn't something she was going to accept.

Her hand automatically reached up to switch on her headlamp, but then realised that it was already on. There was just too much dust in the air for her to see anything.

'Everything okay?' Weird, this voice. Katie immediately knew who was bending over her. Paul.

'The tunnel's collapsed!'

Only now did Katie feel the body next to her, and remembered pulling David down with her.

'David?'

A shadow next to her.

'David, are you okay?'

No reply.

'Are you hurt?'

'I'm fine. But Julia ... '

Katie was relieved to hear David's voice becoming stronger and clearer. He stood up, his horrified expression looking like a grimace in the cloud of dust.

Katie leant forward.

'Chris? Ana?'

'Here.' One after another they emerged, unhurt, from the darkness. Their faces were black with dust, and Katie couldn't see their expressions. She could imagine them, though.

Chris sounded choky as he pushed his way towards David. 'You stupid idiot.' He was hissing rather than speaking. 'So now whose fault is it if something bad happens to Julia?' He took a deep, gasping breath. 'Just get this: if anything's happened to her, then *I'm* the one who'll kill *you*!'

He lunged at David, but Katie flung herself at him. The last thing they needed down there was two boys fighting.

David sank down. 'We have to look for her,' he said desperately. 'Now. We mustn't lose any more time.'

'Forget it.' Paul couldn't stand up completely; his head

bumped against the ceiling with every movement. 'We can't go any further forwards. The rockfall has blocked off the tunnel ahead of us. We just felt the tail end of it back here.'

David pushed past him. 'We'll have to dig a way through.'

'What with? Your hands?'

David didn't reply but crawled past him. Chris followed him, stooping.

'I know just how it feels when the life of someone you love is on the line,' Katie heard Paul's whispering voice again. 'And so do you. What do you reckon, Katie? Do we ever get over it?'

He knew.

Paul Forster knew what had happened to Sebastien and the part that Katie had played in it. And, no, she would never be able to get over it, but she couldn't change her past. The only thing she could do was help David.

Until now she hadn't realised that David was in love with Julia. But that was what happened if you tried to act all saintly and stuck to the rules. Rules were walls that cowards hid behind.

The irony, though, was that he was now shoulder to shoulder with his arch rival, crawling through rocks to the place where the fall had blocked the tunnel from floor to ceiling. The light of his lamp flickered to the rhythm of his desperate attempts to make a path through the debris.

'Hey, watch out,' Katie heard Benjamin grumbling as she crawled over his legs. 'I don't want my camera getting damaged.'

'I don't give a shit about your camera, you jerk,' she hissed. 'It's reality that counts, not video technology. See Julia's dead body with your own eyes and you'll never give a toss for a single image produced by that gadget of yours.'

'We were almost through,' came Ana's clear voice in the darkness. 'Julia might already be outside.'

'Maybe,' replied Katie. 'But maybe not.'

The reply was just a quiet yelp.

'What's wrong? Ana? Are you okay?'

'Fine,' came the halting reply.

Katie had no time to check whether this was true.

She started digging.

I hope Julia's still alive. Please don't let anything have happened to her.

Katie could smell the dust and decay, and her heart was pounding with exertion. Beads of sweat stood out on her forehead. She removed one stone after another, putting them to one side.

God, it was so airless, and so utterly exhausting. She couldn't feel her arms any more, and her fingers were hurting. She could already feel blisters forming on her hands. Would they actually manage it?

She could only take in air through her mouth now: breathing through her nose was impossible.

Were they completely wasting their time? They didn't have even the faintest idea what was on the other side. How many stones might have fallen?

A muffled rumbling was becoming louder and louder.

'Hey,' David whispered next to her. 'Be careful. Just take the higher stones, and don't do it too quickly. We don't want another rockfall.'

He seemed to have calmed down. His voice sounded calmer, at any rate. Wasn't that the reason why she'd been so set on him coming? His sense of perspective, his ability to keep a clear head. Although clearly frantic with worry about Julia, he was again displaying great calm, and this was having its effect on Katie too. Quite unlike Chris, who was rummaging around wildly in the stones, making no progress and causing more damage.

'We need to take turns,' she heard David saying. 'There isn't space for all of us.'

'Since when were you the boss around here?' Chris was now bristling with naked aggression.

Katie felt a surge of anger. After all, he was the one who had set this whole deadly chain of events in motion. *He* had made Julia run away.

'David's right,' Ana interrupted. 'Chris, there's no point doing what you're doing. You take Katie's place. We'll form a queue behind you and pass the stones down the line.'

'I'm not going anywhere ...' Katie resisted, but Ana interrupted again.

'We'll take turns, it'll save energy. Let Chris go up to the front.'

Katie capitulated and crawled back on all fours. Ana and Paul pushed past her and piled the stones up behind them.

Katie sat down next to Benjamin. He was sitting with his back against the tunnel wall, holding his torch. It was casting a pale beam of light onto the four who were immersed in their work.

'Don't you want to help?'

Benjamin laughed – a shrill and horrible sound in this musty tomb.

'Someone,' he said, 'has to take care of the lighting.'

'Can you hear that?' Ana sounded tense.

'What?' Chris asked.

'That noise?'

'I can't hear anything.'

'Stop. Just be quiet. I can hear something!'

Chris and David stopped work and they all listened breathlessly to the silence.

Katie shut her eyes and tried to concentrate.

'Can't hear anything,' she heard Chris saying again.

Katie nodded.

But then David whispered, 'I can! Ana's right.'

'What do you think it sounds like?'

And now Katie could hear it too. 'Someone's on the other side!' She stood up quickly and banged her head on the ceiling. Dust tumbled down.

Julia.

It had to be Julia!

CHAPTER 17

The world had caved in behind Julia.

As the stones rained down, she had just managed to save herself by hiding under a jutting rock. Her arms clasped protectively around her head, which she had jammed between her knees, she had waited for the torrent of rubble to stop.

She was unhurt. Thank God. For several seconds, she was relieved, almost euphoric. God, that could have been the end of her. But her euphoria only lasted until she remembered the others.

Her headlamp had gone out, and she could press the button as often as she liked: it simply didn't work any more.

She found herself in utter, dust-laden darkness. She couldn't even see her hand in front of her face. Even if there *were* such a thing as a light at the end of the tunnel, there was no chance of it penetrating the swirling dust. That was when it hit her. She had been completely cut off from the others.

Oh God, she'd just gone storming off without thinking. How could that have happened to her of all people? She had trained herself always to think before she spoke, to consider her next step carefully. It could mean the difference between life and death.

Today, though, she'd lost it. Maybe it was all because she had repressed everything for so long, because she had had to deny her past ever since she and Robert had been given new identities as part of the witness protection programme. But the scrawls in the cave had been too much. She hadn't seen any alternative but to run away.

She couldn't tell anyone the truth. No one at all. Nobody knew that the name Mark de Vincenz, carved on the memorial stone to the eight missing students, was the name of her murdered father.

But panicking had been a terrible mistake. She was realising that now in the worst possible way.

The tunnel that she'd crawled through had been the very epitome of horror, but she had gritted her teeth and hadn't turned round. Turning round would have meant having to put up with the looks of all the others. Chris, who specialised in getting under her skin and could drag her down so easily with his fickle moods. David, whose longing looks had become ever more intense over the past few weeks.

And so she had noticed the rumbling sound too late. The black dust started raining down almost immediately, like nuclear fallout. She was covered in it. And then that noise again, which caused her to freeze. It seemed almost as if the mountain were replying to her cry.

From then on, Julia hadn't dared to move or utter a sound. She pressed herself against the wall beneath the jutting-out bit of rock and just sat there, shutting her eyes and trying to think herself into another place where the air wasn't about to choke her, where the damp wasn't seeping through her clothes, where her rucksack wasn't bruising her back.

There was a time when Julia Frost had been a perfectly normal girl called Laura de Vincenz, whose greatest pleasure in life was buying outlandish clothes from edgy shops in Kreuzberg. And the worst crime she had ever committed was shoplifting a Pure Color 'Ku'Damm' lipstick that xKarenina had recommended in her YouTube make-up tutorial. But that was then, and now was now.

There is clearly some kind of state that humans can drift into that is comparable to the way reptiles stiffen up in the cold: time and place cease to have any relevance, and your thought processes slow down, as if the batteries in your brain were about to run out. This was the state that Julia was in: a kind of stand-by mode. But she instantly snapped out of it when she heard a scraping and scratching sound from some-where ahead of her. Something told her that it wasn't an animal. Rats could never have found anything to eat down there. And it didn't sound like more stones falling from the rocky walls.

It had to be something else.

The others?

This time Julia thought before moving. She cautiously shrugged off her rucksack and turned around on all fours. She was listening the whole time, trying to find out which direction the scratching and scraping was coming from. Concentrating hard, she felt her way systematically along the pile of rubble, realising as she did so that it reached up to the ceiling. She couldn't stand up fully but, stooping, she set about removing the stones one by one.

It reminded her of the game that she and Robert had played as children. She couldn't remember its name. But so what: she hadn't enjoyed the game then, and the very thought of it was horrific now. First you had to build a tower of wooden bricks, then you had to take it in turns to remove one piece at a time and place it on the top. The game ended when the tower collapsed.

One bad choice, one thoughtless move, and the mountain would collapse on top of her.

Jenga, she remembered.

The stupid game was called Jenga. And who was it who always lost?

She had.

She took the next stone but then stopped, daunted. Exhausted, she stared at the pile of rocks ahead of her in the darkness. She couldn't see the extent of it; she could only guess.

And then she saw something flashing. As if the stones were glittering. At first, she couldn't see what it meant.

Then she understood.

Light.

Light was coming from the other side.

Light was showing through a tiny gap at the top of the pile.

CHAPTER 18

They hadn't heard any sound coming from the other side for a long while now. One or other of them coughed every now and then; the air was becoming ever more stuffy.

Katie was hoping.

She was hoping with every fibre of her being that Julia was on the other side, that she could see the light, that she could hear them moving the stones, carefully pulling them out and putting them to one side.

Benjamin was a fair target for criticism, for sure: his were the only arms not hurting, his the only hands not covered in weals and blisters; but at least he had never stopped flashing the light to try to signal to Julia.

At some point, a rhythm developed naturally. Without any great discussion, they relieved one another. When Katie wasn't pulling out the stones, she was kneeling further back, receiving them. Then she would lean, exhausted, against the wall once more, and her thoughts would become ever more slow and automatic.

She couldn't have said how long they worked away in silence. While she had lost any real sense of time, she could feel the minutes slipping away. Or was it hours?

'I can't feel my fingers any more. We surely have to make

a hole in this heap at some point,' she heard Chris murmuring. 'I think we're digging in the wrong place.'

'Then stop thinking,' Paul retorted. He glanced over his shoulder. 'Your turn, Katie.'

Katie slid to the front. Her trousers felt damp and dirty like old dishcloths.

Benjamin's torch was shining on the place at the top right where Paul had just been working.

Stooping there with an uncomfortably bent back, she reached her hand up as high as she could.

Don't think about it.

Switch off the pain.

She shut her eyes briefly, concentrating, and her fingers found a stone; she could just reach the edge of it. Then she heard a muffled sound. She stood on tiptoe and pushed her hand further forward – but just as she was about to grab the stone with her fingertips, she found herself reaching into empty space. Her hand was in a hole.

Where had that rock gone? She leaned forward, and her hand found nothing to hold on to. And then – or was she just imagining it? – she felt a breath of air on her hand. Then something else. Something touching her. Something soft was stroking the back of her hand.

Fingers.

No doubt about it: she could feel fingers.

'I'm here! Here! Get me out!' They could hear Julia repeating the same words over and over again.

'Don't worry, Julia. Everything's going to be fine. We can do it. We won't be long now.'

It was David who was speaking through the small hole

that connected Julia to the rest of them. But maybe Julia hadn't heard his voice, or maybe it wasn't really David she wanted to speak to. At any rate, she just kept on whispering one name alone: 'Chris, please. Please, Chris. Get me out of here.'

David let Chris push him aside, even though he, David, was the one who had been working non-stop.

'She shouldn't be talking so much. Never mind starting to shout,' Ana murmured. 'Tell her that. She just needs to sit down and keep quiet.'

'Julia, stay calm,' Chris said softly. 'I'll be with you any second.'

'I can't stand it! It's pitch black in here. I can't even see my hand in front of my face.' Julia's voice was rising.

'Julia, keep your voice down. All this stuff only fell down because David went around bellowing. So just stay quiet, okay?'

One stone after another was set aside and slowly but surely the hole became bigger. Julia didn't say anything more, but every now and then they could hear her whimpering.

David managed to manoeuvre himself into a half standing position. 'Okay, that ought to be it,' he said. 'Julia, here's my hand. Can you feel it?'

'Yes.'

Katie could hardly hear Julia.

'Now take a few steps back. I'm afraid of the whole pile of stones collapsing.'

'Okay.'

'Let me through.' Chris took a step forward. Benjamin's flashlight shone in Julia's face.

She was cowering on the floor, and looked dreadful. Her face was black with dust and stained with tears. Katie did something that was so unusual for her that she surprised even herself. Before David, Chris or any of the others could do anything, she had already crawled through the stones to the other side, where she took her friend in her arms and didn't let go of her even when Chris tried to push her aside.

I know why I'm doing this, she told herself. I just can't stand the thought of those two lovesick idiots wrapping themselves round each other again.

But she knew she was just trying to fool herself. For if she was honest, Katie had been panicking the whole time that she might lose the only friend she'd ever had in her whole life.

'Okay,' Ana said after a while, her voice sounding warm for the first time. 'You can let go of her now. Or aren't you in a hurry any more?'

There was no time to rest. Ana was driving them on, and knew no mercy. 'Come on! It can't be far now.'

'I don't think I'll ever be able to walk straight again,' Benjamin murmured ahead of Katie. 'I'll spend the whole of the rest of my life as the hunchback of Notre Dame.'

There were stifled giggles at this. The atmosphere had suddenly changed, and all the irritability, the suppressed tension and nervousness had vanished at a stroke. Normally only the weather in the valley changed with such rapidity. Come to that, Katie fervently hoped that the sun would still be shining outside. And something suddenly dawned on her. Something she had often read about but had never experienced.

As a loner, she had never previously understood that the dangers in the mountains – the weather, one's dwindling strength, the wrong paths that one might choose – were just one side of the coin. The other side of the coin was the people, the team. If the team failed, that could be even more dangerous than an avalanche.

But they had overcome this particular nightmare. What could happen now?

The group ahead of her came to a halt.

'What's the matter now?' Katie peered impatiently into the dim glow of their headlamps.

Benjamin shrugged.

But before he could reply, Katie realised two things. Firstly, they had reached the end of the tunnel. Secondly, she had completely forgotten about her claustrophobia for the past few minutes.

She screwed up her eyes, trying to see what was going on.

Unlike at the entrance to the tunnel, there wasn't a cave or any kind of larger space. Instead, the tunnel simply ended at a massive wall of rock. But before her fear could return, Katie saw that Chris was already setting up a ladder that had been leaning against one side of the tunnel.

'You first?' Paul said, turning to Katie.

Katie nodded gratefully and felt for the first rung. She had never climbed a ladder so fast in her life, and she could have hugged the whole world when she finally crawled out through a crack in the rock and into the fresh air.

'Straight from hell into heaven,' she heard Benjamin calling as he appeared behind her. The others followed one by one, and their shouts of joy were the best thing that Katie had heard in a long time. They looked like a group of madmen who had just been let out of captivity. Benjamin wasn't the only one dancing for joy. The others, too, were yelling themselves hoarse; their laughter could probably carry all the way to Fields.

The whole thing really was laugh-out-loud funny, with their faces as black as if they had just dropped down a chimney.

'Just look at you!' Julia gasped. 'You look like total freaks. Scary!'

'We are freaks.' Chris grabbed Julia and swung her up in the air.

'Yeah!' Katie punched the air triumphantly. If they could get through that, they could get through anything.

Tomorrow she, Katie West, would be standing on the summit of the Ghost. And nothing and nobody could stop her now.

Once the initial euphoria had worn off, they started to look around. The tunnel had led them to the rear of the mountain range. To the left, they were looking down into an extremely narrow side-valley enclosed by sheer cliff faces and mountain peaks.

They had wound up right in the middle of the mountains. Rock faces cut through the air and the slopes were strewn with boulders. They seemed already to have left the treeline behind them. The only things growing at this height were stunted trees and sparse bushes.

And then there was the sky. After the darkness of the cave, it was a radiant blue, so blue that it deserved a name all of its own. There wasn't a cloud to be seen. Not even the rounded summit of the Ghost, rising up to their left, was shrouded in a veil of cloud, as it so often was. Katie dropped to the ground and took her rucksack off. On this side of the mountain, the breeze took the edge off the sun, making the air feel almost springlike.

Katie stared up at the broad wind gap. She couldn't see the summit behind the Ghost, but at the sight of the White Soul in front of it, Katie felt her confidence growing. She could do it. The actual challenge would come once they had crossed the glacier. The south ridge, which could be clearly seen from their position. From here, it looked razor-sharp and extremely steep, but it did Katie good to see their route at last and to know that she could rely on her own instincts from this point onwards.

No more surprises.

Above all, no more tunnels.

Katie tilted her head back and gazed upwards. It was crazy, but she really felt as if she was much closer to the Ghost, even though they had only just been inside the mountain.

'We've gone six hundred and fifty feet up since we went through the gap,' she heard David saying at that moment. He was standing near to the hole in the rocks that marked the tunnel exit. 'Assuming my altimeter hasn't gone crazy.'

'I told you the way through the mountain was easier. Now all we have to do is climb up to the bridge.' Ana pointed to the slope higher up, which consisted mainly of rubble. 'The cabin's up there.'

'I can't see a path.' Julia put her thick jacket into her rucksack and put on her sunglasses.

'That's because there isn't one. We have to find one for ourselves.'

Katie sensed someone dropping onto the ground close to her.

Paul.

'How are you feeling?' he asked.

She beamed at him. 'Like the king of the world.'

It was a moment before she realised that she had said words she had sworn never to repeat in her entire life. She had shouted those same words to Sebastien the very first time she had leapt from a bridge.

Even though there wasn't a proper path and the boulder-strewn terrain meant they had to tread warily, they quickly gained altitude. Katie soon found herself taking off her Gore-Tex jacket followed shortly afterwards by her fleece. She wasn't the only one sweating with exertion. But after the narrow tunnel, this meant true freedom. It wasn't the same as real climbing, sure, but it came pretty close. She could feel her heart beating hard and rhythmically, and all the muscles in her legs were starting to work. And, most importantly, every step was taking her closer to her goal.

Katie kept stopping and looking up to the right, where the glacier began. The broad, white expanse shimmered in the sunlight. The higher they went, the more often they crossed snow gullies, then ever larger snowfields. The brightness was starting to hurt Katie's eyes. She took out her polarised sunglasses from the side pocket of her rucksack and put them on.

'Look, there it is!' Julia stopped and pointed. 'The cabin!'

She was right: a dark roof was clearly visible high up behind the edge of a cliff. Benjamin, Ana and Julia, who were in the lead, speeded up slightly. Katie wondered how they had the energy, after all their exertions: they had been walking for hours now. But just the fact of being out in the fresh air once more and being able to move unhindered seemed to be a tremendous spur to all of them, not just Katie.

She looked at her watch. It would probably take them around two hours to reach the cabin.

'Ben won't be able to walk a single step tomorrow,' Katie heard a voice in her ear. Paul again. Since leaving the tunnel, he had been walking close to her the whole time. Whatever she did – whether she hung back or raced ahead, overtaking him – she would feel his presence again just minutes later.

'He knows what he's doing,' she replied, although she wasn't entirely sure of that. For Benjamin was like a dog, constantly running backwards and forwards, camera in hand.

'No he doesn't. He hasn't got a clue what awaits him tomorrow.'

I don't give a damn, Katie thought. I don't care about tomorrow. This wasn't the time to start having negative thoughts. Only one thing mattered now: getting higher up the mountain and reaching their objective.

She looked around and was pleased to see how far they had come. The stunted trees that were grouped around the tunnel exit looked like something from a model village from up where they were now. Katie could feel the air becoming thinner and harsher. The wind was no longer a springlike breeze: it had whipped up and was sweeping across them as if it wanted to blow them away from this wasteland of stones, boulders and snowfields. But that didn't bother her either. For she was now starting to realise that her feeling of euphoria wasn't just to do with the Ghost.

It was because she and the others had managed to leave the valley behind them.

They had escaped from Grace Valley by their own efforts.

Katie was on the other side of the wall and this time nobody had been able to hold her back.

It was magic.

But this magic was suddenly interrupted by a sound that was familiar to Katie – but one she had never yet heard around here and which, for some reason she didn't understand, she found strangely threatening. She stared up at the sky. The first thing she saw was a broad vapour trail as if the glacier, which stretched through the mountains like a white motorway, were reflected in the sky.

And then she saw the plane.

It was just crossing the mountain range opposite, heading right towards them.

'Hey, do you see that?' Benjamin yelled from the front of the line. He started jumping up and down and waving.

They all stopped abruptly.

The plane was losing height. Its wings were glittering in the sunlight. They could clearly see the windows.

'What on earth is he doing? If he goes any lower he'll crash straight into the Ghost!'

Benjamin was right. The plane was heading straight for them and, once above them, it seemed to hang immobile in the air for several seconds. Then it tilted to one side, did an about-turn, shot upwards, looped the loop, and turned away to the north. Bewildered, Katie and the others watched it until it was out of sight. All that remained was the vapour trail in the sky.

'What on earth was that all about?' Chris said. 'You'd almost think he was out to get us.'

'The pilot was probably just wondering who these lunatics were up here,' Benjamin said. 'I hope I got it all on film.'

'I've not seen a single plane in the valley since we came here. Has anyone else noticed that?' David frowned.

'It's just not on a flight path.'

'No.' Paul shook his head. 'There's a flying ban over the valley.'

'A flying ban? Why?'

Paul shrugged. 'You lot don't know anything, do you?'

'What do you mean?' David demanded.

'Nothing.'

Paul's face, though, had a mocking, almost cynical, expression. For a moment there was silence, then Paul asked sarcastically, 'So, no more questions?'

Please don't ask, Katie thought. Just don't ask. She at any rate wasn't going to show herself up, and nor was she going to give Paul the satisfaction of lording it over them.

'Oh, for God's sake,' Ana said at that moment. She reached behind her and pulled her water bottle out of her rucksack. 'Being out with you lot is like being in charge of a group of three-year-olds. As if none of you had ever seen an aeroplane before.' She took a sip of water and wiped her mouth. 'Can we finally carry on now? This path might not exactly be a challenge for real climbers, but I would like ...' Ana suddenly pulled a face and shut her eyes briefly.

'Is something the matter?' Julia asked nervously.

'Why would it be?' Ana put the bottle away and turned round. 'I just want to get there, that's all.'

That's what they all wanted, Katie thought. After all, that was why they had set off in the first place.

CHAPTER 19

Benjamin was first to reach the stone cabin. Katie was genuinely starting to wonder where he found all his energy. There wasn't a trace of exhaustion about him. As they went up to it, he was already standing on one of the benches that were grouped around a big table on the terrace, looking down the lens of his camera and shouting, 'The team reaches the cabin at 6.07 p.m.! They have struggled up the last few feet in a state of total exhaustion!'

The cabin stood above the wind gap on the nearer summit, in the wind shadow of a gigantic overhanging crag. As the others dropped onto the benches or the ground, loosening their rucksack straps and groaning, Katie walked around the cabin and found herself suddenly standing in front of a chasm. A chasm that stretched deep down into the valley.

The view was all-encompassing. Mirror Lake was immediately below them. Mysterious and dark, it stretched out before them. Directly opposite the lake, they could see the college building in the warm reddish light of the evening sun.

There was Solomon Cliff and, so tiny it was barely visible at all, the boathouse. They looked as if they were hidden in the forests of the Rocky Mountains, as the most spectacular panoramic view of icy peaks that she had ever seen opened up around Katie. And there it was, rising up ahead of her: the steep face of the Ghost. Huge, almost vertical. The wall to end all walls.

'Oh my God.' Benjamin appeared next to her. 'What an awesome view. I've never seen anything like it. You could get addicted to this.'

'Just you watch where you're standing,' Katie warned him.

'You're a born party pooper,' he teased her. 'Are all Koreans so grumpy?'

'I'm American,' she retorted.

'But you were born in Korea, right? Did you ever climb the mountains there?'

'No.' Katie turned away from the camera. It was amazing how quickly you got cold if you weren't moving. She suddenly felt hungry for the first time that day. We need a hot meal, she thought, and went back to the cabin, where the others hadn't moved a muscle.

'It's darned cold up here,' Chris grumbled, pulling the zip of his fleece up to his chin.

'Just you wait until you're up the Ghost tomorrow,' grinned Ana. 'You'll be freezing your cute ass off then.'

'How do you know it's cute?'

'It's been in front of my nose all day.'

Katie laughed and went over to the door. The cabin was built of rough stones and its roof was covered with grey slates.

'Doesn't exactly look like a luxury mountain hotel,' Chris muttered, pulling Julia towards him. 'Is there a double room for us?'

'The only thing that matters to me is that it survives the

night. It looks pretty ancient. Do you know when it was built?' Julia looked enquiringly at Ana, and Katie wondered why she wanted to know.

'No idea. It's just a cabin, not a tourist attraction. The main thing is that the roof doesn't leak and won't blow off in a storm. That's all I'm bothered about.' Ana pulled a face.

'So what are we waiting for?' asked Katie. 'Is the door locked?'

'No idea.'

'So why haven't you gone in yet?'

'No energy,' groaned Chris.

Katie went to the door, put her hand on the handle and moved it. The door immediately swung open.

Before her was one single room. A row of narrow windows faced the valley. In front of them was a large wooden table with a corner bench. To the right was an oak cupboard with numerous drawers; to the left, a huge old stove that was evidently heated with wood.

'Cool. This is the life.' Julia had come to join Katie.

Benjamin came racing in behind them. 'Wow, this is brilliant!'

'Have you been upstairs yet?'

Katie hadn't noticed the narrow staircase leading to an upper floor.

'I'm just going to bag the best sleeping place before anyone else can grab it. You girls can start cooking.'

'What century are you from?' Julia asked.

'None. I'm a creature for whom time doesn't exist.'

'But you're hungry, aren't you?'

161

'Precisely. And I need a pee too. Is there a loo anywhere? If not, I'll pee out of the window. I've always wanted to piss on the valley.'

You could say what you liked about Benjamin, but he was guaranteed to put everyone in a good mood. At any rate, they were all laughing.

'Remember the double room's reserved for Julia and me,' called Chris. Katie noticed David giving Julia a look, which she ignored.

'Hold your horses. There are only two bedrooms.' The narrow staircase wobbled under Benjamin's weight as he ran back down. 'So, what about this food?'

'How about an Italian tomato soup?' Ana was waving a carton in the air.

'Huh, I'd been thinking more of a steak,' grumbled Paul, starting to open the cupboard doors. He emerged holding a can of something. 'Here we go. Forget your tomato soup.' He started to list the provisions. 'Crisps, chocolate biscuits and – wow! Monster Energy drinks. I've not drunk that stuff since for ever.' He pulled out a can and opened it with a loud hiss. 'Cheers. Here's to our first day.'

'Is there anything to eat to go with it?' Julia asked wryly. It was almost impossible to tell that she had nearly been buried alive only hours before.

Benjamin went over to join Paul. He reached into the cupboard and immediately found something. 'Of course there is! Specially for the heroine of the day: your favourite meal in a tin, Julia. Campbell's New England Clam Chowder Soup. Clam chowder to heat up. Guys, we're so well provided for here that we might never want to leave again.'

Julia shuddered. 'Yuck. I already have nightmares about that stuff. I think it's the only food they know at Grace.'

They all laughed.

'How about ... hang on,' Benjamin pulled out another tin, 'how about Hamburger Helper Cheeseburger Macaroni for a tasty cheeseburger macaroni pasta bake? There's nothing to beat American gourmet recipes.'

'I'll go for the macaroni,' said Julia. 'How many tins are there?'

'One ... two ... three ... seven!'

'Okay. If you let me off the clam chowder, I'll make everyone a pasta bake.'

Moments later, she had found a huge dish in a small low cupboard by the stove.

'Could someone fetch me some wood?' Julia was opening the door of the cast-iron stove. 'Hey, someone's been here,' she said, surprised. 'Ana, is it in the rules that you have to put fresh wood in before you leave the cabin? There are even brand new matches here.'

'No idea.'

'You really don't know?'

Ana shook her head. 'I've never been up here before.'

They all stared at her. 'Never been up here?'

'No.'

Katie could feel her mouth gaping open. Surely that couldn't be true! She mentally replayed all the conversations she'd had with Ana. Ana had said she'd often taken groups across the glacier. But if Katie remembered rightly, she had always been evasive when it had come to giving any details about these trips.

She looked at the others. Should she tackle Ana in front of them all? Was that really a good idea?

'Hey, Katie.' Someone was nudging her shoulder. 'Are you coming to fetch some wood?'

She stood up and followed Chris and David. Outside the cabin, Chris clapped a hand to his forehead. 'We're being idiots,' he said. 'We left the treeline behind us ages ago.'

'You're right,' David replied. 'There isn't even any juniper up here.'

'Don't say that,' Katie said. 'I can still smell the stuff.'

David grinned. 'I think I'm right in saying that juniper has a diuretic effect.'

'You mean that's why Ben keeps having to pee?' Chris laughed. His bad mood had evidently passed, and even his anger with David seemed to have faded away. 'I'd prefer it if it switched off his language centre or had some kind of narcotic effect on him.'

David looked around. 'But, guys, the wood in the stove has to have come from somewhere,' he mused. 'Those weren't just random branches – they were properly cut pieces. I'll go and have a look.'

Chris dropped down onto the bench. 'A man's gotta do what a man's gotta do.'

Katie looked up at the Ghost, trying to work out the route that they would take tomorrow. The glacier looked harmless with its broad tracks, but that was true of many glaciers. You couldn't be too careful with ice fields. Given all the cracks and crevices, they could be infinitely more treacherous than they looked.

She remembered again that Ana had suddenly declared

that she'd never been in the cabin before. What if she didn't know her way around the glacier either?

Whatever. If need be, they could find their way together across the ice fields. That didn't seem impossible to Katie.

After the glacier came the rocky ridge that led to the summit. They could do it if they all had the necessary focus and stamina.

'Sorry for how I was earlier,' she suddenly heard Chris saying behind her.

She turned round. This was neither the time nor the place for confessions or therapeutic conversations. And, more importantly, she was the wrong person for him to be talking to.

'It's Julia you ought to be apologising to,' she replied.

Chris scrutinised her with his grey eyes. In the light of the evening sun, he looked unashamedly chilled out. Just like Sebastien, he was good looking – but in such a perfect kind of way that Katie always found it slightly off-putting. His bronzed features were absolutely even, and his ruffled hair and three-day stubble looked as if some stylist had artfully created them for an advertising photo shoot entitled some-thing like 'nature boy in front of mountain backdrop'. Any minute now, he'd be looking into Benjamin's camera, waving a granola bar.

'What if I'd prefer to apologise to you?' Chris didn't take his eyes off her.

Katie shuddered. 'You can be a bit scary sometimes,' she said bluntly. 'We can't be doing with that up a mountain. And above all, you need to leave your feud with David down in the valley. That's where it belongs.'

'You're friends with Julia. Do you think she loves me?'

'When I'm six and a half thousand feet up, I'm only friends with myself,' Katie replied brusquely. 'There's absolutely no room for feelings like jealousy, love and hate. Just look around you.' She pointed across to the summit, already shrouded in dusk. 'This is a completely different world here. We're so small when we're down in the valley.' She gestured with her fingers. 'And we're correspondingly mean. But up here, where there isn't even any juniper ... ' She grinned. 'We can feel so big that everything becomes unimportant. Apart from experiencing it. That's all that counts.' Katie took a deep breath. Sweet Jesus, she had no idea what had come over her. She normally restricted her answers to one sentence, two at most.

'Who's talking about experiencing stuff when it's actually about surviving ... ' said Paul, who was coming out of the cabin and had just caught the last bit of the conversation.

David saved Katie from having to reply by appearing from behind them, calling out, 'There's a shed back there with heaps of wood for burning. Our cosy evening in the cabin is saved.'

'Too right.' Benjamin appeared in the doorway, grinning from ear to ear. 'Watch out!' He threw a can of beer each to Chris, Paul and Katie. 'Some kind soul really has provided us with every conceivable kind of fuel. Thanks, whoever you are.'

The good mood continued. Katie couldn't believe that the rivalry between David and Chris had almost cost Julia her life a couple of hours ago. All trace of it had vanished.

Julia had put the macaroni in the oven, and half an hour or so later a delicious aroma was floating through the cabin.

Katie's stomach was rumbling, and the others seemed to feel the same way. As they ate, the setting sun bathed the mountain scenery in a red light. It looked as if the warm fire in the stove were reflected in the sky.

'What do you reckon? Should we call Debbie and give her a fright?' Benjamin took a long swig of beer.

'I expect she's already asleep,' Julia said. She grinned at Katie. 'With her hair-curlers in.'

Benjamin pulled the mobile from his trouser pocket and asked Julia to tell him the number.

'Put it on loudspeaker,' Chris called.

The sound of the phone ringing seemed completely out of place here in the middle of the mountains – and then it simply stopped.

'No reception,' said Benjamin. 'Pity. I'd have enjoyed winding her up a bit.'

Afterwards they all sat around the fire and only once the first pieces of wood had burnt down to glowing embers and people had started yawning widely did Katie start to feel her spine tingling. A strange feeling was giving her goosebumps. It's just tiredness, combined with all the day's excitement, she told herself. But something had caused it. It might have been the moment when Paul suddenly produced the map and, with an exaggeratedly concerned expression, had said, 'Guys, today was just child's play. The real test comes tomorrow.'

'Tesht?' The alcohol level in Benjamin's blood was already so high that his speech was noticeably slurred. 'Hey, are you your father? Haven't you got any other word for it? It's not a

167

tesht tomorrow, it's a path that makes the difference between life and death. D'you think I was doing my butt in today for some stupid tesht? That's why I'm at Grace. Because I didn't have to do an entrance tesht.' He laughed.

Nobody else did.

Katie winced. She, too, hadn't had to do the entrance exam that was regarded with such awe at Grace. The exam was notorious far and wide, since only a small proportion of candidates managed to pass it and secure a treasured place at the college.

Katie had assumed that she hadn't had to sit the exam because of her grades. Benjamin, though, was a completely different matter. His performance at the college was average at best, although, to be honest, she had never seen him doing any work. He only ever went to the library because, so he said, it was the quietest and warmest place in college. He mostly sat on the floor, poking around in books about films or video technology, or he would lie between the shelves, listening to music.

Katie's gaze wandered back to Paul's map, which was spread out on the table.

'What do you actually want with these scraps of paper?' Benjamin broke in again. 'That revolting swamp's not on it, and neither's the cave entrance that we squeezed through. It's only any good for wiping your butt. Where d'ya get it from anyway?' He turned drunkenly to Paul, who had stood up to put some more wood in the stove. 'D'ya find it in your father's stuff? Had he hidden it in some book? In one of the countless Proust volumes that he's used to ruin the lives of generations of students?'

Paul didn't reply. Katie couldn't see his expression as he was kneeling by the stove with his back to her. Benjamin jumped up, pulled a lighter out of his pocket, flicked it on, and held it under the map. 'Ha! Or we could just as well burn it.'

'That's enough, Ben. Stop it,' said David. His voice was surprisingly sharp.

'Why? He just wanted to get round Katie with his crappy bit of paper.'

'Nobody gets round me,' Katie retorted.

'Oh, I'm not so sure.' There was a malicious grin on Benjamin's face. 'You spent months looking for a map. I watched you. In the library, in the computer department – you trawled through every atlas, website and book about this area and you didn't find anything. Did you?'

Katie shrugged. She had no desire to quarrel with Benjamin, especially not when he was drunk.

'But that's what happens if you just rely on your brain. You need to use your eyes too. The eyes are the senses that tell you the most. If you use them properly.' He paused. 'Like I do.'

'You of all people.' Paul stood up and returned to the table. 'You spend your whole time either stoned or drunk or hiding behind your camera. You're the one who doesn't see any-thing.'

'Oh yeah, so that's what you think, is it? Well, you couldn't be more wrong.' Benjamin had jumped up and was climbing onto the table. 'Then I've got something to show you. You'll piss yourselves laughing when you see it. I'm the guardian of the truth! I've got you all on film. I know you all better than you know yourselves. Whenever you think you're alone, I'm there somewhere, burning your faces onto this thing here.' He held up his camera.

'David, for example.'

David looked at him, baffled. 'What about me?'

'Thirteenth of January last year.'

David turned pale, but before he could say anything, Benjamin was ploughing on. 'Or what about your brother, Julia? What kinds of dreams does he have? Why does he squeal at night like a stuck pig? And what about you, Katie?'

'Just shut up, Benjamin,' she said, trying to stop her heart from pounding.

'What goes on in the mind of someone who sets off in the middle of the night to go cliff-climbing without ropes or hooks? That kind of person is completely insane, isn't she? You risk your life whenever you get a chance. I just wonder why.' He made a sweeping hand gesture. 'Guys – these are the true stories. The stories that interest me. What's behind all your façades. What's really going on down there' – he pointed to the window – 'in the valley. It's your eyes that you have to trust. And it's my eyes that found the money bag in the swamp. And something else.' The next moment, Benjamin was waving a piece of paper high in the air.

'What's that?' Julia asked.

Benjamin lowered his voice to a dramatic whisper. 'It's something I found here in the cabin. Something you don't want to see.'

Before Benjamin had chance to react, Paul had grabbed the fragment of paper from his hand with one swift movement.

'Hey, you give that back!'

But Paul turned and stared at the piece of paper.

'What is it?' Julia asked.

'Just another old photo.'

'Just another old photo? Like hell it is! Do you know where I found it? Up in one of the bedrooms.'

'So?' Chris shrugged.

'Give it here, Paul!'

Paul put the photo on the table in front of them. It was of eight young, smiling faces in front of the cabin that they were in now. The sun was shining. Behind them rose the rounded summit of the Ghost.

'You know what that is, don't you?' Julia said tonelessly.

David shook his head firmly. 'Rubbish. It can't be. It's obviously a Polaroid photo. Did they even exist back then?'

Benjamin raised his hand as if he were trying to stop the traffic. 'The first Polaroid cameras came in in 1972.'

Chris sounded hoarse. 'Julia's right. That must be the last photo they took before they set off.'

Katie stared at the faces, feeling the goosebumps now spreading across her whole body. Something incomprehensible was happening to her. She wanted to run away, to scream loudly.

'And have you noticed? Don't you see?' Benjamin seemed semi-hysterical. 'This girl looks almost exactly like you, Katie. Is that just coincidence? Or is it fate?'

CHAPTER 20

That night, Julia slept fitfully, constantly jerked awake by the images that came crowding in on her. She was lying between Katie and Ana in the middle of a horribly uncomfortable double bed. She could feel the rickety frame beneath her, which constantly seemed as if it might collapse.

Chris had given her a look when they'd gone to bed. She knew he'd been counting on them sleeping in the same room. But when all was said and done, the cabin only had two bedrooms. Smirking, Benjamin had offered to take her place between Katie and Ana in order not to deprive the young lovers of their happiness. Was there any such thing as happiness? Since the business in the tunnel, Julia was more unsure than ever. Something had changed inside her. But why on earth was Chris so moody and irritable?

Actually she had worked him out long ago. He was someone who wanted everything. He wanted her heart and soul. And that was precisely what he couldn't have. For her big secret still stood between them.

Her big secret.

She first had to deal with having seen her father in the photo. She was still so completely taken aback that the shock of it hadn't yet hit her.

She jumped as she heard the door creak. It was pitch black

in the room. Not even the moonlight shone through the narrow window.

And yet the moon had stood in the sky like a giant disc when she'd gone to bed. Its pale yellow glow had coloured the horizon a strange shade of blue. It had been somehow unreal. Completely surreal, Benjamin would probably call it.

Julia stared into the darkness.

Nothing. There was nobody there.

She must have been mistaken. Or was she? Hadn't they closed the door when they went to bed?

God, it was so cold! Julia pulled her sleeping bag up to her chin. She should have put on her fleece and her socks.

Had they closed the door or not? She tried to remember, but instead she found her mind whirling. She should have said no to that final beer.

There was a rustling sound coming from somewhere.

Next to her, Katie was fast asleep. The only actual sound was the snoring coming from the next room. It wasn't Chris: she had slept with him so often during the past few weeks that she'd certainly have noticed if he snored.

David? No, David was Mr Perfect. People like David didn't snore or belch or do anything at all that could be construed as embarrassing.

It was presumably Benjamin. On a drunkenness scale of one to ten, he'd probably reached a nine that evening.

Julia jumped. There it was again – the rustling sound. Was it coming from the landing? From outside? No – Julia sensed somehow that it was coming from the wall.

'Hey, Katie.'

Her friend didn't stir.

'Katie!'

No reaction. She reached for her shoulder and shook it gently.

Nothing.

Of course: people like Katie slept like logs. Any halfway normal person fell into a deep sleep after a day like that and two bottles of beer. Particularly Katie. Julia had once gone into her room and found her asleep on the floor. Not in bed, but on her bare bedroom floorboards. Okay, so that wasn't normal either.

She turned to Ana on the other side of her.

'Ana?'

No reply from Ana either.

Damn. Was she the only one who could hear these noises? As if someone were scratching long fingernails down the wall.

You're just imagining it, Julia.

Maybe it's the wind. Branches tapping against the cabin.

Branches?

This cabin was on bare rock; the treeline was far below them. An animal? Birds sitting on the roof of the cabin, pecking away at the black slates with their beaks?

My God, Julia, you really must be going crazy. Why would birds start pecking holes in the slates?

Bats?

No. Bats flew quietly, moved noiselessly through the darkness, and if they needed to communicate with one another, it was all done by ultrasound.

Julia listened into the darkness. The scratching in the walls ebbed away for a moment, then started up again, accompanied by a pitiful whimpering.

Oh God. What was that?

Was she about to lose it? Turn into a weirdo like Robert, who heard voices? Please, not that. Anything but that.

Trembling, Julia crawled out of bed. She wrapped her sleeping bag around herself, then put her shoes on and slipped through the crack in the door.

She crept quietly down the narrow wooden stairs, almost tripping over the sleeping bag on the last couple of steps. She just managed to hang on to the banister. The cabin door was wide open.

One of the others was obviously outside. Benjamin had probably gone to puke. Did he really have to fill himself up to the limit with beer and then scare her to death?

Julia went outside.

After looking out of the bedroom window, she had expected pitch-black darkness, a starless gloom into which people could disappear, where they could dissolve, because they could no longer work out where the hell they were. Like in that tunnel yesterday.

Instead, the horizon was bathed in an unreal light, as if the summit opposite Julia were glowing from within, turning the sky green. Blue, she could have understood. But green?

She didn't have time to wonder about it, because she heard the whimpering sound again. And amidst the whimpering, she thought she could make out individual words.

Help.

Help me.

Help.

The voice was clearly audible now. Horrified, Julia stood rooted to the spot. It was a girl's voice, that was for sure. But Ana and Katie were sleeping peacefully in their sleeping bags. So she must be wrong.

Julia shut her eyes for a moment, forcing herself to think logically. That was her great strength. Whenever her brother Robert had one of his hallucinations, she always tried to bring him back to earth with logical arguments.

She had to do the same with herself now.

Okay, Julia. You almost came unstuck in that tunnel yesterday afternoon. And then there was that exhausting hike up here. Then the photo yesterday evening and the prospect of the climb to the summit tomorrow. No wonder you're losing it.

Julia took a deep breath.

She didn't have to go up there. What did she hope to discover on the Ghost that she didn't already know? What did she want to prove?

She wasn't going to find her father's body up there on the summit. She could remember only too well the way he had died a year ago. Not ten thousand feet up, but crammed into the boot of his Mercedes. Murdered.

What about me?

Me?

Me?

Was she the one who was calling – or was it the voice again?

What if Benjamin were actually prowling around the cabin? He'd think it was a great joke, scaring the life out of her.

She turned round abruptly, banged the door of the cabin behind her, and ran straight across the room and upstairs. She made no attempt to be quiet. Her footsteps clattered up the wooden staircase. The noise would surely have to wake someone up.

Julia wrenched open the boys' bedroom door, expecting to hear howls of protest, but all she heard was the sound of snoring.

There was no bed in there, just mattresses on the floor.

She bent down over the sleeping boys. While there was hardly anything to be seen of Paul and David beneath the thick blankets, she immediately realised that Chris was completely outside the covers. She could hear him breathing. It was such a familiar sound. She should just lie down next to him, cuddle up to him. Then everything would be fine; she'd be safe.

However, a loud snore cast all such thoughts aside. Benjamin was indeed right next to Chris. He wasn't outside the cabin. He wasn't the one making the noise.

Her mind was racing. Where was his camera? She felt her way along the bedcovers and found it right next to his head. She knew it. If anyone were ever to invent contact lenses that also took videos, Benjamin would be the first to take advantage of the new technology.

Without pausing to think, Julia took the camera. At the door, she hesitated briefly, but then shook herself and went back outside.

The cold air hit her in the face. She listened carefully. The whimpering – had it stopped?

Yes. Everything was silent.

Deadly silent.

Julia breathed out, relieved, and felt herself relax. Okay, she had concrete proof. It had all been in her imagination. Her mind had been playing tricks on her after their completely crazy day.

She was just about to turn and go back to bed when she heard the girl's voice again. Once more, it was crying for help – and once more, Julia jumped as if she'd had an electric shock.

This time she didn't hesitate for a second. She turned to her left, in the direction of the summit. In the direction of the Ghost, where the voice was coming from, and set off at a run. Did the mountain get its name because there were creatures up there that could send you insane?

Go back to the cabin, Julia. Don't do it. Wake the others. Chris or Katie.

She remembered her brother.

Robert had prophesied that something would happen.

And the picture of her father.

Had he gone the same way as her? In the middle of the night?

Help me!

No, that wasn't him.

It was a girl calling.

Julia had by now reached the ledge that marked the ascent to the glacier. The snowfield beneath her was still bathed in a greenish light, but she wasn't interested in that now.

Instead, she was trying to find the way down to the slope. At first the snow only reached up to her ankles, but with every step, it was becoming more difficult to move. Julia gritted her teeth. Damn it – this didn't feel like snow. If felt more like that blasted swamp.

She raised her right foot with difficulty.

She could still hear the whimpering, but she could no longer place it precisely. She turned round uncertainly. Was she going the wrong way?

And then all of a sudden she stepped into nothingness – or, rather, a hole that must have been hidden beneath the snow.

She tried with all her might to pull out her foot, but she was stuck. Just as badly stuck as she had been in the tunnel.

Why hadn't she just stayed in her sleeping bag? Did she really need to get to the bottom of everything? Had it ever done her any good? No: people like Benjamin were the ones who survived. Stoned or drunk they may be, but they survive. Benjamin shrugged everything off, but she, Julia . . . She could feel the cold creeping up her legs from her toes to her calves. She couldn't take a single step further; she couldn't move her legs. She could feel each of her toes freezing, and if someone didn't come soon to get her out, then . . .

'Help!' Julia cried. 'Help me!'

CHAPTER 21

It was freezing cold. The kind of cold you get in September in the Rocky Mountains.

But this wasn't why Katie suddenly sat bolt upright, wide awake. Someone was shouting loudly for help. Right next to her. Julia.

Katie grabbed her shoulder and shook her hard. 'Hey, Julia. Wake up! You're dreaming.'

Julia opened her eyes and stared at her in confusion.

'My God, you gave me such a scare. Do they run in the family, these nocturnal screaming fits of yours?'

'Dreaming?' Julia murmured. 'Was I only dreaming?'

'Only? Nice one.'

'It was horrendous.' Julia shook herself. 'Did you put something in the food? I had the worst nightmare of all time ever. And it seemed completely real.'

Katie sighed. 'I think you need to go back to sleep. You look like crap. Black rings round your eyes might be the height of cool in some funky London club, but you're really not fit to climb the Ghost.'

Regardless of whether Julia had understood her or not, she turned onto her other side and, seconds later, she was fast asleep again.

In the dull grey of dawn, Katie heard a rattling sound. She

listened. Had someone opened a window? There was obviously a strong wind outside. Was that why it was so horribly cold in here?

The thinnest trickle of light was coming through the tiny windows into the narrow room. Katie rummaged for her mobile in the side pocket of her rucksack, which was next to the bed. She was sure she'd put it in there the previous evening, but she couldn't find it now. Whatever. Her inbuilt sense of time, which she could normally trust one hundred per cent, told her it was time to start getting up. The earlier they set off, the better.

She could hear one of the boys snoring in the next room. She suspected that Benjamin had been so drunk that he'd have thrown up outside the cabin at some point.

He would clearly be a safety hazard on the mountain – but she hadn't wanted to leave him behind because he really did possess the ability he'd been boasting of the previous night.

He kept his eyes open. He was inquisitive, and he noticed things that others didn't have eyes for – though he could also use this same ability to throw everything into turmoil.

He had spotted the money bag with the photo in the swamp, and he'd spotted the second photo too. Katie had lain awake practically the whole night after she'd realised who it was in the photo. How could she possibly have slept, even though she knew she had to gather together all the strength she could muster?

The room was stuffy; the smell of old socks and sweat was becoming increasingly overpowering. As the minutes ticked by, Katie felt more and more imprisoned in the warm security of the bedroom. She crept out of her sleeping bag.

She flinched as her bare feet touched the floorboards. Quickly, she put on her socks and soft shell jacket. One look at Ana's sleeping bag told her that Ana was already up.

She presumably hadn't been able to hang around waiting for the day to begin any more than Katie could.

Ana was like her. Someone who preferred doing to talking. But Katie could never become friends with Ana – unlike with Julia. Ever since the cave, Katie felt a new closeness to her flatmate.

Maybe I should talk to Julia about that photo. But would Julia actually want that? She hadn't said a single word about the picture last night, and yet Katie was convinced that the business with the eight students was the reason why Julia had joined in with their trip at all.

Eight students, vanished? Lies, thought Katie. All lies. At least one of them had survived. Did she want to know what that meant? No. But she couldn't just ignore it. It had been a kind of shock, seeing that face. She was still baffled by it all, and all she could hope was that she could just push all thoughts of it out of her mind when she set off up the Ghost. The last thing she needed was problems. Her mind had to be completely clear and focused.

The room downstairs was empty, and there was no trace of Ana. David – considerate, thoughtful David – had made sure that there was enough wood the night before, so rekindling the fire in the stove was child's play. Katie put a pan of water on to boil. Okay, if Julia really was something along the lines of a friend, then Katie should just tell her that David might not set anyone's heart racing, but he was probably a better bet than Christopher Bishop and his irritability. Katie had noticed the sullen look on Chris's face when he'd realised that Julia was going to share a bed with the other girls. Had Chris really thought that he and Julia would be getting the best room just because he didn't want to spend a night without her?

The water was boiling. Katie took the pan off the stove-top and was hunting in the cupboards for tea or coffee when she happened to glance out of the window.

Oh my God, I don't believe it.

Katie raced to the door and wrenched it open. She stepped back, horrified. An icy wind was howling around the cabin. No. This couldn't be happening. The landscape had completely changed since the previous evening.

Somewhere behind the clouds, the sun was rising above the mountain ridge, but its light couldn't manage to break through the dark clouds. It was unbelievable. The cabin was surrounded by whiteness. There must have been more than three feet of snow during the night, and big flakes were still falling.

Damn it. Yesterday, radiant sunshine. Today, the mountains submerged in snow.

Was a full-blown depression on the way? Was it going to carry on snowing like this all day? She started to feel scared. What if they had to abandon the whole enterprise?

'So much for online weather forecasts. You might just as well have asked a shaman.' She whirled round. Paul was standing behind her. She could tell by his expression that he was as shocked as she was.

'Well, it looks as if that's the end of our big adventure. We can't go up the mountain in this sort of weather.'

Katie didn't answer. She had to ask Ana's advice. Ana would know what to do.

Katie pulled her jacket zip up to her chin and tramped around the cabin.

Perhaps Ana had gone to fetch some wood. Or maybe she was at the back of the cabin, checking the wind direction.

But wherever she looked, she found no trace of Ana. After a quarter of an hour, she went back inside the cabin. She must have been mistaken. Ana can't have got up yet.

Paul was busy at the stove. 'Do you want a coffee?'

Katie didn't reply, but murmured anxiously, 'Have you seen Ana?'

'She can't do anything about the weather either.'

'When I got up, I thought she wasn't in her sleeping bag. But she's not down here, and she's not outside either.'

Paul shrugged. 'She probably looked out of the window, saw the weather, and pulled her sleeping bag back over her head. She's right. We've had it for today. We might as well sleep the day away.'

Katie said nothing, but went up the narrow staircase and opened the door to the girls' room. Julia was getting dressed.

'God, I've had it after last night. And I'm frozen solid. Was it this cold yesterday?'

Instead of replying, Katie asked, 'Where's Ana?'

'Already up.' Julia thumped the sleeping bag next to her. 'At any rate, there's no one in there.'

Katie turned wordlessly and headed for the stairs, where she almost clattered into David, who was rubbing his eyes. 'What a night. Benjamin snores like a bulldozer.'

'Ana's disappeared,' Katie said.

'What do you mean, disappeared?'

'I can't find her anywhere.'

'Calm down. Nobody can just disappear up here.'

But shock was written all over their faces.

Benjamin was still fast asleep and had no idea what was going on. The others, however, had all gathered downstairs.

'Where on earth can she be?' Julia was sitting at the table, leaning against Chris, staring out into the leaden sky. It had stopped snowing.

'I haven't got the faintest idea,' replied Katie.

'Didn't you hear her getting up?' asked David.

Julia and Katie shook their heads.

'How could anyone be crazy enough to set out on their own, in this weather?'

'I think Ana knows what she's doing,' Paul said from over by the window. 'She does know her way around here, after all.'

'That means nothing,' David retorted. 'You can have as much experience of mountains as you like. Take as much care as you like. But one mistake, and you've had it. The weather turns, or there's an avalanche or a rockfall.'

'Okay.' Katie stood up. 'We'll have to go and look for her. The weather's starting to calm down. She can't be far away.'

The others looked at her uncertainly. Katie could well imagine that none of them much fancied going out into the freezing cold to look for someone who had managed to rub them up the wrong way more than once on the previous day.

David, though, was his usual reliable self. 'I suggest we divide into groups of two.'

Katie pondered. She and Paul were the most experienced mountaineers. The best thing would be for them to head off towards the glacier together. They could discount Benjamin, as he'd be chronically hungover. He could stay in the cabin with Julia, who didn't exactly look the picture of health. That left Chris and David. Katie didn't like the idea of letting them go together, but felt that she had no choice.

'Okay,' she said, turning to David. 'Then I suggest you and Chris go back the way that we came yesterday. Paul and I will go down the wind gap to the glacier.'

'What about Benjamin?' Chris asked.

'What about me?' Benjamin was standing on the staircase, stretching and yawning widely.

Katie ignored him. 'He's staying here with Julia in case Ana comes back. We'll take our mobiles so you can ring us,' she declared.

'If they work, that is,' said Paul. 'Remember yesterday night. And when I tried earlier this morning, there was no reception again.'

Katie wondered who he was trying to ring at that unearthly hour.

'Hey,' Benjamin held up his arms. 'Can someone tell me what's going on?'

'Ana's disappeared. We have to look for her,' Julia replied.

'What?! Something exciting happens, and you don't even wake me up? And then I'm supposed to sit around here on my ass all day, holding hands with Julia?' he grumbled. 'That's Chris's job.'

'You're staying here, and that's that,' Katie said firmly. 'The rest of you, put on everything that you've got.

Remember your crampons and ice-picks. In case Ana ...'
She trailed off.

'Just in case there really isn't any reception here, and we
need some other way to communicate,' said David.
'Something that will make a lot of noise, in case we need
help.'

'How about this?' Paul went over to the cupboard, pulled
out two saucepan lids and banged them together. 'That
should do. You'd hear that from miles around up here.'

Katie nodded. 'Right. Let's go.'

Progress was slow. They took a couple of steps at a time,
rested, then carried on. A couple of steps. Pause. A couple of
steps. Pause. It had stopped snowing, but the wind was whip-
ping Katie in the face and blowing the hard, cold snow into
her body. The snow stuck to her clothes, and she sank up to
her knees with every step.

They wouldn't get far like this. It was clear to Katie that
they would have to turn round soon. The snow was already
nearly two feet deep, and they stood no chance of spotting a
glacier crevice.

She looked at Paul, whose mop of sandy hair was hidden
beneath a thick hat. She wondered once again what had
driven him to join them. Was he really just craving adventure
in the way that she did? Did he just want the challenge of the
mountain?

And then there was the stuff about him having been in
prison. He'd admitted it to her quite openly.

On top of that, she couldn't work out what he thought of
her. On one hand, he kept on trying to wind her up – but

then it would appear as though he was genuinely concerned about her. That's how it had seemed yesterday in the tunnel when he'd noticed how upset she was.

People were far too complicated, Katie thought. The bit of her brain that dealt with social skills really didn't seem to be very well developed. She was useless when it came to giving advice or being diplomatic. Either she said nothing at all, or spoke her mind regardless of how tactless it might sound.

As she was thinking this, she heard herself asking, 'Why?'

Paul turned to look at her. She could see his breath, white in the cold, as he asked, 'Why what?'

'Why were you in prison?'

'I knew you'd ask me that eventually.'

'So why didn't you tell me before?'

'Why should I?'

'Go on, then. Why?'

He took off his glasses, and his yellowy-brown eyes suddenly looked distinctly dark. 'I killed someone.'

Katie caught her breath. Was that supposed to be a bad joke? No: the expression on his face was enough to convince her that he was telling her the truth.

This was decidedly not the place for that kind of confession. They were completely alone out there in this snowy desert.

'You ... you killed someone?' she stammered.

They were silent for what seemed like an eternity.

Footsteps. Pause. Footsteps. Pause.

'So why are you out?'

He looked her in the eye. 'I was given a reprieve.'

Katie breathed again. Okay, he'd just wanted to shock her.

Of course he hadn't killed anyone. A murderer wouldn't get a reprieve.

'There was a procedural error during the trial,' Paul continued, fingering the scar on his face. 'The police supplied evidence that turned out to be false. Just some stuff happened that was unlawful. So they had to let me out on probation.'

Another long silence.

That wasn't the answer that Katie had been expecting. And she really didn't want to ask the next question.

The wind was whistling around them.

'Procedural error,' she said. 'Does that mean ... ?'

'Yes, it's true. I killed someone.' Paul was staring fixedly at the snowy wasteland. 'A boy at high school. His name was Michael. I stuck a knife into his stomach, and he died on the way to hospital.'

Katie shuddered. 'Was it self-defence?'

Paul laughed shortly. 'No. I wanted to do it, you know? I did it deliberately.' Katie could hear his voice becoming louder, angrier. 'And I'd do it again.'

He put his glasses back on, hiding his face. 'There are still people I'd kill for today. You, for example.'

Katie stared at him in disbelief. What the hell was he talking about?

'It was about a girl, Katie. You know?'

They had reached the bottom of the glacier. But the foothills of the huge ice field that began there were hidden beneath a gleaming white treacherous layer of snow. Katie couldn't tell where the scree slope ended and the ice began.

'No footprints,' said Katie, trying with all her might to concentrate on the actual reason why they were there. 'Nothing.

If Ana really did go up here, then ... ' She left her sentence unfinished because the thought was too horrific to say out loud. 'Let's go back.'

She turned to Paul, who had taken off his polarised glasses again. His eyes were bright now; the darkness in them had vanished and they looked amber once more.

At that moment Paul slid across to her with one of his characteristically lithe movements, put his right hand behind her neck, suddenly pulled her to him, and kissed her on the mouth.

Katie was taken by surprise – but only for a second. Perhaps two. Then she pushed him away with both hands. 'What's the matter with you? Have you gone crazy?' Her voice was hoarse with shock.

He shook his head. 'No,' he whispered. 'Definitely not. I wanted to do that the first time I ever set eyes on you.'

CHAPTER 22

'Don't you ever do that again!' Katie had found her voice, and was yelling at Paul. Then she turned and ran back to the cabin. Well, she didn't exactly run. Running was impossible in these conditions. Instead she tramped through the snow and up the slope, trying to keep her balance. An icy wind was blowing in her face and burning her eyes. At one point she got her foot stuck in a hole, and struggled to get it out again. She had no idea whether Paul was following her, and she didn't care either.

The wind wasn't clearing the sky. Instead, new dark clouds were heaving their way across the summit and Katie couldn't work out where the sun was. It had to be late morning by now.

Anger propelled her forwards even faster than the wind. Anger and a feeling of confusion. Maybe the kiss had been completely harmless. Just a try-on. Nothing more.

What would her father say if he knew that she was hanging out with a convicted murderer? That she had kissed him and – stop there, Katie. That's not true.

He had kissed her. But the fact was that Katie hadn't found it unpleasant. She could deny it all she liked, but she knew herself that it was true. He had most definitely kissed her. A demanding kiss, and one that presumed aquiescence. Could a killer really kiss like that?

As if that had anything to do with it. Katie suddenly realised that she had involuntarily clenched her fists inside her gloves.

It had been a shock, feeling his body so close to hers. She had felt his warmth even through the thick layers they were both clad in. Or was her imagination running away with her? When you were freezing your ass off, you would probably imagine that even a stick was giving off warmth.

Paul hadn't kissed her in the way that Sebastien had.

The first time Sebastien had kissed her had been after they had jumped off the bridge for the first time.

They hadn't slept together until much later on. And the goodbye kisses he'd always given her had been different too.

Long, tender.

Infinitely long, infinitely tender.

Katie speeded up and promptly stumbled. She just managed to stop herself plunging into a snowdrift. Angry, she struggled upright and carried on. The last thing she needed was Paul's help.

She couldn't stop herself sighing with relief when she finally saw the compact silhouette of the cabin in the dim light. It was snowing again, and only now did Katie realise that she had lost track of why they'd set off in the first place.

Ana. Had Chris and David found her? Or had she come back of her own accord?

But as she opened the door, her hopes were dashed. She could see at a glance that Ana was still missing.

Benjamin was leaning on the left-hand wall next to the fire

that was crackling in the stove. He was pointing his camera at Julia who was leaning against the cupboard, strangely pale, as Chris and David stood in the middle of the room, glaring at one another.

Katie opened her mouth to ask about Ana, but before she could say a word, Chris was speaking in a menacingly low voice. 'I'm warning you, David. Don't you ever lay a finger on her again. Got it?'

'I only . . .'

'Shut up. I'm speaking. You just stay away from her. You're obviously bad news for her. You almost killed her yesterday.'

'Stop it, Chris!' Julia cried. He ignored her.

'People like you really piss me off.'

'You don't deserve her,' David replied calmly.

'Deserve her?' retorted Chris. 'People don't deserve love. It's just there. Like a law of nature.'

'Oh yeah?'

Julia's eyes were brimming with tears. Katie felt like crying too, but tears weren't part of her emotional repertoire.

'Oh yeah?' Chris jeered, mocking David's tone. 'You listen to me. I just don't buy this Mr Nice Guy act. So turn off the spiel – I saw through you ages ago.'

'And you reckon your designer stubble and Marlboro Man act are going to work long term?'

'If you need someone to warm up your bed, David, then order a nun.' Chris's voice was distinctly louder and sharper. 'That'd fit in with your holier than thou image. But not Julia. You're the type who's best friends with girls – but nothing more. Nice men and nice girls can't be happy. It's like in physics. Two positives repel one another. What kind of girl wants to sleep with a psychotherapist or a priest? You just keep your hands off my girlfriend.' Chris took a step towards David and grabbed his shoulder. 'Or I won't be able to restrain myself.'

David made no reply. Katie wondered how on earth he managed to maintain this weird composure.

'Come on, you wuss. Hit me.' Chris gave David a push in the chest.

Katie heard Julia gasping. Then Julia leapt forwards, grabbed one of the coffee cups from the table and threw it at the wall, where it broke into hundreds of pieces.

'Wow!' Benjamin called, lowering his camera for a moment. 'Isn't broken china supposed to be lucky or something?'

'I'm so sick of this!' Julia yelled 'Don't you get it? I don't want either of you. I just want to be left alone.'

'Julia, that's great.' Benjamin was filming away like mad. 'You go for them. And just keep on crying. You look fantastic with your face all tear-stained. It gives you the ultimate smoky eyes.'

Julia ignored Benjamin and ran upstairs.

Katie dropped down onto the corner seat. What on earth was going to happen next? First the business with Ana, then the kiss, and now there was war in the cabin.

Oh well, it did at least take her mind off Paul's unexpected pass at her.

'Congratulations. Well done, you two,' she said tiredly.

'You keep out of it. You haven't got a clue what you're talking about. I bet you've never even had a date,' Chris replied scornfully, flinging himself down on the bench.

Katie rolled her eyes.

'To hell with it,' said Chris. 'Put the camera away, and let's have a beer. There's nothing else we can do today anyway. If this is what the weather's going to be like, we're presumably going to be stuck up here until spring anyway.'

For once, Ben turned off his camera. Katie watched him as he went to the store cupboard and took out four cans of beer. He threw one across to Chris, who caught it deftly.

'Want one, David?'

David shook his head silently.

'Katie?'

'Beer before lunch? No thanks.'

Katie wondered whether she should go up and see Julia – but comforting people wasn't exactly her strong point. She'd be better off making sure the boys didn't go completely crazy.

She looked out of the window. The snow was falling more heavily again. She took a deep breath. 'Okay, guys. Let's get back to what really matters. What's happened to Ana? Did anyone find any trace of her?'

Chris opened his can of beer with a swift movement. 'Nothing.'

'Julia said she took all the stuff out of her rucksack, apart from her crampons,' David added. 'She surely wouldn't have tried to . . .'

'No way would she have been that crazy,' replied Katie. 'She knows what she's doing. Don't forget she's a ski instructor as well as a mountain guide.'

Could she really be that certain? No. If she was honest, she knew Ana just as little as the others did. She remembered her unquestioning assumption that Ana had been up there before.

On the other hand, Ana had talked about instinct.

Katie felt a cold draught on her back and turned to look. When she saw Paul's silhouette in the doorway she turned back round abruptly.

She was on the point of telling Benjamin that she'd have a can of beer after all – but alcohol had never been a help for her, and anyway she needed to keep a clear head, even if nobody else did.

Instead, she went over to the stove and poured herself a coffee.

It must have been sitting on the hob for hours. It was incredibly strong and tasted revolting. But at least it was fairly warm. God, she was frozen solid.

She had ignored Paul, but she could feel his gaze boring into her back. Her teeth clenched, she slid back onto the bench and quickly downed her coffee. Her nerves were frayed practically to breaking point, and she was almost starting to count the snowflakes. There were more and more of them, as if they were being cloned as they fell.

This could go on for ever. Hours. Days. Maybe even a week. Going back down to Fields would be more than difficult – if, that is, it was possible at all. And she had remembered something else. Their absence would be noticed by the college. Rose and Robert might be able to cover for them over the weekend that the Governor General was there. But what would happen after that?

Then there was Debbie. You could never count on her – she'd been the one who'd reported a forbidden party to the Dean in order to make herself look good.

The atmosphere in the room couldn't have been much worse. David was staring gloomily at the staircase, but Julia didn't appear. Chris had assumed his poker face and was sipping his beer, and Paul had turned his back to Katie and was poring over the map that was spread out on the table in front of him.

Benjamin was the only one with any energy left. 'Hey, guys,' he called. 'I've got a joke for you. A mountain guide leads a group through the dense mountain forests of the Rockies; they've long since lost their way. The group eventually starts grumbling and the guide admits he's lost. One of the group asks, "How could you be lost? You're supposed to be the best mountain guide in America." "Yes," he says, "but we're in Canada now."'

Benjamin giggled hysterically and Chris murmured, 'When we get back down, I'll put you up for *Canada's Got Talent*. As a top-flight clown of the future.'

Benjamin still couldn't stop. 'Okay, this one's for Paul,' he continued. 'Two hikers find themselves by a crevasse. One says to the other, "My guide fell down there last week." "And you're not bothered?" "Well, it wasn't the most recent edition and there were already a couple of pages missing."'

Katie rolled her eyes, irritated – but a moment later Benjamin was completely forgotten.

The door was flung open. Cold air streamed into the room and the wind banged the door shut again. Ana was standing in front of them. Her clothes were sodden and she looked completely exhausted.

They all stared at her, each of them waiting for some kind of explanation.

'She's back – the lost daughter of the Cree tribe,' Benjamin said mockingly as his camera whirred.

Instead of offering any kind of explanation, though, Ana merely said, 'I'm starving. Is there anything to eat?'

'For Christ's sake,' cried Chris. 'Where were you?'

Ana, however, didn't reply. She didn't even deign to look at him. Instead she pulled a chair up to the stove, sat down, and took off her shoes and socks. Then she put her right leg on her left knee and started massaging her foot.

Katie's heart almost stopped. It was now quite clear that Ana had in fact been telling the truth. She had experienced more in the mountains than the rest of them put together.

If, that was, you could judge by frostbite.

Ana was missing three toes.

Ana didn't reply to any of their questions. She just kept shrugging. It seemed to Katie almost as if she had taken some kind of vow of silence. And Julia didn't reappear at all.

It didn't stop snowing even as morning turned into afternoon. In places, the snowflakes were invisible in the gathering fog. And despite the fact that Ana had returned safely, Katie didn't feel any better.

Quite the reverse. This waiting, trapped here in the cabin, was almost as bad as being in the tunnel yesterday. Having to wait: that was the perfect breeding ground for unwelcome thoughts.

Benjamin broke the silence with a belch. 'Sorry,' he said, 'but someone had to say something.'

Paul was the first one to laugh. He seemed to have relaxed over the course of the past few hours, almost as if a heavy burden had been removed from his shoulders. Was it his confession? The kiss? Both? Did he perhaps fancy his chances?

Benjamin reached for his camera, stood up, opened the window behind him and held it outside. 'My God, it's cold out there.'

'With a bit of luck we'll get a warm chinook wind, and the temperature will shoot up,' Paul responded.

Benjamin put the camera back on the table and leaned backwards out of the window. Then he opened his mouth and let the big snowflakes melt onto his tongue. They could barely hear him although he was shouting. 'So why've we got all this glacier equipment if we're waiting for the snow to melt?'

'God, Benjamin,' Chris sighed. 'You must have driven your parents crazy with your constant *whys*. Use your brain. We won't be able to see the crevasses because they'll have got snowed up.'

'I sent my parents crazy just by existing.'

'I'm not surprised.' A smile was spreading across Ana's face. What was up with her all of a sudden? Just like Paul, she had seemed much less tense since returning to the cabin.

Benjamin pulled his head back in. 'Hey, Ana, you Native Americans are famous for being the best weathermakers on earth. Can't you do us some kind of rain dance?'

Ana got up, went over to the cupboard and took out a tin of tomatoes. 'No, but I can cook you something.'

'Come on, you must know some kind of saying or magic spell to drive out demons.'

Ana grinned at him. 'Yeah. Don't you know what the Sioux said when they went into battle at Little Big Horn?'

They all looked at her expectantly.

Ana raised her eyebrows mockingly.

'Tell us.'

'Today is a good day to die.'

Katie caught her breath.

Before every jump, Sebastien had said, 'Today's the day we might die.'

CHAPTER 23

At some point Julia pulled herself together and decided to go downstairs. Or, to be more precise, the smell of cooking wafted up to her and her stomach reminded her quite insistently that she hadn't even had any breakfast. It must be well after midday by now.

What on earth's the matter with you? she wondered. You're not normally this sensitive. This is the second time in two days that you've gone flouncing off like a silly toddler.

But somehow it was all just too much for her. The exertion of the past few days, the experience in the tunnel, the nightmare, Ana's disappearance and not least the weather, which was making her anxious.

But the worst thing of all was that Chris had seemed like a stranger ever since they'd left the college. Or was he the same as always, and she was the one who had changed?

Her thoughts drifted back to that morning. Chris and David had returned from their fruitless search for Ana, and Chris had gone straight up to change into something dry. David had stayed downstairs, and she had sensed that he wanted to talk to her, although he'd just hung around clutching his hot coffee, not saying whatever it was he wanted to say. It had finally irritated her so much that she'd asked what was wrong.

'It's just yesterday. The rockfall. It was all my fault.'

'How could it be your fault?'

'Ana warned us not to make a noise. She said something like that might happen. But then ... ' he broke off.

'What?'

'I ... I was just worried about you. And I was so angry with Chris.'

'I was angry with him too.'

'But when I called you ... the stones suddenly started crashing down from the ceiling. You'd disappeared into the darkness and I couldn't stop myself. I had no idea where you were or whether something had happened to you. Do you see? I'm the one who put your life in danger.'

'David, it's fine. You didn't do it on purpose.'

They were silent for several minutes.

'I just don't understand what you see in him.' David hadn't looked at her. 'He's so ... so unpredictable.'

'Everyone's unpredictable.'

David shook his head vigorously. 'That's just an empty cliché. I don't buy it.' David had come over and planted himself right in front of her, looking at her intently. It had been completely crazy. Because she, Julia, had withstood the challenge. She had been able to look David in the eye without embarrassment, without nervousness, without fear.

It had felt so ... familiar. *He* had felt so familiar. And for a moment she had thought: you could tell him everything. Your whole story. All your secrets. And he'd keep them for ever. No doubt about it.

And then she had moved, and a strand of hair had fallen across her face. David had instinctively raised his hand to tuck it back behind her ear – and all of a sudden Chris was standing there, and all hell had broken loose.

She could still tell David. But she sensed that the moment had passed. Unlike him, she believed in the cliché, however old it might be. Today more than ever.

Everyone was unpredictable. And feelings could lie to you. Feelings were just as unreliable as your supposed best friend.

Julia sighed and got out of bed.

She slipped her shoes on and went out onto the landing. She hesitated once more at the top of the stairs, then shook herself and went down to the ground floor, where the others were sitting around the table.

'Okay, let's talk facts. When are we setting off?' she heard Chris asking.

'First thing tomorrow morning,' replied Katie. 'The earlier the better. We need to reach the summit by midday.'

'What about the weather, Katie?' asked Paul. 'Did the Ghost whisper to you that it'll have improved by tomorrow or something?'

'There are always two options,' Katie said. Julia could hear something in her voice that she couldn't quite put her finger on. 'You either figure on every new day being another chance, or you quit before you've even started. I've got a plan in my head and I'm sticking to it.'

Julia admired Katie. She knew what she wanted and she made sure she got it. Unlike Julia herself. Which was presumably because she didn't actually know what she wanted.

'Total risk, that's *my* motto.' This was Benjamin. 'Don't you know the story of ... what was his name? Damn, I can't remember, but there's a film about him.' Benjamin raised his can of beer, shook it, and said, 'Huh – empty again.' Then he got up and went to the store cupboard. 'So, what do you reckon? We've got precisely four cans. Either we can down them today on the hope principle: because the sun's going to shine tomorrow and we'll be leaving our five-star hotel. Or we can ration them out. One shared between all of us each evening. What do you think?' He returned to the table, unexpectedly thumping Chris on the shoulder. 'I know! He was called Chris, like you. Christopher McCandless. Let's drink to the guy. He was a hero.'

Ana snorted. 'He was an idiot.'

Julia glanced at her. How long had Ana been back? And where the hell had she been?

'Who on earth are you talking about?' Katie asked.

'McCandless was from a wealthy East Coast family,' said Benjamin. 'Well, he would be, wouldn't he?' He laughed. 'He was a bit of a screwball, had all these crazy fantasies, like surviving in the wilderness. Yeah, right. He crossed America first, then hitched to Alaska. He changed his name and trekked off into the wild on his own. Exactly four months later a group of elk hunters found his body. Crazy, eh? Well, he did at least end up as the subject of a Sean Penn film. Not bad if you ask me.' Benjamin paused for a moment. 'You know what impressed me about his story? Right at the end, when things were really bad, he must have stayed really cool not to have done himself in.'

A shiver ran down Julia's spine. There was something in Benjamin's voice that she recognised. The great longing to leave everything behind.

Ana was the only one to respond. 'Crap,' she said calmly.

'Christopher McCandless starved to death a couple of miles from Park Highway. He tried to live off wild berries. He didn't even have a map. If you ask me, he was stupidity personified.'

'Hey, he did it in order to be free.'

'Free?' Ana laughed sarcastically, tapping her forehead. 'Up *here* is the only place you can really be free.'

CHAPTER 24

It was still dark when Katie got up. She could instantly sense that something was different. The sky was still pitch black, but the storm seemed to have abated. They had given up all hope the evening before. One after another, they had disappeared off to their sleeping bags early. Nobody had mentioned the weather or expressed any anxiety about the storm that was sweeping across the cabin. Nobody had said aloud the thing that Katie was most afraid of. That on the following day, too, the dark snow clouds from the north would push their way across the summit, leaving them with no choice but to return home.

Katie got up quietly, squeezed past Julia, and ran downstairs in her thick woollen socks.

She opened the door and stepped outside into the cold air. The clouds had gone. She was greeted by a clear night with a pale moon lighting the dark blue sky. On the horizon she could see a thin strip of light, as if drawn with a ruler. The horizon was the only straight line in nature. Sebastien had once told her that.

Katie looked sideways up the Ghost. There was a mild breeze, and the air was so clear that she could see the round summit without any problem. She took a deep breath. Paul had said it so blithely yesterday, but what he'd said had come true.

The chinook had saved them. The temperature had risen

markedly, and water was crashing down the rocks some-where behind her.

Katie had heard several stories about the chinook, the warm mountain wind that the Canadians also call the Snow Eater. It was possible for the temperature to rise from −22 degrees Fahrenheit to +55. If this happened, then the snow-drifts on the glacier would have melted by this morning at the latest.

It was incredible. Katie's heart was pounding. She had to wake the others. No, on second thoughts, too early. It'd be better for them to be well slept and fit for what lay ahead of them.

Katie was just about to turn round when she spotted what looked like grey marks in the corner of the wooden verandah floor. They were stones.

Had they been there yesterday?

She couldn't remember.

She reached them in two paces. No; she couldn't fail to notice the pattern. These stones ... one, two, three ... Katie counted ... twenty-four ... they hadn't just got here by acci-dent. Someone had put them there on the verandah. Lots of stones with unusual shapes and colours.

Katie stared at the pattern. There were two circles, eight stones in each. A bigger circle with a smaller one in the middle. And the other eight had been made into the arms of a cross, which linked the two circles together.

Who had put them there? When?

It must have been one of the others.

Was it one of Ben's crazy schemes? Or had Chris put them there in a fit of jealousy to scare everyone?

No.

There was a black feather in the middle.

The whole thing looked like a message.

Katie shivered suddenly.

Then she leaned over the stones, picked them up one after the other, and hurled them towards the boulder-strewn wilderness that led down to the wind gap. It took less than a minute to destroy the whole arrangement.

But Katie couldn't forget the words that had come to mind when she'd seen the pattern.

Today is a good day to die.

And something else was sending a cold shiver down her spine. What had the voice in the lift whispered?

Someone will die up there. Do you hear me? Katie? Katie? And it will be your fault, Katie. Your fault, your fault ...

No.

That wasn't going to happen.

An hour later, it was noticeably lighter. The sun wasn't yet visible on the horizon, but Katie could already tell that it was going to be a magnificent day.

After a quick breakfast, they had all gathered on the verandah. Like Katie, the others were almost euphoric in the face of such fabulous weather.

'I don't believe it,' said David. 'The chinook has melted most of the snow.'

'Which doesn't mean to say that climbing to the top's going to be child's play,' Ana replied, firmly tying the laces of her mountain boots. 'This thaw will make the glacier and the firn-ice on top of it damned slippery, and some of the crevasses will still be covered with snow where the sun can't get to it.'

'Yeah – but who'd have believed it? Did anyone really think it was possible? Snowstorms yesterday, and today ... God, it's unreal, like some kind of computer animation.' Benjamin ran up and down outside the cabin, arms outspread. 'Believe me, this is all unreal. It's a dream.'

A snowball hit him all of a sudden. 'Does that feel unreal?' called Chris.

'Hey, you're going to regret that.' Moments later, a snowball fight had broken out. The only ones not taking part were Katie, Ana and Paul, who was last out of the cabin.

As on the previous day, Katie was keen to keep as far away from him as possible – but she couldn't help noticing that he was standing there motionless, just as she was, gazing up at the ridge that led up to the summit.

This close, Katie could for the first time make out the extent of the challenges posed by the mountain. A route led from the wind gap over the glacier, which looked scary from where she was standing. And once they'd managed that, they still had to get to the summit.

The start of the ridge looked relatively harmless, but further up it became terrifyingly narrow, and so steep that they would have to climb rather than walk. It would demand total concentration from all of them.

But once they had that stretch behind them, it would be only a few more feet to the top.

Paul took a couple of steps towards Katie. 'The gradient on that lower section must be almost one in two,' he said, as if he had been reading her mind, 'as for the last few feet up to the summit ... I don't know how the others are going to manage that.'

Katie paused for a moment's thought, then decided simply to act as if nothing had happened the day before. 'We need to cross the glacier first,' she said.

Paul adopted the same tone. 'After the fresh snow yesterday, we might find that there are colder pockets where we could easily miss crevasses that are still covered with snow.'

'What's wrong?' Katie asked. 'Are you chickening out? Do you want to give up?'

Paul gave her a sidelong glance. 'I'm only giving up if you are.'

Katie shook her head. 'No chance.'

She turned back to the others.

'How long will it take?' Julia asked, putting on her gloves. Like the rest of them, she was bundled up in her Gore-Tex jacket and was wearing a hat.

'Four hours at least,' replied Ana, stroking her left hand across her right arm. She grimaced for a fraction of a second. 'Depending on how fit you are. But you've had a whole day to relax. It'd be best if you pack your things in such a way that you don't have to spend ages trying to find your crampons or your harnesses. And I hope you've had enough breakfast. Once we're on the glacier, we'll need strength and concentration. There won't be another break until we're up on the summit.'

Her good mood of yesterday seemed to have been wiped away. When she'd stepped onto the verandah, her face had darkened, and her customary sergeant major tone had returned.

Julia put on her sunglasses, even though the sun hadn't yet risen. 'I wonder whether she's ever got to the summit?' she asked quietly, and Katie realised that she had never asked that question herself. She had somehow just taken it as read.

'Maybe there's a guest book up there, with all their names in it for posterity. That'd be really creepy.' Benjamin grimaced exaggeratedly.

'Oh my God,' David murmured. 'I shouldn't have taken the blue pill.'

They all laughed. Only Ana gave him an irritated look.

'*Matrix*?' Benjamin prompted her.

'I haven't got a clue what you're talking about,' Ana insisted.

'You've never seen the film?'

Ana shook her head impatiently. 'I haven't got a television.'

'You're kidding!' exclaimed Benjamin in mock horror. 'We're entrusting our lives to someone who doesn't own a television!'

'That's enough, Ben.' Ana sounded as if she were struggling to contain her anger. 'Rule number one for crossing a glacier: always rope up. We'll have two rope teams. Benjamin, Julia and me. The other four of you can go together. And make sure you put brake knots in the ropes.'

Chris, though, didn't seem to like this suggestion. 'Hey, I want to go with Julia,' he protested.

'I'll decide who goes with who.'

'But I . . .'

Ana ignored him. 'Stay at least thirty feet apart. Any less, and there's too big a risk of one of you pulling another down into a crevasse before you can even shout out a warning. And don't forget that the rope mustn't scrape against the glacier. David, Paul – you both go ahead. Match your speed to the person following you. No going off elsewhere, and as for your camera, Benjamin . . .'

'My camera? It's nothing to do with you.'

'Oh yes it is. You'll have to do without it.'

'Are you crazy?' Benjamin stared at Ana. 'My only reason for coming was to find the story of a lifetime up there. Reckon I could make a fortune selling that sort of stuff.'

'You'll have your hands full making sure you don't disappear down one of the crevasses up there.'

'I'm not going without my camera.'

Ana shrugged, unconcerned. 'Then you're staying here.'

There was a pause.

'We all ought to stay here.' Paul broke the silence.

They all stared at him.

'But you were desperate to come,' said Chris.

'But not at any price. And especially not if the conditions aren't exactly ideal.'

Chris jabbed at his watch. 'Not the best? When are we going to go if we don't go now? It's almost half past six. We'll be up there by eleven, six hours for the descent, well, maybe an hour more, and it's all over.'

'You do what you like. But you need to make a decision. We haven't got time to sit around talking.' Ana looked at them all. 'I'm going first. The rest of you, try to keep to my footsteps. Bear in mind once you're on the glacier that not being able to see the gaps doesn't mean they're not there.' Ana shouldered her rucksack and went down the verandah steps.

Katie followed her, kicking aside as she did so one of the stones from the weird circle that she had destroyed during the night.

The circle had been made of eight stones. Just like the eight faces in the photo that Katie had tried so hard to forget about.

One face had indeed looked like her own, as Benjamin had pointed out.

It was the face of Katie's mother.

The sun was becoming warmer by the minute, and the remaining snow of the previous day soon melted. Water was flowing in all the rocky gullies and trickling down the cliffs in little streams. As they made their way down the boulder-strewn wasteland to the wind gap, Katie tried to think. Had her mother said anything about her decision to go to Grace? No, not a word. But that was nothing new. Her mother was the most reticent person she'd ever known. Well, she could make fantastic conversation when she had to; in fact she could have easily invented the whole concept of small talk. Her favourite topics were the weather, and the best restaurants in DC.

'Ah, so you've never met Nora? Her restaurant in Florida Avenue is *the* place for those in the know. You absolutely *must* go there; I couldn't recommend it more highly. Do mention my name when you book a table. Wait a moment – I just happen to have their card here.'

'Just happen to'? Yeah, right. Katie's mother had business cards in her handbag for every restaurant worth knowing about.

And Katie suddenly remembered with blinding clarity the reason why she had decided to accept Grace's offer at all.

It had been the shut doors.

Katie had grown up with shut doors. And the voices behind them. The voices of her parents, which drowned out even the pounding of her heart. She always knew when it was about her. She had made a habit of checking out the rooms in which these secret conversations had taken place, as if there might be clues there, words that her parents had accidentally left behind – and it was after one such conversation behind the library door that she had discovered the letter.

It was an invitation to Grace, including the information that in view of her good high-school grades she wouldn't need to sit the entrance exam. The letter was addressed to her – but her father had opened it, as he did with all her post.

Katie manoeuvred around a water hole formed by the thawed snow. Paul was ahead of her. He had adopted the even tempo set by Ana and was moving down the slope with the same athletic ease as Katie herself.

Around the halfway mark, Ana changed direction and struck off on a curving route that led towards the eastern side of the glacier bottom. Katie glanced at the view, noticing that she could get a brief glimpse of Grace Valley, thousands of feet below them.

Still shrouded in shadows, it had a gloomy, ominous air, while the Ghost and its companions gleamed in the almost unreal light of the rising sun.

Heaven up above.

Hell down below.

Katie's thoughts returned to her mother.

If that really was her mother in the photo – and she was quite sure it was – then what did that mean for Katie? Why wasn't her name on the memorial stone for the missing students?

And why hadn't she stopped her daughter from going to Grace, of all places?

Yeah, why, she thought sarcastically. Because she never goes against *him*, that's why. And anyway, what arguments could she have come up with? Katie couldn't imagine her father knowing about what Mi Su got up to at college. Otherwise there was no way he'd have agreed to his daughter going to Grace. It was inconceivable.

But her smooth, polished, oh-so-perfect mother had a secret.

For a heartbeat, Katie's head felt completely empty. And she felt deceived. But this feeling was quickly replaced by another. Katie couldn't quite name it at first. The only word she could think of was satisfaction.

Ana was calling something from further down, and Katie could see that they had almost completed the descent from the wasteland. The wind gap, which joined the Ghost's secondary peak to its main one, was right in front of them.

'Have you seen? Down there?' Julia waved to Katie. She had already reached the bottom of the glacier and was now standing directly by the offshoots of the glacier. 'Amazing, isn't it?'

Katie completed the last few feet.

Julia was right.

To her left, the boulder-strewn wasteland stretched up to

the cabin. To her right was the white glacier, and above them was the narrow ice ridge that they were going to conquer today.

The valley lay below Katie's feet. It was no longer wreathed in shadow.

Mirror Lake was shimmering blue through the thin trails of mist that rose from the water. The bright college buildings were directly opposite. From up here, they looked tiny like toys – yet the air was so clear that all the details were still visible.

Katie didn't feel intimidated now. On the contrary. She had found it: the chink in her mother's armour. She had been looking for it for years. And Katie knew exactly what it meant for her future.

Power.

For the first time in her life, she had power over her mother. And the valley had given her that power.

The valley was on her side. Katie could feel it clearly. It was going to take her to the summit.

'Okay!' Ana's stentorian voice interrupted her thoughts. 'Buckle up your harnesses, get your crampons on, and rope yourselves together.' She gave David and Paul an auxiliary rope each. 'Here you go. From now on, you are responsible for your partners.'

'Why do we need the ice-pick?' asked Julia.

'So that we can chop one another up into steaks if we run out of food,' replied Benjamin.

CHAPTER 25

How tiny Katie felt in the face of the enormous masses of ice that had accumulated over the course of centuries. Layer upon layer.

Although the snow of the previous day had all but melted, there was still a thin covering on the ice. The glacier was gleaming with a bright, almost uniform white, making an unreal contrast with the blue sky above them, across which occasional clouds floated. They had plunged into a fairy-tale world. A fairy-tale world, enclosed within the cliffs and mountains, more sublime than Katie had ever imagined. Maybe it was because the play of light and shade made the panorama of mountain-tops around her look as if it were constantly changing.

The steep face of the Ghost rose up to their right. The melt water collected in narrow channels and gushed down the bare rocks.

And the clouds above them were performing a shadow-play on the dark grey wall.

'This isn't a sightseeing trip,' Ana said, pushing them onwards.

Katie was amazed by the surefooted way that Ana was leading them through the mountain terrain. Her steps were sure and even, and she set a pace that they could all manage. She was similarly astonished by Ana's ease in finding her way across the bizarrely formed ice fields, past awe-inspiring snow cornices and immensely long snow-drifts.

She circumvented every crevasse, not hesitating for a second. She seemed once more like a mountain guide who had led countless groups across the glacier. So why had she said that she'd never been to the cabin before?

Now and then she bent down and used stones to mark out particularly striking features for their return journey.

Katie's respect for Ana was growing by the minute. Up here she seemed to be in her element, at one with nature – a nature that seemed more beautiful than ever. At that moment, she couldn't imagine a single place in the world where she would rather be.

The others seemed equally awestruck. Julia in particular was glowing beneath her alpine glasses and thick hat.

'Wow, wow!' Benjamin couldn't stop exclaiming. 'This is so awesome. It's like some gigantic film backdrop. I could fall to my knees and worship this!'

He was the one who surprised Katie most by appearing unfazed by the exertion. What's more, he seemed to feel a respect for the crevasses and snow cornices that she would never have expected from him, and he kept his place in the line with an unwonted sense of discipline. He even made sure he kept the rope between himself and Julia taut.

The others, too, were acquitting themselves better than Katie had ever dared to hope. They had been walking for a good two hours now, and were rapidly approaching their destination.

The rounded summit of the Ghost arose ahead of them, casting its half shadow on the vast icy surface of the glacier. Katie had imagined that the particular shape of the mountain, its similarity to a ghostly face that she could see from the college, was just an optical illusion created by the distance. Up here, though, the similarity was, if anything, even greater.

'Creepy, eh?' Benjamin called at that moment. 'That thing in front of us in the wall really does look like a huge eye.'

'Big Brother's watching you,' laughed Julia, as Ana turned round briefly and said:

'My ancestors painted that eye on the rock face.'

'You're not serious?' asked Katie.

Ana didn't reply.

Presumably the whole thing was just a legend. Katie turned her attention instead to the particular difficulties posed by the southern ridge that they would have to climb to reach the summit.

First, though, they had to finish crossing the glacier. The sun was now high in the sky, and they had to watch out for the melt water in the sunnier parts of the glacier. In the shade, though, the air was noticeably colder than it had been an hour ago, and some of the snow bridges had frozen so solid that Katie felt as if she were walking across tarmac.

Ana held up her hand as a signal to them to stop. Then Paul passed her order down the line. 'Five-minute break.'

Katie would normally have been impatient – but she was so close to her goal now. Today was the day on which she would be standing up there.

How could she have been so wrong? She had thought that the route up to the cabin would be straightforward and that the serious challenge would follow afterwards. But compared to the tunnel, the glacier seemed like child's play. She was in her element now.

Ana was right to let the group have a short rest. They would need to be completely sure-footed and clear-headed to tackle the razor-sharp rocky ridge ahead of them.

Katie took off her rucksack and pulled out a granola bar and her water bottle.

Paul, a good twenty-five feet away from her, did the same. Katie had been concentrating so hard on their ascent, and had been so captivated by the scenery, that she hadn't given a moment's thought to yesterday's kiss, despite the fact that Paul was just ahead of her the whole time, attached to her by the rope. Was it deliberate or just a coincidence that his pace was almost completely in sync with hers?

They had barely exchanged a word. Was he regretting having told her about being in prison? Had he hoped that the kiss would lead to something? If so, he should have kept his confession and his kiss to himself.

Katie pushed her thoughts aside. Ana was now signalling to them to set off again. Before they did so, though, she advised them all to put their helmets on.

'I'd never imagined you'd get cold so quickly when you stop walking,' Katie heard Julia saying as she detached her helmet from her rucksack.

'You'll soon warm up once we start going uphill,' Chris called across to her.

'But I don't want to think about getting back down again.'

They tramped onwards, and before long Ana raised her hand again. 'You see the frozen rocks ahead of us?' she called. 'After that, it's only two hundred yards to the ridge.'

She set off, curving round slightly, and they passed the rocks that blocked their view of the entrance. Barely were they all on the open ice field once more, though, when Ana called out a warning.

'What?' Katie heard Paul calling back.

Benjamin, who had stopped at the same time as Ana, turned his head and shouted, 'Crevasse!'

'So? It's not the first one today,' Katie called. They had already avoided at least six or seven crevasses, and Katie had been astonished every time by how deep they were.

'But this one's truly massive.' Benjamin began stamping his feet, then started jumping up and down. 'Stop moving for one second and it's so damn cold.'

'Carry on any further and you'll be stone-cold dead.' Ana's voice came sharply across the snow field. 'Keep your distance. This crevasse is horrendous.'

'I'll be fine.' Benjamin took another couple of steps further forward. The rope was sagging down now.

Paul was by now on a level with Benjamin. And now Katie too was so close that she could see what the others meant. Ragged at the edges, the crack was more than seventy feet deep and extended like a gigantic jagged fault line right across the glacier. It was more than fifteen feet wide in some places, and in others it appeared to be so narrow that you could step across it. Katie, though, had developed something along the lines of an eye for the shape of the edges and the consistency of the ice and knew that it was impossible to be certain that the ice around the edges would hold.

'So how are we supposed to get round this one?' Julia sounded anxious.

'Hey, Chris, David, could you just keep hold of Benjamin?' Before Katie knew what was happening, Ana had taken off her rucksack. She was still wearing the rope which attached her harness to Benjamin's. She took out her ice-pick, held it firmly, took a run-up and suddenly jumped across to the other side of the crack, landing in the snow. As her feet started to slide away from her, she struck out with the ice-pick and rammed it hard into the snow to stop herself from falling.

Benjamin found himself suddenly pulled forward, and stumbled towards the crack. David grabbed him wildly by the shoulders and pulled him back.

'Hey, are you crazy?' For the first time since Katie had known him, Benjamin was as white as a sheet. 'You almost pulled me into the crevasse.'

Ana shook her head. 'No I didn't. But it's time you learnt a lesson. So that you finally see what you're contending with up here.'

Ana was rubbing her right arm.

'Are you okay?' called David.

'Fine.' Ana looked across at them. 'So. You first, Ben.'

Icy silence.

'What's the matter?'

'If you think I'm doing that, you're very much mistaken,' he said. 'It's lethal. I was always a dead loss at long-jump.'

'Well, it seems to me that the alternative is that you climb down into the chasm and back up the other side. Or that you take a detour that might go on for miles.' Ana was grinning.

Ben turned round. 'One of you others go first. How about you, Julia? You're in the athletics team.'

'Yeah, right.' Ana shook her head. 'You're second on my rope, so it's your turn. And we need two people here in case one of the others doesn't manage it.'

'And what if *I* don't manage it?'

'Oh, you will, believe me. It's your choice. Either down there' – Ana pointed into the chasm – 'or you jump over here into my arms. Now shift your ass!'

Benjamin hesitated. He looked so pitiful and unhappy in his purple Gore-Tex jacket that Katie almost felt sorry for him.

Chris, David and Julia exchanged anxious looks.

'There are no stuntmen around here. These action scenes are for real. Just jump, okay.'

Benjamin put down his rucksack, stepped a few paces back, took a run up, and jumped.

It wasn't far – not for a practised sportsman, at any rate – but barely had he landed safely on the other side when he started going totally crazy. 'Hey, I did it. I did it! I jumped over the crevasse. How wide is it? What do you reckon, Ana? At least eight feet, don't you think?'

Katie was sure that the crevasse would take on biblical proportions as soon as they were back at Grace. Benjamin would be showing off, making out he was on a par with Moses. Only he'd have led his people across a glacier rather than across the Red Sea.

Ana looked around. Not far from where she was standing, a huge, solitary frozen stone rose up from the snow field. Ana took the rope and tied it around the stone.

'Okay, the rope's secure. God must have sent us that rock.'

'Don't you lot call him Manitou?' Benjamin was so ecstatic that he was scraping the bottom of his joke barrel, or so Katie thought at any rate. Ana ignored him. 'I'll throw the rope across to you,' she called across to the rest of the group. 'You attach your rucksacks to it, slowly let them down into the gap, and Benjamin and I will pull them back up. Make sure they're all closed and that the zips are done up. You don't want to lose anything. Once the rucksacks are safely across, then you jump in the order in which you're attached.'

Julia was next. She hesitated briefly, and David took a step forward as if to help her. But then he thought better of it.

Ahead of him, Chris gave a mocking snort. 'You can do it, baby,' he called to Julia. 'And remember I'll be right behind you.'

Julia didn't seem convinced.

Katie moved forward. 'It's all in your mind, Julia,' she said. 'You can't bring yourself to do it because it looks so deep. But the actual jump is child's play. Just imagine that there's a net underneath you. Not air, but fabric, silk, some fantastic hammock ... imagine whatever works for you. Then you'll do it as easy as anything.'

Julia shut her eyes for a moment, opened them again, and nodded. 'Yes, that works,' she murmured.

Then she took a run up, leapt over the gap, and didn't even need her ice-pick on the other side.

David, Chris and Paul followed her. They all made it look effortless.

When Katie's turn came, she felt completely confident. How was this crevasse any different from the bridges that she and Sebastien had jumped off?

She concentrated and took a run up. Her right foot caught the edge of the crevasse. She could feel the ice giving way beneath her, and she caught her breath for a moment. But a second later, once she was in the air and looking down into the chasm, she felt as happy as she had felt then.

Until she realised.

There was no water for her to dive into.

Nothing to catch her.

No. Beneath her was nothing but sheer ice. And a blue chasm. For a fraction of a second she felt herself losing her balance, but then she landed safely on the other side.

She was rewarded by Benjamin dashing up to her and throwing his arms round her – something that she could have done without.

Once they had finally regrouped and had detached the rope from the rock, something had changed. Katie knew exactly what it was. Like her, the others were buzzing. They were all on a high with adrenaline.

How often had Sebastien twirled her round in the air after a jump? 'This is cooler than any drug in the world, isn't it? What could be better than getting drunk on your own endorphins?'

*

Almost immediately beyond the crevasse was the entrance to the rocky ridge. Its steep edge led up to the summit, and was the greatest challenge of the whole expedition.

'We're going to go in pairs on a short rope,' Ana said. 'You can take off your glacier safety line.'

'I don't need a rope ...' Katie began.

'Maybe you don't, but so far as the others are concerned, I'm playing it safe.'

And then they finally set off.

Katie was still unfazed by the challenge and Paul, too, seemed to be having no trouble. Following their climb, though, Ana now adapted her speed to that of the weaker members of the group.

Katie had to force herself not to become impatient. Remember the tunnel, she kept telling herself. You had to rely on the others then.

'Just imagine if we'd had to bring Debbie with us.' Julia stretched out her hand and clambered over a jutting-out bit of rock that blocked the ridge. After her initial hesitation, she seemed to be enjoying the whole thing. She looked around her, and Katie could see her broad grin even from a distance. 'She gets vertigo on the bank of Mirror Lake.'

Katie laughed.

'Watch out – extremely narrow bit coming up!'

Chris, his face red with exertion and excitement, turned to Paul. The ridge narrowed down from a foot and a half to the width of their shoes. To their left and right, the cliffs dropped away into nothingness, and there was nothing to hold on to.

Paul nodded and followed him nimbly. He looked as if he were going for a stroll down Fifth Avenue.

226

Katie couldn't help but admire his technique. She knew an expert when she saw one. Every footstep was exactly right, and as soon as they had to start climbing his movements were so lithe that it looked as if he'd spent his entire life doing it. Or maybe not – it was more as if his body were weightless, as if he were flying from rock to rock.

What had he said?

He'd wanted to kiss her ever since he set eyes on her.

The only question was: where had he first set eyes on her? When she'd gone into the sports hall equipment room?

She remembered what had happened in the lift on her way there, and she was suddenly no longer sure whether it had actually happened. If an extreme sport like climbing could create an excess of endorphins in your body, then surely that could cause side effects as well? Like losing your grip on reality.

On the other hand – he had confessed to her that he was a murderer.

That he had killed – for someone else.

What had the voice in the lift said?

Someone will die up there. Do you hear me? Katie? Katie? And it will be your fault, Katie. Your fault, your fault …

She could hear it again. She could hear the voice again.

She started to sway.

'Watch out.'

Paul sounded quite calm, but Katie bit her lip. She was more than ten thousand feet up. To both sides of her were sheer drops hundreds of feet deep.

Concentrate on the present, Katie. Switch off your thoughts. Stay in the here and now.

With difficulty, she pulled herself together and looked around. Far below her was the icy blue glacier with the various summits as its backdrop. At the bottom of the glacier, she could make out a dark speck: the cabin.

'My God, it's a long way down,' she heard Benjamin calling from up ahead. 'That's just awesome.'

Katie shook her head. She'd lost count of the number of things that Ben had found awesome since they'd set off.

She followed Paul across the narrow pass that Chris had warned them about. From there, they had a fantastic view of the summit, which was now directly in front of them. Katie quickly estimated how far away it was. Probably about ...

Unbelievable! Probably about twenty minutes, half an hour at most, and then they would be at the top.

Only now did she discover that the thing that looked like a face from the valley was in fact notches in the otherwise smooth wall which fell away down into the swamp. The giant eye some six hundred feet below the summit was even more clearly visible. Had it really been created by Ana's ancestors, as she had claimed? Katie doubted it. This rock face looked as if it could only be climbed with super-modern equipment. The eye was presumably just a fluke of nature.

'What the hell do you think you're doing?'

Katie jumped as she heard David's voice ahead of her. He sounded angry.

'What do you think I'm doing?'

Katie groaned. Oh no. Benjamin was rummaging in his rucksack and pulling his camera out.

What an idiot.

'Hey, I've earnt this.'

She had to watch helplessly as Benjamin put the strap round his neck, bent down, and clambered down the rock face to their left. His head disappeared for a moment, then popped up again.

'Stop that!' Ana yelled. 'Do you want to pull me down with you?'

'Ben, stop it this instant!' There was an edge of panic in Julia's voice.

Katie stopped behind Paul and now saw that Benjamin was standing on a narrow ledge jutting out from the smoothly polished wall of the Ghost, around three feet below the ridge they were standing on. Beneath him was a yawning chasm several thousand feet deep.

The rope that attached him to Ana was pulled taut and ...

'Yeeee, haaaaaa!' Benjamin threw his arms into the air.

The echo came back to them.

Yeeee, haaaaaa!

Benjamin started laughing his head off, then began to bawl, 'Always look on the bright side of life!'

'Are you drunk or what?' Chris snapped.

'No, just a favourite of the gods.' Benjamin stretched out his arms. 'I'm Prometheus. I'm chained to the rock.'

'You'll be jelly in a minute if you don't watch out,' Paul replied.

'If I fall, you can all pull me back up.'

'I wouldn't bet on it,' growled Chris.

'You're my friends – I can rely on you.'

He reached for his camera.

'What's that dumbass doing now?' Paul snapped.

But everyone who knew Benjamin – and Katie had come

to know him very well by now – knew what he had in mind.

'Leave it, Ben,' Chris said warningly.

Benjamin swayed slightly on the narrow ledge. Katie heard Julia gasp, but the next moment he was removing the lens cap.

'Proof!' he called. 'We're not going to suffer the same fate as the seventies students. The truth will be in my camera.' He held it up and started filming. '12th September. At a height of . . .' He looked up. 'How high up are we?'

Nobody answered. Ben carried on. 'Whatever. We're just three hundred feet below the summit. After a sensational jump across a glacial crack, down which I could see into the eye of the Ghost, I managed to reach the other side. The side that's going to take me up to the top of the mountain. And all of us . . .' he panned across the horrified faces above him, 'We're all hoping to find it there. The truth.'

'This is the last time I'm going to say it. You're risking our lives as well as your own,' hissed Chris.

Benjamin ignored him, instead reaching round to his back pocket and pulling something out. 'The last piece of information we got about the vanished students was this photo. We haven't found a trace of them since then.'

Ana's mouth was set in a grimace as she took a step forward directly towards the chasm. She reached for the rope and pulled it with one hefty jerk. Benjamin lost his balance for a fraction of a second, but he didn't lose his composure.

Only once David joined in did Ben seem to realise what was going on. 'That's enough, Ben,' David said quietly. 'Come off there. You've scared us enough. I'd like to get to the top now.'

Benjamin duly stuffed his camera back into his rucksack and returned from the ledge to the rocky ridge.

They climbed on in silence until Julia spoke. She evidently couldn't get Benjamin's performance out of her head. 'You know what? We haven't got any proof that they ever made it to the top.'

'Does that matter?' asked Chris.

'I think it does.'

'Of course it matters,' called Benjamin. 'The whole thing's just a game, isn't it? We're competing against the past.'

'What do you mean?' asked Julia.

'Well, let's assume they got to the summit. So if we get there and return safe and sound, we win.'

'Crappy game,' murmured Chris.

'And what if they didn't get to the top?' asked Paul.

'Then we've hit the jackpot. We get to the top *and* we get back to college safe and sound.'

'And hope that Debbie's kept her mouth shut and hasn't reported us to the Dean,' Katie muttered.

'What? You can cope with coming up here, and you're afraid of the Dean?' David laughed.

The last stretch passed as if in a dream, and Katie slipped into a trance-like state that she wouldn't have missed for the world. The perfect rhythm of arms and legs. Her muscles working together. The interplay of the senses. The shutting out of all conscious thought. It was what other people called meditation. No, it was more than that. It was total self-surrender.

231

The only thing that disturbed her trance was the pace set by Ana. It was too slow, much too slow. Even Benjamin could keep up perfectly well. Julia wasn't flagging either.

The group ahead of her stopped before the summit.

'What's wrong?' Katie shouted.

'Ana wants to attach a couple more safety devices.'

'Hey, Ana, is that really necessary?' Chris was becoming impatient now too. 'There are only fifteen, twenty feet to go.'

'Those fifteen to twenty feet could cost you your lives.'

Katie paused only briefly. Then she pushed past Paul, pulling several pitons, wedges and safety slings to the front of her harness.

'Is everything okay?' Katie had reached Ana. She could see the sweat trickling out from under Ana's hat.

'Fine. I just don't want to take any risks. A couple of extra precautions can't do us any harm.'

'Let me do it,' said Katie. 'I'll put in a couple of hooks. That'll be plenty.'

To her surprise, Ana immediately gave in.

Paul came up to them. 'What's wrong with Ana?'

Katie shrugged.

He looked at her thoughtfully with his brown eyes for several seconds. 'You paid her, didn't you? You paid her to bring us up here.'

She turned away and put her hand on the rock face.

The way Paul said it, it sounded calculating. But it hadn't been like that.

Her right foot found a narrow crevice. She tested the rock by giving it a few gentle kicks. It was fine. She then pushed two wedges into a cranny in front of her and made herself a firm hold. She could now secure Paul.

When she'd first met Ana in the sports shop in Fields, a woman had suddenly come storming in, interrupting their conversation. She looked older than Katie's grandmother in Korea, but Ana had called her 'Mom'.

'Mom, Mom, what are you doing here? Is something wrong?'

'Your grandfather . . . '

And then they had vanished. Four weeks later, Ana had appeared at Grace, asking to speak to Katie.

'Do you still want to go up the mountain?' she had asked.

'Absolutely.'

'Four hundred dollars up front.'

'Four hundred dollars? What for?'

'Do you want to go, or don't you?'

'Of course I do.'

'And we're not going on our own. Running around on a glacier, just the two of us, would be crazy.'

Four hundred dollars.

What for?

Katie hesitated briefly, then found a fingerhold in the rock above her and started to pull herself up. How much further until she reached the top? No more than fifteen feet. Two more wedges. That would do it.

Katie was totally focused on her task. The voices of the others below her seemed to melt away. She had never given up hope, not even down in the tunnel, but being so close to her goal was something else altogether. And it was something different again, taking those last steps and finally managing it.

The feeling was overwhelming.

The exhaustion, the doubt, the fear. They had all evaporated. Now only one thing mattered: reaching the summit. Standing on top of the mountain. On the Ghost. The moment when the world would be at her feet. Katie shut her eyes, took a deep breath, and let out a cry that echoed around the valley.

One by one, the others followed suit.

Benjamin, of course, had only one word for it.

It was awesome.

Completely awesome.

The most awesome thing ever.

They flung their arms around one another, yelling We are the champions!

Over and over again.

We are the champions!

And now they could all laugh again at Benjamin tramping through the snow, his camera in front of his face, delivering his usual commentary. 'None of your dopy grins. Laugh. Laugh as if you've mainlined a happy hormone straight into your veins. Get it? You're in the realm of the gods, and it should show in your faces.'

Katie let them have their fun – but she knew that there was only one real champion. Her. Without her, without Katie West, none of them would have made it up there.

But what about Ana?

'Ana?' Katie called.

The others looked at her in surprise.

'Where's Ana?'

David looked around. 'Isn't she here?'

'Where did you last see her?'

'She wanted to be last,' said Benjamin. 'To be sure that we all made it.'

The ensuing silence portended disaster. Even Benjamin had stopped leaping around like a madman.

Katie was gripped by a terrible fear.

She bent over the summit and stared downwards. Down below lay Ana Cree. She wasn't moving.

CHAPTER 26

'Ana?'

The cutting wind sweeping across the summit of the Ghost suddenly seemed even colder to Katie than it had done only moments before.

She stared aghast at the immobile figure beneath her. Had Ana fallen off the cliff, or hadn't she even started to climb up?

'Ana!'

Ana didn't stir.

The wind was whistling shrilly in Katie's ears. Why did this have to happen now? When they'd finally reached the top?

'What's happened?' David appeared by Katie's side.

'You tell me! When I climbed up to put the safety stuff in place, everything was fine.'

But had it really been fine? Hadn't Ana been behaving strangely for the past few hours?

David opened the bottom compartment of his rucksack and fished out his first aid kit. Then he stood up, tightened his harness, and made for the chasm. 'I'm going to climb down. Will you hold me?'

'Oh my God,' Julia was whispering next to them. 'Ana! Did she fall?'

Katie hesitated. If Ana was no longer able to lead the group then she, Katie, would have to take over. She couldn't afford for any of them to start freaking out up there.

'I'm going with you,' she said.

Paul secured them from above and minutes later David had reached the bottom and was kneeling beside Ana. As Katie landed next to him, she heard him asking over and over again, 'Ana, can you hear me? Ana?'

'What's happened to her?'

'No idea. Concussion, maybe?'

'What's going on?' Paul called from above.

Ana had opened her eyes and was staring at them, but Katie wasn't sure whether she was actually conscious or not.

David removed Ana's helmet. There was a deep scratch on her temple.

'She's banged her head. But it doesn't look too bad.' He felt her pulse. 'Ana,' he said again. 'Did you fall, Ana?'

Ana finally responded. She shook her head and tried to speak, but evidently found it too hard. She tried to get up, but barely had she struggled to her feet when her legs gave way. She fell to the ground again, and her body suddenly started to shiver uncontrollably.

David bent over her anxiously. 'Concussion doesn't make you shiver like this. It must be something else.'

Ana's teeth were chattering as she struggled to speak. 'I'm fine. But we have to ...'

'Don't worry.' David took off his jacket and wrapped it around her shoulders. 'Everything's going to be fine.'

As Ana raised her right hand to pull the jacket more tightly around herself, she winced with pain.

'What is it?' David reached for her arm.

She hastily withdrew it. 'Nothing.'

However, David's suspicions were aroused. He was already undoing the velcro on her climbing glove and taking it off.

Ana screamed.

Katie stared, horrified, at Ana's hand. It was like a punch in the stomach. Ana's right hand was red and swollen. Katie was amazed that it had even still fitted into the glove.

David turned her hand upwards and pointed to a gaping wound on the palm. 'How long have you had this?'

'Since that goddamn ... tunnel.' Ana's teeth were chattering more than ever. 'Something ... metal.'

David cursed. 'Why didn't you tell me? I could have disinfected the wound. With some of that spray-on plaster, you wouldn't even have noticed it within a day.' He rummaged around in his nylon first aid kit. 'Have you had a tetanus vaccine?'

Ana shook her head.

'Let's hear the latest news,' Benjamin was on the edge of the summit, pointing his camera straight at them.

'Please,' Ana murmured. 'Get him to stop.'

'How bad is it? Can she carry on? Will she even manage to get back down?'

Katie could feel an explosive mix of frustration and anger boiling up inside her. It felt as if the wind, which blew nonstop at this height, was fanning her flames.

'Why didn't you tell us?' she shouted at Ana. 'You came up here with your hand in that state. That's insane! You've put us all in danger!'

'Shut up, Katie,' David murmured. 'This isn't the time or place for accusations. We need to get back as quickly as possible.' He stood up and called to the others. 'Hey, listen up all of you. I'm afraid the sightseeing's over.'

'But we've only just got here,' Benjamin called back, his camera glued to his eye. 'I've not bust my ass to spend five seconds up here. Not with this awesome view. 3-D films are crap compared to this. Honestly, when you're standing up here, you start to think there's a fourth dimension. Give me at least five more minutes.'

'Sorry, Ben. Ana's in a bad way. We've got to go.'

'What about our mission? What about the missing students? We've not even started to look for anything!' There was something in Julia's voice that made Katie sit up. Despair? Frustration? She couldn't quite work it out.

David didn't reply. Instead he turned to Katie. 'Don't breathe a word to the others about how badly injured she is,' he whispered. 'Otherwise there's going to be total panic.' Then he knelt down beside Ana once more. 'I'll see to the wound, so far as I can, and I'll give you some pain relief. I'll give you an antibiotic too.'

'David, how's she going to get back down in that state?' Katie pointed. The rocky ridge seemed even steeper and narrower from up above than it had seemed when they were on the ascent. She looked again at Ana, who was leaning against the cliff wall, her face chalky white.

'You and me, Katie. We'll get her down between us.'

The others reached them more quickly than Katie had anticipated.

'What's wrong with her?' said Julia. She had evidently

accepted that they had to leave sooner than expected, and was now just concerned about Ana.

'Nothing too serious,' David said casually. 'Nothing that a bit of paracetamol can't sort out.'

As cool as a cucumber, he put the first aid supplies back into their pouch.

Chris scrutinised Ana suspiciously. 'Are you taking the piss, David? Ana looks as if she's about to fall unconscious at any moment. Getting her down from here could put all of us in danger.'

Katie could feel Paul coming to stand next to her. His voice betrayed no hint of emotion as he said, 'Ana's a native. Her grandfather was in charge of the Mounties for years. You may be shit-scared of the mountain, but Ana will get down it just fine.'

'And that was the sound of Mr Paul Forster Junior. Mr Forster, what would your father say if he heard that kind of talk from you?' Benjamin said mockingly. 'Would he hang, draw and quarter you? As a punishment for ...'

'Shut up!'

Julia, David and Katie all said it at the same time.

'While I'm at it.' The camera panned to Ana, who stood up with difficulty, using the cliff to support herself. 'Ladies and gentlemen, Ana Cree, expedition leader.' Then he added, 'My God, you look real bad, d'you know that?'

Ana stuck it out.

Katie took over as leader. Ana followed her, supported by David. Roped together as a threesome, they stuck close to one another, holding the coiled rope that they needed to stop

240

anyone from falling. David kept having to help Ana, who was struggling to keep her balance and who staggered dangerously close to the chasm more than once.

Katie noticed that David was constantly trying to stop the others from realising how unwell Ana really was. Fortunately his first aid measures were gradually starting to take effect, and Ana was starting to look slightly better.

They didn't speak much, instead focusing all their efforts on trying to progress as rapidly as possible while also helping Ana. It was arduous and gruelling, and their nerves were frayed by the time they reached the glacier.

The afternoon sunlight flooded the giant ice field that they had already crossed once that day and that they now had to negotiate for the second time.

At its entrance they all dropped down one after the other, exhausted, and took off their rucksacks. David alone stayed on his feet, looking anxiously at the glacial crevasse.

'Don't make yourselves too comfy,' he called, passing Ana a bottle of water.

'Since when have you given the orders?' Chris protested. 'Have you elected yourself as mountain guide? What happened to democracy?'

'I've never been keen on democracy,' Benjamin interjected. 'Democracy means losers choosing losers. I'm an anarchist.'

'Loser?' Chris raised his hands. 'Am I a loser?'

'Since when have you been standing for election?' asked David.

'Do you think Ana can make it across the crevasse?' Paul appeared at Katie's side once more. His ability to make himself invisible then suddenly reappear was truly astonishing.

He looked anxiously across at Ana. She was leaning against the rocks, her eyes shut.

'I don't know. She's doing pretty well, but leaping over the crevasse ... ' Katie shook her head.

'Maybe we should circumvent the crevasse after all.'

Katie shook her head. 'We'd lose too much time. And she wouldn't have the strength.'

Paul nodded. 'You're right.'

'Can you help me a minute, Paul?' Julia called. 'My carabiner's stuck.'

As Paul went over to help Julia, Katie glanced back at the summit of the Ghost, trying to suppress her anxiety. She had done it: she had conquered the summit. But she hadn't made a single inch of progress so far as her mother's secret was concerned. Who had she climbed the mountain with? Why? And why was she recorded as missing, when she was now alive and well in Washington DC?

I'll ask you one day, Eomma. Her mother had always wanted Katie to call her Mom, but she had steadfastly refused.

Katie turned to look at the glacier. She could see the cabin on the mountainside opposite them, tiny in the distance. In her state, there was no way Ana could make it to Fields. But they had to reach the cabin at the very least, and that was Katie's responsibility.

It was still only early afternoon and the sun was shining with all its might, but the wind had strengthened, and it was considerably colder. If the meltwater froze again, they would only be able to proceed very slowly across the glacier.

'Listen up, guys.' Katie turned to look at them. 'We've got

to get over the crevasse. You know what that means. Here's the plan. Paul belays with an ice-pick and Chris jumps across and belays on the other side. Then we fix a rope across the crevasse. We attach Ana to the rope with her harness and get her across the gap that way. Ana, do you reckon you can do that?'

Ana shook her head. 'No, I can jump ...'

David shook his head vigorously. 'No way. Far too risky.'

Chris folded his arms in front of his chest. 'And attaching her to a rope isn't?'

'Does anyone have a better suggestion?' Katie looked from one to the other.

'I trust Katie,' Julia said, reaching for her rucksack. 'I'll jump first.'

'No – I will!' Benjamin interjected. 'I've had so many Monster Energy drinks in the last few days that I could do all the stunts in *Superman Returns*.'

For a moment they all laughed, and at once the mood lifted.

Once we're back, thought Katie, I'll treat him to a slap-up meal. It was beginning to dawn on her that mankind couldn't survive psychologically without clowns like Benjamin.

Paul had rammed the ice-pick in and was now tamping down the snow to make the anchorage more secure. The sun was diagonally above the summit of the White Soul and was shining directly into Katie's face – but that wasn't why the sweat was pouring down her forehead. What if her plan didn't work? What if she wasn't strong enough to hold on to Ana?

'Okay, here we go.' Paul snapped the carabiner on to Ana's chest harness. 'I'm afraid you'll have to hold the rope with both hands. Ignore the pain. Don't think about it. Try to think about something else. I know you can do it.'

Ana managed a feeble grin. 'You mean like "An Indian brave knows no pain"?'

David stood up and waved to Chris, who was standing on the other side of the crevasse, holding the rope taut.

'Let's get started.'

Barely had David spoken when things did indeed get started. But not in the way they had planned.

At first, it looked perfectly harmless: a silent, fluid movement miles away from them on the western slope of the White Soul; a slab of snow coming loose. But moments later they heard a distant whooshing sound that soon became a deep rumble as it raced towards them.

'Avalanche!' yelled Katie. She was about to shout a warning to the others to dive for cover, but the words died on her lips, as the safety rope suddenly snaked through her hands and she was dragged forward. At the same time the thunderous sound echoed from mountain wall to mountain wall, sounding as if they were in the midst of an explosion. The rope slipped unchecked through her wet gloves, and pulled hard on her harness. Katie was jerked onto her front and found herself sliding headlong towards the crevasse.

Everything flashed before her eyes. Katie's icy hands tried in vain to find something to hold on to. Her crampons were throwing up fragments of ice, which rained down onto her face.

And then she was pulled down into the crevasse. Her head was flung backwards and hit something hard.

It's over, she thought, and then she lost consciousness.

When Katie came round again, she was completely bewildered. Her mind was empty. Instead of remembering what had happened, she felt as if she were still falling. A never-ending fall. As if real time had stopped.

But then she realised what had happened. Her legs were in the air; her body was bent double; and her chest was pressed against a cold, hard surface. Her left cheek seemed to have frozen onto the glacier.

She opened her eyes and found herself staring into a bright light.

A memory stirred in her. Muffled rumbling. A slab of snow breaking from a rock face. A mass of dirty whiteness thundering down the mountainside.

There had been an avalanche. But not here. Not on the Ghost, but on the mountain opposite. She moved her head. Her cheek grazed the ice, and she stared into a dark blue chasm.

The crevasse.

Ana.

Ana?

Ana must have fallen into the crevasse.

Because she, Katie, had allowed her mind to wander for a fraction of a second. Because she hadn't been concentrating.

'Katie! Are you okay?' Paul's horrified face appeared above her.

As if he were air and then became human, Katie thought.

It's creepy. But he's always there. Always around me. Like a guardian angel.

Guardian angel, Katie?

You have to be your own guardian angel.

'Where's Ana?'

Paul didn't reply. 'God, you were lucky that David reacted so fast. He just managed to hold on to you before you were dragged over the edge.'

'But ... Ana ...' Katie tried to look round.

Paul looked at her, and there was something indefinable about his golden yellow eyes. An expression that she didn't immediately comprehend.

'It wasn't your fault, Katie. The rope – it just broke. She's gone.'

Katie stared at him. 'What do you mean, it just broke?'

'I mean exactly that.'

The rope had broken, just like that. Katie stopped breathing for several seconds.

'Katie? Katie?' Paul's hand was on her shoulder. His eyes were searching for hers. Katie suddenly found herself gasping, trying to pump as much oxygen as possible into her lungs.

'Calm down, Katie. Deep breaths. In. Out. And again. That's it.' He called something over his shoulder that she didn't catch. 'Okay, we're going to pull you up.'

The same question again, just a name in fact. The only one that mattered. 'Ana?'

Again, he didn't reply.

'Katie, you have to understand that it all happened so quickly. David held on to you and Ana both, but then the rope snapped.'

'We have to help her.'

'Let's pull you up first, then we'll see to her.'

She felt her upper body being pulled across the hard ice, and instinctively tried to stop it from happening.

'Ana?'

She craned over the crevasse. Her voice echoed dully around the icy walls.

'Ana, can you hear me?'

No reply.

It seemed in fact to Katie as if the steep icy walls were themselves rumbling. No: it was the reverberation of the avalanche which still hadn't entirely finished.

'Ana?'

Nature was quiet for just a second – and then Katie heard it. A pitiful sound coming up from the depths.

Katie's heart stopped.

It didn't sound like Ana.

It sounded like the nameless despair of someone who had been swallowed by the crevasse and had given up all hope.

The dying roar of the avalanche rang out from the depths on the opposite side.

CHAPTER 27

'I'm going down there.' Katie was sitting on the ice. David was bending anxiously over her, and she pushed him away.

'You're in shock. Let someone else do it.' But the sympathetic note in his voice provoked the opposite response.

'Who?' she snapped. 'Who can do it apart from me?'

'I can. I'm a trained paramedic.'

'But you've got no climbing experience. And I need someone up here that I can rely on.'

'I could go down!' interjected Paul. At least he wasn't kneeling down next to her. She couldn't bear the thought of any more sympathy. 'And you can rely on me just as much as on David, Katie. No matter what.'

Could she?

Katie glanced across at the other side of the glacier where Benjamin, Chris and Julia were leaning over the crevasse. Shock was etched on their faces, and for once in his life Benjamin had the decency to put his camera away.

'I was supposed to keep her safe, so I'm going down. End of story.' Stubbornness: that had been her big thing ever since she'd been a child. She zipped up her jacket, which David had undone. 'You'll have to let me down on the rope.'

'It must be at least eighty feet,' David warned her.

'No further?'

'You'll need twice as much rope if you're abseiling,' said Paul.

'We can knot them all together.'

David shook his head impatiently. 'We can only guess how far it is. What if we haven't got enough?' He paused. 'It's insane, Katie.'

'I'd be insane if I didn't try. So are you just planning to leave Ana lying down there? Are you trying to tell me it's not worth it; that she's going to die anyway? Is that what you're trying to tell me, David?'

He shook his head.

Katie stood up shakily. Her body hurt. She must be covered in bruises, and was lucky not to have broken a rib. But her hands – she stared at her shredded gloves – her hands at least seemed to be okay.

'I'll do whatever it takes, okay! Have you got that?'

Katie was yelling now. She was yelling so loud that the entire world could surely hear her. Yes, let them all hear it: she wasn't giving up this time. She was going to do the right thing.

'Stop it.' She could barely hear Paul's voice. Maybe it was the wind. But then his hands grabbed her shoulders. It felt as if she and Paul were the only ones there. 'Stop it, Katie. Don't you see? You can't make up for stuff you've done before.'

'That, coming from you?' she cried. 'D'you know what really makes someone a murderer? It's not killing someone. It's not having done everything you can to stop someone dying.' Katie banged her hand against her chest. She couldn't stop doing it. She didn't want to. 'It's my fault. It's in here. It was my plan. And you can bet your life that I'm going down and making sure Ana gets back home.'

'You can't make that decision on your own,' she heard Chris calling coldly.

Katie stared across the crevasse at him. 'Oh yeah? Can't I?' She ran past Paul, grabbed her rucksack, unzipped it, and pulled out the rope that she had been carrying around with her for the past couple of days.

'Katie.' Paul was still trying to stop her. 'Let's just all calm down and think about what to do.'

Chris's voice came across the crevasse once more. 'We don't even know if she's still alive.'

Katie was freaking out now. 'And what about the voice I heard? Are you telling me it was her ghost talking?'

Benjamin looked up. He was as white as a sheet beneath his mountaineering glasses. 'Katie, do you realise how far down it goes? Falling down there ... ' He broke off.

Julia reached for Chris's hand. 'What we're trying to say' – her voice was trembling – 'is that we can't hear Ana any more.'

'Right, so that means she's dead?' Katie looked around for Ana's rucksack. 'You know that for a fact, Julia? You know that for an absolute fact? Or is it one of those intuitions that reveals the magical powers granted to the Frost family? Can any of you guarantee that she's dead? Are you ready to sign her death certificate? Well I'm not.'

She bent down and started to unroll the rope with trembling hands. Her fingers were numb with cold and pain. But she didn't give up, and she eventually succeeded. And as always when she was focusing on what to do next, she started to feel calmer.

She stood up again. 'So. Who's going to let me down?'

Nobody replied.

The wind was still howling around them.

Julia, Benjamin and Chris were standing close together on the opposite side of the crevasse. Chris stared at her, his fists tightly clenched in his pockets. Benjamin shifted nervously from one foot to the other, and Julia looked close to tears.

Shoes crunched on the frozen ground next to her, but David and Paul weren't saying anything either.

Katie knew full well that it wasn't the wind or the cold that had silenced them.

She finally turned round.

'David?' she asked.

He hesitated.

Katie didn't say anything, but she kept repeating the same words to herself:

Please don't leave me in the lurch, David. Please don't leave me in the lurch.

David didn't leave her in the lurch. He nodded.

'I'll help too.' Paul looked Katie straight in the eye. He's doing it for me, she thought. Only for me. He killed for one girl, and he's doing this for another. He doesn't have any morals. He only acts in his own interest. But that didn't matter for now. The only thing that mattered was having allies.

'What about you guys?' Katie could hear that the despair had left her voice. Instead, she put as much arrogance and contempt into her words as she possibly could.

Chris shook his head. 'Count me out. I'm not standing here and watching you direct your own suicide. If David and Paul want to watch you and Ana die, they're very welcome to do so. But I'm going. And Julia's coming with me.'

'Can't Julia decide for herself?' Katie yelled against the wind.

Her eyes sought Julia's, and she watched helplessly as her friend hesitated. 'Katie. It's already gone three o'clock,' she called. 'If you actually manage to pull her up, we've got to get back across the glacier. And who knows what kind of state Ana will be in. I think we need to get back as quickly as possible and fetch help. Anything else would be suicidal.'

Katie was aghast. 'Help couldn't get here until tomorrow at the earliest, as you well know. That would be far too late for Ana.'

'So you'd prefer to risk all our lives?' snapped Chris. 'Night falls faster up here than you think, and it gets a lot colder than you can possibly imagine. We haven't even got a bivouac tent. What if it starts snowing again? Then we'll all freeze to death.'

'And what if the world ends? What if the ground opens up and sends you straight to hell?' Katie could hear her voice cracking. 'You know what you are, Christopher Bishop? A complete and utter asshole.'

Chris shrugged. 'If you say so. But I'm going anyway.' He turned round. 'Ben, you coming?'

Benjamin hesitated. For one second. Two. 'Chris is right,' he said. 'And anyway, Ana brought it on herself. Remember the way she was acting before?'

Katie snorted. She couldn't believe the way the boys were behaving.

'How about a helicopter?' Julia called desperately. 'We could try to contact the mountain rescue team in Fields.'

'The mobile won't work up here any better than in the cabin,' said David.

'At least try.'

'I already have done.'

Katie grasped the rope. 'Oh, piss off, the whole lot of you. I wouldn't leave her even if I were here on my own. We're wasting time.'

She moved towards the edge of the crevasse and stared downwards. She thought she could make out a dark silhouette on the ground, but may just have been imagining it.

'Ana?'

Silence.

'Ana, can you hear me?'

A biting gust of wind was coming down from the Ghost. It blew through Katie's hair, strangling all sound.

She looked up.

Five faces were staring at her, pinched with cold and tension.

Then Chris reached for Julia's hand. 'Come on,' he said. 'We're going.'

Julia looked at him, then at Katie. For a moment she held Katie's gaze, then lowered her head.

Without looking up, she called across the crevasse, 'We're fetching help, Katie. Okay?'

Then she turned and followed the two boys.

'Right. Here we go.' Katie pulled her rucksack towards her.

Her hands were trembling as much as her voice, but she quickly got a grip on herself. She wasn't going to let anyone see how Julia's betrayal had wounded her. 'I've got some ice screws somewhere. We can make a stand with them and the ice-pick and a rucksack. I'll abseil down until the rope runs out, then I'll jump.'

'What about coming back up?' asked David. 'How are you going to get hold of the end of the rope if it's too short?'

Katie didn't reply. Instead she stared at the three heavily clad figures quickly disappearing across the glacier.

It wasn't the first time she and Sebastien had been to the Arlington Memorial Bridge. But it had been a special day. Christmas Eve.

Katie had leaned over the parapet and had felt her throat tighten at the thought of climbing over and jumping off. Her thoughts had wavered between 'I'm jumping come what may' and 'No way am I ever doing that'.

'I can't do it,' she had said. 'Not today. Not tonight. I've got a weird feeling, and it's freezing cold.'

'Hey, Katie,' he had said gently, kissing her. 'It's the same as always.'

'It's Christmas Day tomorrow.'

'Exactly. And this is our present to each other.'

Sebastien had roped up, as always. He had put his helmet on, as always. He had climbed onto the parapet and had stretched out his arms. He had yelled, 'Happy Christmas, Katie!' And then he had jumped and she had laughed and laughed and ... then came the silence. The long silence. At first Katie hadn't noticed what was different this time – but then she realised. Sebastien hadn't said what he always said: 'Today's the day we might die.'

'What's wrong, Katie?' A voice brought her back to reality. She looked up into Paul's face. 'Shall I go instead?'

She shook her head. 'No.'

'Katie ...' He gave her a penetrating look. No, not just a penetrating look. It was more as if his amber eyes had some strange capacity to keep her there, to see into her soul. Okay, Katie, you're exaggerating. But she had no choice but to return his gaze. At the same time, he was speaking.

'The boy I told you about ...'

'Yes?'

'He killed that girl. That's why I killed him.'

Katie stuffed David's first aid kit into her jacket pocket, did up the chin-strap of her helmet and checked the safety rope and the knot on her climbing harness for the hundredth time. Then she took several steps back until she reached the edge, and leaned back into the rope.

She had chosen the side of the wall that she, David and Paul were standing on. So far as she could tell, the descent from there would be easier than from the wall nearer the valley, where the ice looked more jagged.

Slowly she let her legs down until her stomach was pressing against the edge and she could feel the resistance of the icy wall against her crampons. She leaned back and as the rope tightened, she let her chest and shoulders down over the edge.

Magical. That was the first thing she thought as she disappeared into the crevasse. The wall opposite her was shimmering in a bizarre jumble of huge icicles and protrusions, like a stalactite cave. In the light of the setting sun, everything was glowing in endless shades of blue.

But then it struck her that beauty could be deceptive.

Deadly.

Resolutely she raised her foot, dug her crampon into the wall, and began her descent.

It was long, and seemed endless, much further than eighty feet. Eighty feet, during which her mind wouldn't switch off. And so she decided to talk. She talked to Ana, constantly calling her name.

That night two years ago, Katie had waited in vain for Sebastien to call her name. For him to call, 'Cool jump!' or 'Do you want to fly? Then jump!'

She had waited in vain for him to hammer the ascenders into the bridge piers.

Had hoped in vain that he would appear over the parapet, smiling crookedly, triumphantly.

But he hadn't come back, and the night had been so dark and freezing cold. She had wasted minutes waiting. Wasted minutes hoping that everything was okay.

After all, what could have happened?

Where was the risk?

What had Sebastien told her? That nothing can go wrong when you're jumping off a bridge – unless the rope breaks.

Katie was clutching the rope tightly with both hands as she went further and further down the crevasse.

Freezing. It was freezing. She must already have frostbite on her hands despite her gloves. At least she couldn't feel the injuries she had sustained when she fell. Presumably due to the adrenalin.

Don't look down. Don't look down.

She did look down, and stared into a chasm that seemed to become darker the further she went. It was as if a dark shadow were forcing its way across the beauty of the upper regions. She dimly registered the vertical icy walls all around her as a ray of sunshine found its way into the depths, turning the ice a shade of dark aquamarine.

Her thoughts, like her hands and feet, seemed to be frozen. The deeper Katie went, the colder the air became. The crevasse was becoming increasingly narrow too.

She kept stopping for a rest. Each time she did so she called Ana's name again and again, but there was no reply. And each time, she was gripped by a sense of infinite loneliness.

Faster, Katie, faster.

She had abseiled hundreds of times before. It was a matter of concentration and coordination. She mustn't waste her energy; she would need it to help Ana and to climb up again.

But it was exhausting. The expedition hadn't brought her the one big prize she had longed for: that amazing feeling of freedom and the unbelievable adrenaline rush that she had experienced with Sebastien. At times over the last few days she had felt on the verge of it – but something had always intervened.

They had made it through the swamp, only to find themselves almost wiped out in the tunnel.

They had reached the cabin, only to find themselves trapped in a snowstorm.

They had reached the summit, and moments later Ana was unconscious.

What if the feeling she had so loved had gone with Sebastien? What if it had just been part of her love for him?

Katie hadn't realised that night that the rope had snapped. How could she have realised? It had been brand new.

Later on, the police had asked her about it over and over again.

How often had you used the rope before it snapped?

How can you explain the rope snapping?

There was no answer to these questions.

It was an accident.

But the others wanted answers.

The police, the insurance company, her father, Sebastien's parents, the press. The press more than anyone.

The only one who had never asked any questions had been Katie's mother. Katie suddenly thought she knew why. Because the same thing had happened to Mi Su. Up here on this mountain.

Katie glanced downwards, and she almost screamed. In the glow of her headlamp, she could make out an outline in the darkness below her. Ana's dark brown jacket. She speeded up and could soon see the shape quite clearly. Ana was lying on the ground in a bent position. She wasn't moving.

'Hang on in there!' she called. 'I'll be with you in a minute. Only a couple more yards.'

But the next moment she realised that she had been overoptimistic. The wall she was hanging on to wasn't actually a wall, but an ice gully that broke off lower down. What's more, Ana was further down than she had thought. The rope wasn't going to reach. And there was another problem. The ice gully wasn't as stable as an actual wall of ice. She now had to proceed with extreme caution, digging her crampons only into the surface of the wall.

The choice had been hers. The choice between this wall and the one on the other side, the side where Chris, Julia and Benjamin had been standing. And she had chosen the wrong one.

Why *had* she made this choice?

Emotion. Misreading the situation.

It had been the wrong decision. The ice gully ended around eighteen feet above the ground. And the rope would stretch another three feet.

What then?

You'll have to jump, Katie.

You're like a cat, aren't you? You have seven lives. If you're careful, you land on your feet.

The only question was whether she could get herself and Ana back up again.

Was she doing the right thing? Or was it another mistake, as with Sebastien? She had climbed down the bridge pier to help him instead of calling an ambulance. And she had lost valuable time.

Ten more feet.

Six more feet.

She had never been afraid of jumping into the depths. And when that psychologist had asked if her negligence weighed on her, she had retorted, 'It wasn't negligence. Don't you get it? It was the rope. The rope snapped.'

Katie had run out of footholds. She had reached the end of the gully. The rope was dangling to and fro.

Okay, Katie. Jump. Just let go.

She jumped.

Her helmet banged against the lowest edge of the icy wall. Everything went black for a moment. As she landed on the ground, she tried to turn so that she could roll onto her back, but at the last moment all she could do was clasp her arms protectively over her head.

A cloud of snow and icy shards rained down on her.

Then darkness.

For several minutes, she didn't move. She simply lay there. But with every breath, Katie realised that her worst fears hadn't materialised. She wasn't buried beneath a layer of snow. Within seconds, she had managed to free her face from the shards of ice.

Her headlamp had gone out. That was all that had happened. She pulled herself together, wiped her eyes, crawled across to Ana and touched her cautiously. 'Ana?'

But there was no answer.

CHAPTER 28

'Ana?'

There was silence.

A deadly silence.

And it was dark.

The scratches on Katie's palms smarted as she pulled off her gloves. The whole time she had been climbing down, the adrenaline had masked her pain and her fear. But the strain of the last couple of days was now taking its toll. And then there was the cold, and this almost unreal shadowy world. It wasn't completely dark down here, but there was no trace of the magic that she had seen higher up. Instead, everything was a dirty blue-grey that served only to remind Katie that she was completely surrounded by ice.

The lamp. Her headlamp. Without it, Katie was truly stuck. Her hand reached up and felt for the switch. But nothing happened.

Damn.

'Katie? Katie, are you okay?'

Katie thought at first that Ana had finally spoken. But then she realised that the voice was coming from up above, where Paul's light grey Gore-Tex jacket merged with the edge of the crevasse. He seemed to be miles away.

'I'm fine,' she called, but she had no idea whether he could hear her.

Her hand reached up again, again in vain. She pulled the lamp off her head and ran her hands across the plastic case. No batteries. They must have fallen out when she jumped.

Okay, Ana was first priority. She could worry about light after that.

She bent down to the wounded girl and felt her cheeks. They were icy. Too cold? Or just normally cold?

Why hadn't she paid more attention to her first aid course? She felt her way down to Ana's neck. Where on earth was the pulse? Had it stopped, or was Katie just looking in the wrong place?

If only she could see what she was doing.

She had an idea. Ana's headlamp.

Where was it? In her rucksack? Or, if Katie was lucky – and she'd already had enough bad luck to last her for the rest of the day – it was in her jacket pocket.

As Katie reached into Ana's right-hand pocket, Ana moved for the first time. Then she groaned briefly.

Katie felt a great wave of relief flooding over her.

Ana was alive.

Seriously injured, maybe; perhaps incapable of getting out of the crevasse by herself – but she was alive!

Lucky. She had been incredibly lucky.

Now Katie needed to find the torch.

A moment later, she tracked it down. Ana had attached it to her trousers. Relieved, Katie unhooked it and found the little switch. She flicked it on and LED light glowed so brightly that Katie, disconcerted, involuntarily screwed up her eyes.

Moments later, though, she could see clearly.

The first thing she looked at was Ana's injuries, so far as she could see them.

Ana was curled up, her knees pulled up to her chest, her head on one side, almost as if she had been tied up. Her mouth was half open, her eyes weren't completely shut, and it looked as if her eyelashes had frozen solid.

Her skin was a worrying bluey-white colour, as if she were lacking oxygen. Or was it the harsh LED light reflecting off the pale grey ice walls?

Panic was threatening to overwhelm her. David had been right. She had no idea about first aid. She simply wasn't cut out to play the Good Samaritan – even if she'd have given anything to have David's knowledge at that moment. She tried desperately to recall the instructions that David had dinned into her before she had abseiled down, but the only things that came into her head were all the things she could do wrong.

As she had done with Sebastien.

One mistake, and Ana ...

Don't undo her helmet.

Don't move her.

Okay – so what now? Holding her hand wasn't the answer.

Recovery position? But Ana was already on her side.

The fear was rushing so loudly in Katie's ears that she wasn't sure whether she could hear Ana breathing or not.

Katie had an idea. She pulled Ana's right glove off her fingers. Her hand was still swollen and red from the injury that had caused this whole catastrophe in the first place.

No, Katie, you caused it. You and your crazy idea of climbing the mountain.

Katie bent her face down over Ana's to check her breathing once more, when Ana suddenly opened her eyes wide and stared at her.

Katie jumped, shocked. She gasped. 'Ana. You're awake! Does it hurt?'

Was that a nod?

Whatever. Dumb question. Of course it hurt. You could tell that by looking at her.

And then Katie suddenly noticed the white spots around Ana's nose and mouth. She knew what they meant. Symptoms of frostbite. First of all the skin turned white then grey then, finally, black. She remembered Ana's missing toes and what she had said two days ago. 'Today is a good day to die.'

Warmth.

Whatever had she been thinking of? Of course. She had to keep Ana's body warm. With trembling fingers she pulled the first aid kit from her jacket pocket, talking non-stop to Ana as she did so. 'Today is a crappy day to die. Do you hear me, Ana? I haven't got a clue how I'm going to get you out of here, but I'm telling you this: you're not going to die today. I'm not the life-saving type, like David. I'm pig-headed and irresponsible. You know who said that to me? My father. I've no idea what your family's like, but my parents had a child for the same reason they bought their car. Something you had to have. Something to show off about. A status symbol.'

She paused. There must be one of those little square packets with a first aid blanket in it somewhere in the kit.

There it was.

As Katie tried to remove the wrapper with her right hand, she carried on talking non-stop. 'Listen, I'll get you back up to the others. Paul and David are waiting up there. I promise, okay? I failed once. With Sebastien. He was my boyfriend. The only person I've ever known who I'd have died for. The only one. And then I messed up. But you have to trust me, Ana. I won't let you down.'

The longer she talked, the calmer she felt. It was astonishing. She, who so rarely said anything at all, was chatting away like a champion talker. She finally managed to pull the foil blanket out of its wrapper, and she spread it out over Ana.

One thing done.

And then? Katie hadn't got the faintest idea.

'Katie! Katie!'

The voice sounded like the one in the lift. Or was she so far down that all the nuances of speech were swallowed up, and all she could hear was individual sounds which she struggled to turn into her name?

She took a deep breath, stood up, made her hands into a kind of megaphone, and yelled, 'She's alive!'

Alive, she thought.

Sebastien was still alive too. But only in the eyes of Eve, his mother.

Katie dropped back down onto the ground next to Ana and put her arms round her. She sat there leaning against the icy wall, one question alone whizzing around her mind.

How was she going to get Ana out of the crevasse?

Think, Katie.

Just think.

You'll think of something. This is completely different from what happened with Sebastien. You could have fetched help then. Now it's up to you.

But you're not alone. David and Paul are up there.

Paul. She had been wrong about him. So very wrong.

She couldn't stop thinking about the way his voice had sounded when he had told her why he had committed murder.

And even though it horrified her, it was a reason that she could understand.

Instead of mistrusting him, as before, she suddenly realised that she was beginning to feel she could trust him.

Unlike Chris, Benjamin – and Julia.

Katie stared upwards, where the end of the rope was swinging to and fro fifteen feet above her.

Okay, back to Plan B.

The crevasse itself wasn't as narrow as she had initially supposed. It was more like a long corridor seven or eight feet in diameter, which gave her enough space to find a suitable spot to climb up to the rope. Ana, though, wouldn't be able to do it.

A shadow appeared at the edge of the crevasse.

Paul or David? She couldn't tell.

Time was slipping away. She had to come up with a plan.

It seemed absurd, but something inside her seemed to know that she was going to get out of here.

As this thought was passing through her mind, she noticed a brown mark out of the corner of her left eye. Something was behind the ice gully that she had passed on her way down. Something strange in this glacial cave.

Cave?

Only now did she realise that the space she was in continued to her left. Were the voices really coming down from up above? Or could they be coming from the side?

She glanced at Ana, relieved to see her cheeks looking slightly pinker. Her fingers were still freezing cold, but Katie's first aid seemed to have had an effect.

She looked at the brown mark again.

Katie half stood up and crept towards the darkness on her left.

The mark was getting bigger, and there was something paler on its right-hand edge. There was something peculiar about this. It wasn't the bright, glittering colour of snow or ice; it was matt, and reminded her of marble.

She went even closer, and couldn't believe her eyes.

The thing was a shoe, and in it was a foot.

It took a while for Katie to realise what it was. She still didn't feel able to distinguish between this absurd reality and a ghastly nightmare. But as she finally found the courage to lean forwards, her fears became reality in the light of her headlamp.

Heavy brown shoes with crampons. The same kind of ancient crampons that she had discovered months ago at the bottom of Mirror Lake.

Fabric.

Trousers that might once have been blue. And, several yards above the head, an orange rucksack.

Katie crept slightly further forwards in order to get a better view of the body.

She could hear someone calling again. Paul? David?

It didn't matter who. For the first time in her life, she was looking at a dead body. The dead body of someone who looked as if they were asleep beneath the ice. All she had to do was touch him, and he would wake up.

She could tell from both the rucksack and the clothes that it wasn't the body of a recent mountaineer. A thought started to form in her mind, but then she heard Ana groaning again.

She crept back and took Ana's right hand in hers.

'I'm here, Ana.'

Ana murmured something that Katie couldn't make out.

'Can you talk louder, Ana?'

'My ... leg ... broken.'

And then the voice again from up above. 'Katie? What's going on? Answer me, please!'

She turned her hands into a megaphone again. 'Ana's broken her leg,' she yelled back. 'But she's talking.'

She crawled back again.

The dead body in the icy cave.

It was lying on its back or, rather, strangely tilted to one side, its face turned away from her.

She looked closely at the figure. She could make out several layers of clothes worn on top of one another. They were hanging from the emaciated body as if they were much too big, in the places where they hadn't already completely fallen apart and turned to shreds.

The body itself was astonishingly well preserved. Or maybe it wasn't so astonishing. There were loads of people who wanted to be frozen after their deaths, to preserve their bodies for all eternity. Katie had never seen the point of it. Why bother preserving the outer shell once the human inside was long gone?

The beam from her headlamp showed up tufts of hair. They were standing out unnaturally from the scalp, and some were so long that they came down below the neck. The skin beneath them was shining through like leather – no, like parchment. Folded, creased, coarse. The caricature of a face that had once been full of life.

Following some kind of inner compulsion – or maybe it was just perverse curiosity – Katie stretched out her hand to touch the neck, then instantly recoiled. What if the mummified skin turned to dust as soon as a living person touched it?

She shook her head. This here was reality, not some film or fantasy novel. And yet – she didn't dare. As if there were some invisible barrier between the dead person and her. The barrier between life and death, in which Sebastien was still hovering; the reason why she had never brought herself to visit him again.

Again she heard Ana groaning, and again she crawled back to comfort her. But she couldn't take her eyes off the body. She took in every detail. And then she saw it.

A rope.

It was wrapped round the ice mummy's waist.

Without thinking about it, Katie suddenly found herself touching the dead body. Her fingers reached for the rope and felt their way along it. Right: it was knotted at the front and ... oh God, she could feel the bones under the thin covering of flesh – it felt as if she were touching a skeleton.

Come on, Katie. You can do it.

Katie crawled to the corpse's feet.

The end of the rope had to be somewhere. Yes, there it was. It went between the body's legs.

Katie pulled with all her might and jumped back in a panic as the corpse shifted and tipped forwards so that it was lying on its stomach.

For a moment, she felt sick. It felt as if she were breathing in the scent of death.

Another groan from Ana.

She quickly ran her hands along the rope. Freeing it from its covering of snow took an enormous amount of energy.

How long was it?

Long enough.

'Katie?' The voices from above.

Now all she had to do was undo the knot by the mummified corpse's stomach.

She gritted her teeth and felt her way forwards.

Then she saw something impossible. It couldn't be true. Mustn't be true.

The shock jolted her entire body, splitting her brain in half and simply switching off one part of it.

Pull yourself together, Katie, she told herself. Concentrate on the knot. That's all that matters now.

Katie's fingers, freezing cold and trembling with agitation, tried to loosen the rope. To no avail.

She needed a knife.

Or something else sharp.

She felt sick again. No, she couldn't do it. It was impossible.

She had to.

She bent down over the dead body, shut her eyes, and for seconds everything swam before her.

Katie would have thought this a miracle if she had believed in such things. Maybe luck itself was a miracle.

At any rate, she quickly cut through the length of rope that the dead body had been tied to. Then she climbed the fifteen or so feet that separated her from her own rope. With her left hand, she hung tightly on to the ice-pick that she had driven hard into the wall, and with her right hand she knotted the two ropes together. She had felt a flicker of hope ever since she had discovered the rope and, when she dropped back down to land beside Ana, she could feel that flicker gaining strength.

She secured Ana to the best of her ability, running the rope through the carabiner on her harness. Now Paul and David could hoist Ana up.

If – and this was the big question, her worst fear – the rope held.

The rope had cost Sebastien his life, even if his heart was still beating. But he was never going to wake up again. Sebastien was never going to come out of his coma. He was going to lie there for ever. That was worse than dying – wasn't it?

'Katie? What are you doing?'

'Ready!' she yelled back.

Moments later, she realised that she had been wrong. The worst thing wasn't worrying about whether the rope would hold.

The worst thing was Ana's screams of pain as Paul and David started to pull her up little by little all the way from the ground to the top.

Katie didn't have much time left. She crawled past the corpse without looking at it again, and reached for the rucksack. It was made of rough fabric. A relic from the stone age of mountaineering. It weighed a ton.

Katie's hands felt for the zip. It stuck as she tugged at it, and then the decaying fabric ripped apart. Without thinking, she rummaged around in the contents. Underwear, a plastic bag containing a toothbrush and toothpaste, a canteen, a pullover, striped jogging pants with stirrups. Nothing else.

Her hands searched in the top compartment and felt something metallic. A pocket knife, a small purse. She unzipped it. All sorts of coins. Then she saw the money bag. It was identical to the one that Benjamin had found in the swamp.

'Katie?'

She looked up.

'Ana's safe. She's made it!'

Katie heard the words, but she didn't immediately take them in. For the past few moments, she had almost completely blanked out Ana and the others.

'I'll let the rope down again. Your turn now.'

'Okay.'

Katie stared at the dark crack that separated her from the world up there. Before long, darkness would have fallen across the glacier. They had to hurry. She quickly stuffed the money bag into the inside pocket of her jacket.

Now there was only one thing left to do. She went back to

the place where Ana had been lying, and reached for the first aid blanket. The dead body had been there thirty years, and had known no peace.

Katie carefully laid the foil blanket over him.

'I'll find out what happened to you,' Katie whispered. 'I'll make sure I do – I promise.'

'Are you ready?' she heard the voice from above.

'Nearly!'

She stood up, reached for the rope, and secured it to her harness.

Then she took one last look at the grave in the icy cave. A last ray of sunshine suddenly caught the blanket, making it shine.

Then she yelled, 'What are you waiting for? I'm ready!'

And then she shut her eyes and prayed that the rope that had spent thirty years deep in the glacier with a corpse attached to it would hold for a second time.

CHAPTER 29

Julia ran.

Ana's screams as she was pulled over the sharp edge of the crevasse were still ringing in her ears.

Julia ran towards the setting sun, a fiery red ball hovering just a couple of inches above the horizon.

She ran as fast as she could, up the mountain and towards the cabin.

Katie had said practically nothing – as if she were in shock, so it had almost seemed to Julia. She had fended off every question, every touch, as though afraid of closeness. But the expression on her face when she saw Julia and realised that her friend had come back told Julia everything she needed to know. From that moment, she had stopped regretting her decision to split up from Chris and Benjamin and make her way back across the glacier on her own.

She, Benjamin and Chris were around a third of the way across the glacier when Julia had suddenly stopped.

'What's the matter?' Chris had asked.

'No. I can't do it. It's wrong.'

'What's wrong?'

'We can't just leave the four of them up there.'

'So what's your plan?'

'I don't know.'

'Come on, guys. In any case it's too late to turn back now,' Benjamin had groaned. 'We can't help them anyway.'

Chris and Julia had both ignored him.

'So.' Chris's voice had taken on the sarcastic undertone that Julia hated so much. 'Is this really just about Ana?'

'Of course it is.'

'And not about David?'

'It's nothing to do with David. But Ana – she could die up there.'

'And you're going to change that? How? Have you been hiding a medical degree from us?'

Benjamin shifted from one foot to the other. 'Come on, Chris, let her go back if that's what she wants.'

'Shut up, Benjamin,' Chris muttered.

'How often am I supposed to shut up? Look, I'm the only one around here facing the facts. Ana's as dead as a doornail, that's for sure.'

Chris ignored him. He was staring at Julia with his icy grey eyes. 'Julia,' he said beseechingly. 'We're carrying on. You said so yourself. Maybe we can summon help from the cabin.'

'No.' It was like an inner compulsion for Julia. With trembling hands, she had undone the safety rope from her harness. 'There's no reception in the cabin, you know that as well as I do.' She had shaken her head. 'I have to go back.'

'Why?' Chris had yelled. 'Why now?'

Julia couldn't explain. Couldn't tell him that she now knew what the whimpering noise coming up from the crevasse reminded her of.

'All right then, go!' Chris's arm had shot forwards. 'You know what this means? You've got to go back across the glacier on your own. That makes you just as suicidal as the other three.'

'I know.'

'Hey, Julia.' Benjamin had evidently realised that she was serious. 'Just forget it. Chris is right – it's too dangerous.'

'You're risking your life.' Chris had grabbed her shoulder.

Julia had pulled away. 'I can't just abandon her. It's wrong.'

She had turned round. And as she had searched for their footprints in the white blanket of ice, she had heard Chris yelling. But the whimpering sound in her ears had been louder. It was the same whimpering that Julia had heard in her dreams the night before last.

Strangely enough, Julia hadn't been afraid of making her way back across the glacier on her own. She hadn't been worried for a single second about falling into one of the countless cracks that ranged across the glacier. Every now and then she spotted one of Ana's marks, but most of the time she could follow the trail of their footprints.

It almost seemed as if the cracks in the ice had closed up in front of her, as if a guardian angel were leading her across the icy wasteland.

Her father?

She suddenly remembered that evening at the lake when Katie had mentioned her plan for the first time. She had thought she had seen her father then. She had thought he was coming to fetch her, but maybe he had just been trying to protect her?

Some people win the lottery and others struggle to survive. Those are the rules. Or, rather, there are no rules for happiness or unhappiness. 'Shit happens' is the nearest thing to a rule.

Had she just been lucky? She didn't know. At any rate, she had reached the others just as Paul and David were pulling the injured Ana over the edge of the crevasse.

Now they were all making their way back.

David, Paul and Katie, who were carrying Ana in a makeshift stretcher cobbled together out of spare items of clothing, had presumably reached the bottom of the glacier by now.

Julia had hurried on ahead to fetch Chris and Benjamin from the cabin so they could relieve Paul and David, who were more or less exhausted by the effort of carrying Ana. Every movement had made Ana cry out. It was exactly the sound that Julia had heard in her dream.

Julia ran.

Her feet seemed to find their own way across the boulder-strewn wilderness that led up to the cabin. The sun had sunk so low that the horizon now looked like a narrow slit; the very last rays of sunlight were just managing to make their way through onto this side of the mountain. Not much longer before the slit would close up completely.

Up there, though, was the cabin. That's where they would be celebrating tonight. Not because they'd made it to the top of the Ghost – God, that was an eternity ago, and seemed completely irrelevant to Julia – but because they had managed to get back down safely.

As Julia reached the cabin, something felt odd. She had expected to see smoke rising from the chimney; she had hoped that Chris would be standing on the verandah keeping watch for her.

Love is strange, she thought, hearing herself gasp with exertion. You know, really, that it's over, but you can't bring yourself to let go. You're the one who clings to him; every time he hurts you, you try to find some excuse for him. And you do always find one. Always.

Ever since she had turned back, she had hoped that Chris would follow her. That he would realise he was doing the wrong thing. She had imagined him standing there in front of her, his face finally reflecting his true nature.

She would only have to look at him briefly and she would feel the same sense of calm that she sometimes felt at night, safe in his arms after they had slept together.

But as Julia pushed the door handle, she already knew what to expect.

Cold. Darkness.

Icy silence.

Nobody had waited for them.

Just the wind sweeping around the cabin.

Julia stared, immobile, through the opposite windows, where the crack of horizon finally closed up.

Chris had deserted her. Had deserted all of them.

Her eyes filled with tears. She was completely exhausted and felt more helpless than she had ever felt in her life.

Then, through the half darkness, she saw something on the table. A note!

She flew towards it.

It was too dark to read it. Julia fetched the matches from the stove and struck one.

But all it said, in capital letters, was:

WE SURVIVED!

Julia couldn't fool herself any longer. It sounded like mockery.

CHAPTER 30

'*WE SURVIVED!*' Katie was fuming. 'They have to be joking, don't they? It must have been Benjamin. What an idiot! I swear to God, when I next see him I'll take his camera and smash it into a thousand pieces.' She kicked the wall for the hundredth time. 'We needed their help. We really needed their help. And as for your wonder-boy Chris ...' Katie turned to Julia. 'Can't you see what an asshole he is? He completely fooled you with his macho stuff. Don't you get it, Julia? Men are just a dangerous sub-species of human life. When it comes to it, they leave you in the lurch.'

'Thanks,' murmured Paul.

'They'll send help,' said Julia.

'Oh yeah? So why didn't they write on the note: *WE ARE GOING TO FETCH HELP*? Are they so brainless that they can't spell *help*?'

David came down the stairs. They all turned to look at him. 'Can't you keep the noise down? Ana's just gone to sleep.'

'How is she?' asked Julia.

David shrugged. He looked worried. 'She's in a lot of pain; ordinary painkillers aren't much help. But at least her temperature has gone down.'

'What about her hand?'

David sighed. 'The antibiotic seems to be having an effect, so far as I can tell. I wish I'd thought to bring more with me.'

'I didn't even remember my toothpaste,' Paul murmured.

They all laughed briefly, then immediately stopped when David said, 'There's no way she's going to get back to the valley in her state. I'm amazed she's survived the ordeal of crossing the glacier and getting back to the cabin. She must be in incredible pain. And I'm still not sure whether she has any internal injuries.'

They all fell silent.

'I suggest I stay up here while the rest of you go back down first thing in the morning and fetch help.' David finally suggested.

Back. The tunnel. Katie shut her eyes for a moment. How on earth was she going to manage that again?

It seemed as if Paul had read her thoughts. 'There's a direct route to Fields.'

Katie stared at him. She knew that too. Only she wouldn't be able to find it without Ana. 'So is it on your brilliant map?' she said sarcastically.

Paul shrugged. 'You still don't get it, do you?'

'Get what?'

'This map is over thirty years old ...'

Katie started to speak, but Paul raised his hand. 'And I found it in Fields. The last original map from the seventies, right?'

Katie remembered the money bag she was carrying inside her jacket. She still hadn't told the others about the mummified body in the crevasse. And she still wasn't sure whether she had come across one of the missing students from long ago.

This would be the moment to tell them, she thought.

But she couldn't. She just couldn't. Not so long as she didn't know what was inside the bag. It might give her some idea why her mother was in the photo.

And maybe also an explanation for why she had found the body in the crevasse. The most horrible, most ghastly thing she had ever seen in her life.

Julia wasn't giving up on the map idea. 'If it's an original map, why's it so full of mistakes?' she asked. 'Is it a fake?'

Paul shook his head. 'If you look at it purely geographically, it seems to be the valley. The same size lake. The mountain landscape. Even the college building is there. Everything fits. And yet ... ' Paul pulled the map out of his back pocket. 'Look. On the back it says when it was printed – 1972. But half of it is missing. And the names ... '

'What about the names?'

'They've all got different names now. The Ghost for example. On the map, it's called Blue Mind, and the ones next to it are White Soul and Black Spirit. And the lake isn't called Mirror Lake, but Solomon Lake. And the college is called Solomon College. Why would anyone change the names of an entire landscape?'

The candle flickered as if a sudden draught were blowing through the room, and Katie shivered. It was a mystery, but they would have to wait to solve it. The only thing that she should focus on now was that the route to Fields was shown on the map. All that mattered was getting Ana to hospital.

'I'll set out first thing tomorrow with Paul. Julia and David, you stay with Ana until help arrives.'

Katie stood up and moved towards the door. As she opened it, she stared, transfixed, into the night. Above her was the most incredible night sky she had ever seen in her life.

It was black and silken, and in the light of the stars she was overwhelmed with such a sense of longing that her heart tightened painfully.

She missed Sebastien.

She missed him so much.

But she couldn't talk about it. She'd never tried. Not even with the psychologist, Mr Lebkowski. What could she have said?

Yes, she blamed herself. Not for the reasons that all the tabloids had given. They had pounced like hyenas on the fact that the son of the French ambassador had fallen in such spectacular fashion while his girlfriend, the beautiful and gifted daughter of that glitzy politician in Foreign Affairs, hadn't even thought of fetching help.

No. She had another reason to blame herself. She had heard the crash – the impact of something hitting the bridge pier – but she hadn't realised that it was anything to do with Sebastien. She hadn't realised even when all she heard was silence.

She had done what she was still doing. She had gone to look for Sebastien. She still hadn't found him.

The boy who was lying there in the bed in the expensive private clinic with all the tubes attached to him wasn't Sebastien. It was just his shell. His mother was alone in saying that he was alive so long as his heart was still beating.

But it was a lie.

Sebastien's spirit had long since fled somewhere else. Maybe it was in that shooting star flashing through the sky up there. It would be nice to believe that, but Katie couldn't quite manage it. She simply wasn't the type for that sort of stuff.

She suddenly felt a hand on her shoulder. She could sense it was Paul's.

'What's the matter with you, Katie?' he asked.

'Nothing.'

'It was just a kiss. Nothing more.'

'But you killed someone.'

'Is that why you're avoiding me?'

'Yes. I don't want to have anything to do with a murderer.'

She could feel him stiffen.

And yet he knew as well as she did that it wasn't quite so straightforward.

Not any more.

But letting Paul in ... that was completely impossible.

She had visited Sebastien three times, and each time he had stared at her with those glassy eyes. Since then, they had followed her everywhere. And she knew what it meant. He may have let go of life. But she hadn't.

He still held her captive, with his eyes and with his last words. When she had reached him at the bottom of the bridge pier, he had still been conscious, almost as if he had been waiting for her. And his last words had been, 'Don't leave me.'

A cold gust of wind blew through Katie's hair. When she turned round, Paul had vanished.

*

Katie's sleep was interrupted by a sound that was familiar but disconcerting. Something was not quite right. Maybe she was still trapped in some absurd dream, but it sounded as if a helicopter were approaching. There had always been helicopters circling above her parents' penthouse in Washington. More helicopters than birds, she and Sebastien had always joked. At any rate, Katie had been under better surveillance during her childhood than she would have been in a high-security prison.

Under surveillance, she thought. Not protected.

The tatty mattress she was lying on; the noises around her ... no, she was neither in her room in DC nor in her bed in Grace College. When she opened her eyes Katie felt, strangely, nothing but relief.

Relief, even though she had spent the night aware of every aching bone in her body.

The dazzling ray of sunlight hit her like a laser beam. Suddenly wide awake, she sat up and looked around. Julia's sleeping bag next to her was empty, and Paul's sleeping bag had completely disappeared.

She could hear excited voices from downstairs. Quick footsteps. Clattering. Chairs being scraped aside. A door shutting. Someone calling something.

And the whirring of the helicopter was becoming louder and louder. What time was it?

Too late.

Damn it. They had wanted to make an early start for Fields. Paul had promised to wake her as soon as the sun rose. And now the sun had risen. With a vengeance.

Katie struggled out of her sleeping bag and ran downstairs

in her t-shirt. The first thing she saw was an empty room. The door was open and Katie ran outside barefoot, where she found David and Julia. They were leaping up and down, shouting and waving. Then they flung their arms round one another.

That was when Katie saw the helicopter flying over the cabin, heading towards her. It flew low above their heads before landing slightly away from them on a patch of scree near the cabin.

It was all so overwhelming that Katie, too, could only join in. 'Here! We're here!'

As if the pilot hadn't already seen them. Three crazy people in their underwear, leaping around like mad.

'I knew it. Chris and Benjamin didn't abandon us!' Julia was beaming. 'Look – they sent a helicopter.'

Katie shook her head. Julia was at it again: forgiving Chris for everything. But so what? That didn't matter right now. A weight was lifted from her shoulders, too. She had persuaded the others to join in the expedition, and it had taken her to the limit in every possible way. But she had also managed to get them all back down the mountain. Alive.

She glanced across at the Ghost. Its white summit was gleaming in the sun. Her gaze shifted to the steep rocky ridge that they had climbed up yesterday.

'We did it, guys!' She tried to outdo the noise of the helicopter – and failed. All she could see was David's broad grin and Julia, who was blocking her ears while shrugging her shoulders in puzzlement.

'WE DID IT!'

Katie was screaming it out now. She was telling herself,

not the world, nor even her friends – even though she had now added another name to her friends list. David Freeman. His name was right under Julia's.

And there was another name that might perhaps make it onto her list in the future.

Paul Forster.

She looked around for him, but couldn't see him anywhere.

'Where's Paul?' she bellowed into David's ear.

She could tell from his face that he had heard her.

'Gone!' he yelled back.

'Gone?'

David nodded.

'When?'

'Don't know. He'd already gone when Julia woke up.'

He'd gone without Katie? Just like that?

'Why didn't you wake me?' she yelled.

The noise of the helicopter was abating now that the pilot had switched off the rotor blades.

David shrugged. 'Maybe he went down first thing. Maybe he was the one who told the Mounties. I wouldn't put it past him. He's done his own thing from start to finish. But that doesn't matter any more. God, what a relief to have Ana off our hands.'

'How did she cope overnight?'

David shook his head. 'Let's just say she coped.' He suddenly looked dumbfounded and, moments later, Katie's mouth dropped open too. The helicopter door opened and it wasn't Paul waving at them but Benjamin, pointing his camera at them.

287

'One day,' David growled, 'I'm going to kill him and that stupid camera.'

'If I don't do it first,' Katie replied.

A second face appeared behind Benjamin.

'Chris.' Julia's voice cracked. 'It's Chris!'

Katie watched as her two new-found friends ran off in their separate directions. Her flatmate ran towards Chris and flung her arms around him, and David disappeared into the cabin.

So much for friends, she thought.

At the end of the day, you're on your own.

Chris had lit the fire in the stove. They were sitting around the table in the cabin, waiting for the helicopter to return. It was on the way to the hospital at the moment. David had insisted on accompanying Ana. 'If I start something, I need to finish it,' he had said. Katie, though, suspected that he just didn't want to be in the same room as Chris.

'The helicopter ought to have been back ages ago, oughtn't it?' Benjamin was gyrating around on a chair, trying to capture every detail on film. 'Your faces are a picture,' he said. 'Life has left its mark on you, have you noticed that? Good luck and bad. Life and death.'

'Just ignore him,' Katie sighed. 'He's like a performing monkey.'

'Don't you remember? Three days ago, we were sitting around this table too. But everything looked completely different.' Chris was in the best possible spirits. He had put his arm round Julia, who seemed simply to be relieved that he wasn't the asshole that Katie had said he was.

Katie wasn't so sure. Julia might choose to forget the way that Ben and Chris behaved on the glacier. She wouldn't, though.

'Three days ago, we at least had some beer,' Benjamin called.

'It all worked out in the end,' said Chris. He laughed. 'While you were pulling Ana out of the crevasse, we were making sure she could get to hospital as quickly as possible. That's what I call team work.'

Benjamin nodded. 'Chris is right. It was clear right from the outset who was the director and who was up for the action scenes.' He grinned round at them.

'Since when has being the director meant just running off?' Katie demanded. 'Ana could be dead if we were all as egotistical as you. She wouldn't have survived the night in the crevasse.'

'To hell with your ifs and buts,' retorted Chris. 'Fact is, we went down to Fields to get help. So much for us leaving you in the lurch.'

Katie looked up. 'So how *did* you manage to do it so quickly? You didn't know the way.'

'We should have had Chris as leader all along,' Benjamin said. 'He knew exactly which way to go. And he didn't need a map. I've never trusted that Paul. He's a fake, just like his dad.'

Katie stared at Chris. The faintest trace of a smile was playing around the corners of his mouth. Katie knew arrogance and superiority when she saw it.

'Oh yeah?' She was struggling to retain her composure. 'So why didn't you say at the start that you knew your way around up here?'

'Never heard of secrets?' replied Chris. But he was looking at Julia, not Katie.

He's no good for her, Katie thought. I'll prove it to her one day.

'You know what drives me crazy?' Benjamin ran his fingers through his hair. 'It was all for nothing. We put our asses on the line for nothing. We didn't find anything up there that gave us any clues about the missing students. Not a thing.'

'Apart from the two photos,' Julia said thoughtfully. She suddenly leapt to her feet. 'Have you guys ever thought that things might be secret for a reason?'

'What do you mean?' asked Benjamin.

'Greek mythology. Pandora's box.'

'Hey, put your inner professor away.'

'Pandora's box,' Katie repeated. 'When it's opened, then ...'

'... Then all the crap of mankind comes flying out,' Chris interrupted.

Now, Katie thought. This is my moment. Now I'm going to tell them about the boy in the glacier.

But before she could say a word, they could hear the helicopter returning.

'So why did you write that note?' asked Julia.

'What note?' Chris frowned.

'You know – *WE SURVIVED*. The note that was on the table in the cabin.'

Chris and Benjamin stared at Julia.

'We didn't write a note.'

'Come on, Benjamin, that's not funny.'

But Benjamin's face was serious. 'Let me see it.'

Julia shook her head. 'I think Paul put it in his pocket,' she said helplessly.

Chris shrugged. 'Whatever,' he said. 'Whoever wrote that note, it wasn't us. We didn't come back to the cabin. We went straight down to Fields.'

CHAPTER 31

Lying in the bath, Katie felt as if she had been reborn. Partly because she could finally wash off the filth of the past few days until only the bruises remained. Katie was so bruised that she feared the security guys would report her to the Ministry of Health with some unknown illness.

The crime – so the Dean had called it – of climbing the Ghost had been an experience that Katie would never forget.

She had returned from hell. And after the things that she had experienced there, a simple bath seemed like heaven.

It had been hell, but she had got away from it.

And these were the facts that remained after three frankly endless days.

Number 1: They had reached the top.

Number 2: They were back down.

Number 3: Paul could have been on her list of friends, if

Number 4: he hadn't deserted her.

Number 5: Ana had survived, and was already starting to recover.

Number 6: Unlike the guy in the crevasse.

Number 7: What should she tell the others?

Damn it. Debbie was banging on the bathroom door for the

hundredth time. 'Katie, how long are you planning to stay in there? You'll soon have no skin left, you've been in there so long. I bet you've, like, used up all the soap too.'

Oh no she hadn't. She hadn't even raised a finger to pick up the soap. She had only used the sponge to soak up water which she then squeezed over her face. She could carry on doing that for hours.

'You could try cleaning the hand basin in the loo while you're waiting,' Katie called back. 'It's so full of your hair that your DNA is blocking the plughole.'

'But you've got to see the Dean with the others in an hour.' Nobody could miss the triumphant note in Debbie's voice. 'After all, you ignored the Governor General's visit, you went missing from college for, like, three days and, worst of all, you went up the Ghost without permission. And I'm in this as well, you know? I'm an accessory.'

An accessory? A parasite, more like.

'We can tell the Dean you didn't know anything about it.'

'I *didn't* know anything about it.'

'Blah, blah, blah ...' Katie muttered.

She could just imagine the performance that Debbie would make if she heard what Katie had found in the crevasse.

'So you really didn't find any, like, trace of the missing students?' Debbie called.

'Have you ever wondered what "missing" actually means? It means that there's no trace of them.'

'Oh and by the way, I tried to call you like a thousand times but all I got was your voicemail.'

'I'm starting to think that the college are deliberately

cutting us off from all contact with the outside world,' Katie murmured, squeezing the wet sponge over her face again.

'What?'

'A dead zone,' Katie murmured, submerging herself completely.

As she dried herself, Katie started to sober up. She bent down and pulled out the plug. Exactly the same would happen if she told the Dean everything. She would be opening Pandora's box.

Don't do it, Katie.

Don't do it.

She suddenly remembered the voice in the lift.

Someone will die up there. Do you hear me? Katie? Katie? And it will be your fault, Katie. Your fault, your fault ...

The voice – whoever it might have belonged to – had been wrong. Nobody had died. And Katie had nothing new to feel guilty about.

And yet ... it all added up somehow. She could feel it.

There were too many secrets in this valley, and things happened that nobody could foresee. Not even Robert.

She still hadn't told anyone about the body in the crevasse. She hadn't opened the money bag in her jacket pocket. And one big question kept swirling around in her mind: should she keep it to herself?

Paul.

She still hadn't seen him. He must be avoiding her. None of the others had heard or seen anything of him either.

And yet she was strangely longing to talk to him.

Him, of all people.

She sighed. Why couldn't she just go for some nice, harmless, Canadian ice-hockey-playing guy whose great interest in life was snowboarding down slopes?

You always had to choose. Mr Good Guy or Mr Bad Guy. Having friends or being a loner. Truth or lies.

But the valley wouldn't let you out of its great game. Who had said that?

She remembered.

Ana.

And Ana had been told it by her grandfather, Nanuk Cree.

There was a giant portion of steak and chips in front of Katie, but she doubted whether even that would be enough. She had sought out a seat at the furthest end of the refectory, where she could see the Ghost without attracting the attention of the other students.

Of course, though, Debbie and their other flatmate, Rose, had found her, and Debbie was bombarding her with questions about what the Dean had said.

'Are you being, like, thrown out of college?' she asked, helping herself to one of Katie's chips.

'The way you say it, it sounds as if you're hoping I have been,' said Katie. 'Bad luck, Deb, we just got an official warning. The Governor General's visit was obviously a huge success, and now they're just afraid of getting bad press.'

'That's it?' Debbie sounded truly disappointed.

'You know what it's like here. Batten down the hatches – that's what they do at Grace. How else could they have kept up the rumour about eight students disappearing?'

'They did disappear!'

'All of them?' Katie raised her eyebrows. 'Didn't you say that some of them got back?'

She gave Debbie a penetrating look.

'Me? I didn't say a word.'

'You did. I remember,' said Rose. 'You were the first one to mention the story at all.'

Debbie was reaching out to help herself to another chip when Katie said, 'Debbie, it ought to say on your Facebook profile: untrustworthy.'

'Do you have any idea of the stories I had to come up with to keep your crazy plan secret? Isabel was constantly badgering me about where you'd gone.'

'You don't normally have trouble making up stories.'

'Yeah, and nobody noticed anything until we got the call to say your lives were at risk. All hell broke loose then. Honestly, I thought the Dean was going to put me on the rack to get it out of me.'

Rose frowned and glanced at Katie. Katie could well imagine what had actually happened. Rose and Robert had presumably been the ones who had covered for Katie and the others, while also struggling to stop Debbie from blabbing the whole story.

Katie nodded and Rose smiled briefly. 'I'm just glad that nothing serious happened to Ana,' she said in the soft, gentle voice that suited her so well. 'A broken leg and a hand injury. It seems like a miracle, doesn't it, when you think how far she fell. But she must find it hard that she wasn't at home when it happened.' Her voice dropped.

'What do you mean?'

'Haven't you heard?'

'What are you talking about?'

'Her grandfather died while you were up there.'

'Her grandfather?' Katie stared at Rose. 'Who told you that?'

Four hundred dollars, Ana had said. We still need four hundred dollars for my grandfather's operation.

'David. He's back from the hospital now.'

Debbie was chomping excitedly on her chewing gum. 'And you know what's really weird? Ana's grandfather died at exactly the same moment she fell into the crevasse.'

'Debbie. That's just a rumour.' Rose rolled her eyes. 'You can't possibly know that.'

'Somebody said Ana said so.'

'Oh yeah?' Katie retorted, although her heart was pounding. 'So she looked at her watch when she fell into the crevasse, did she? And that was exactly the same minute that the hospital doctors were recording her grandfather's death?'

'No.' Debbie leaned across, her watery eyes almost exactly the same shade of pale blue as her sickly looking skin. 'She felt it. Get it? She could feel it.' She opened her eyes wide. 'That's what David told Julia, anyway.'

'Felt it?'

'Yes. It was something about a stone circle that had gone in the morning.'

Katie started.

'What kind of stone circle?' Rose ran her hand across her shaven head. 'That's the first I've heard of it.'

Debbie was getting into her stride. 'Okay, listen up. I googled it just now. It's a Native American ritual. You put a stone circle on the ground. The outer circle conjures up the powers of the universe, and the strength within people, and they're, like, connected with the centre, which represents the source of all being.'

'The centre?' Katie repeated uncomprehendingly.

'Yes, they put something in the middle, it might be ... I think David mentioned a feather. Whatever. At any rate, Ana promised her grandfather that she'd climb up to the glacier to, like, carry out this ritual for him. So she went out in the snowstorm in the middle of the night to find stones on the glacier. Unusual stones with, like, unusual colours, but all similar shapes.'

Debbie was prattling on and on, but Katie wasn't listening any more.

My fault, she thought.

Wherever you went on this earth, you couldn't escape from guilt. One false step, and you destroyed a ritual. A ritual you didn't even know about. But how the hell could you have guessed?

Easily.

After all, the stones couldn't have found their way onto the terrace by themselves. And she, Katie, might not believe in it, might reject it as superstition like the altar in her mother's bedroom – but that didn't give her the right to go trampling on it.

'I mean, I'd never put my life at risk for my grandfather.' Katie became aware of Debbie's voice again. 'And he's not even, like, seventy. But Ana's grandfather was more than ninety! He'd have croaked anyway. With or without magic.'

'Debbie. You're bound to get extra credits for empathy this term,' sighed Rose.

Debbie changed the subject. 'Where's Paul gone, anyway? Are you sure he didn't stay up there?' She laughed.

'Hasn't he turned up yet?' Katie asked.

'Well, do you see him anywhere?'

Katie jumped up and pushed her chair aside.

'Katie, where are you going?' Rose asked in surprise.

Debbie called after her, 'Can I have your chips?'

Katie didn't see anyone en route to the bungalows that the lecturers and professors lived in.

She knew now what the problem was.

Not the actual contents of the secrets.

It was the fact that they *were* secrets, had been shrouded in silence, that made them so dangerous.

If Ana had talked about it, if she had told Katie why she had gone out into the snowstorm, then she would have understood the significance of the stone circle. She might still have thought it was all a bit like voodoo, but that was fine; she didn't have a problem with that. After all, Sebastien had always come up with some kind of pre-jump resolution.

He would turn ascetic. He'd stop drinking and smoking. *Everything but sex,* he had once called to her before jumping.

Another time he had resolved to tell his father at long last that he knew about his affair with the embassy secretary.

And on the day that the rope had snapped, he had shouted, 'Today's resolution, Katie: I will love you for ever!'

The white-painted bungalows were red in the low-lying evening sun.

She had no idea which was Mr Forster's, but then she saw the huge dog Ike coming towards her. Following him was Mr Brandon, the Philosophy professor.

Ike stopped and looked at her with his watery eyes as Mr Brandon said, 'Katie West, do you realise how lucky you were up there?'

Katie took a deep breath.

Silence wasn't really an option. It couldn't get you through the whole of your life. But that didn't mean that you had to tell everybody everything.

'Lucky?' she said. 'I wasn't lucky. We survived because we didn't give up.'

Mr Brandon sighed. 'How did I know that you were going to say that?'

'Maybe because you agree with me, Mr Brandon?'

Katie pushed Ike aside and walked on.

After a few yards she turned round. 'Could you tell me where the Forsters live?'

'Last bungalow on the left.'

Katie held the snake's-head door-knocker and banged it three times against the wooden door.

Mr Forster opened the door. 'Miss West? I wasn't expecting you.'

'I'd like to talk to Paul.'

He looked at her, evidently puzzled.

'Who?'

'Paul. Isn't he here?'

'I have no idea what you're talking about.'

Maybe Mr Forster was one of those parents who prefer to

hide their wayward children, rather than admitting that they've failed.

And I kissed him, Katie was tempted to say, sensing that this would make him furious. Instead, she said, 'Paul. He was with us on the Ghost. We were going to come back down from the cabin together, but when I woke up in the morning, he'd gone.'

'What are you talking about? Why are you telling me all this?'

'Why? Because I think you know where he is.'

Mr Forster was becoming impatient and increasingly nervous.

'Who the hell are you talking about?'

'Paul. Your son!'

'My son?'

At last. He was beginning to get it. Some lecturers might be great luminaries in their field, but they were complete idiots when it came to real life.

'There's a problem here,' said Mr Forster.

'What's that?'

'I don't have a son called Paul.'

EPILOGUE

It was one of the last warm days in September, and they were sitting on the refectory balcony, enjoying the sunshine.

Julia's brother Robert was leaning against the balustrade, staring out across the lake. There was a regatta that afternoon, and the white sails seemed to fly across Mirror Lake in the glimmering air.

Like white envelopes falling from heaven, Katie thought. She sighed.

She had heard nothing from Paul. None of them had. That in itself, she could cope with. But what had really shocked all of them, even Benjamin, was the fact that Paul had never been registered at the college. Nobody knew him, and he wasn't on any of Benjamin's video recordings.

Benjamin, wearing only purple shorts, was sitting on a chair with his legs on the table. He was repeatedly rewinding and fast-forwarding. 'I don't get it,' he groaned. 'I'm absolutely certain he has to be on here somewhere. I was filming non-stop.'

'Maybe he was a ghost,' Chris commented. He was hammering away at his laptop. 'What do you reckon, honey?'

Katie couldn't see Julia's eyes behind her sunglasses, but one thing was for sure: Paul hadn't been a ghost. She could

302

remember all too clearly the kiss and what he'd said. 'I wanted to do that the first time I ever set eyes on you.'

'Who actually started the rumour that he was Forster's son?' Julia murmured sleepily.

They were all silent for a while before Rose said, 'It was you, Debbie, wasn't it?'

'No it wasn't!'

'Well, I definitely remember you talking about Forster's son.'

'He said so himself!'

'Does it matter?' asked David. 'It's all over anyway.'

'No it isn't.' Katie started as Robert suddenly came over to her. 'Is it, Katie? It isn't over.'

They all pricked up their ears, as they always did when Robert made one of his odd remarks.

'What are you talking about, Rob?' David asked. Apart from Julia and Rose, he was the only one who bothered with Robert.

'Ask Katie.'

'Ask Katie?' She knew she sounded hysterical. She still hadn't said anything about the boy up in the glacier cave. It was too risky. The college had already had to shut in the seventies because of the disaster. Katie's story would only dredge up the college's past again. Along with her own.

'So, Katie.' Benjamin jumped up and pointed his camera at her. 'What should we be asking you? This would make a brilliant ending to my documentary about you.'

'I don't need a documentary about me.'

'Too late.' Benjamin produced a DVD from his back pocket.

'What's that?'

'A DVD.'

'I can see that. But what of?'

'You.'

'Me?'

'Yes.'

Chris grabbed the DVD and put it into the laptop.

Seconds later, a title image appeared. Katie. Katie hanging from the steep face behind Solomon Cliff.

'Wow!'

'That's so cool! You're not even secured!'

'When did you film that?'

Katie couldn't make out the individual voices. She could have killed Benjamin. 'You filmed me? It was you that morning? You caused the rockfall?'

Benjamin shrugged. 'Sorry babe. I didn't mean to.' He winked at her. 'I still haven't got a really killer ending. I mean, it's a bit tame. After all, I wasn't there when you pulled Ana out of the crevasse.'

Something happened in Katie's brain. It was like an explosion of memories. The voice in the lift. The pictures in the cave. Her name carved into the rocks.

'You want a killer ending?' she yelled. 'A real killer ending? Well, here's a killer ending for you. There's someone in the glacier cave who didn't survive the trip up the Ghost.'

Too late. She had said it. She had opened Pandora's box.

'And you're only telling us now?' asked David, turning as white as a sheet.

Katie looked at him. 'Yes, I'm only telling you now.'

Chris's nonchalance suddenly vanished. 'Katie, we have to go back up there!'

'I don't think I want to.'

Julia, too, was as if transformed. She had taken off her sunglasses, and her eyes were wide. 'But that's why we went up the Ghost in the first place,' she exclaimed in despair. 'To look for clues. The names on the memorial stone. They have to mean something.'

'They're the names of the missing students. And we've obviously, like, found one of them.' Debbie jumped up. ' It's the coolest thing ever. This really is a story for the *Grace Chronicle*. I must go straight to the computer department and put it on Twitter.'

'No!' Katie replied firmly. 'Not a word. Don't say anything to anyone. Especially you, Debbie.'

'I'm not having you tell me what goes in the *Chronicle*.'

'Maybe not,' said Katie, 'but you've got no proof. Nothing. Bear in mind our star director started shitting himself as soon as he took one look into the crevasse.'

'But the Dean! We'll need to report it.'

Chris flared up. 'Do you really think he's going to do anything, seeing that the Governor General is going to give Grace an "excellent" for next year?'

'Have you spared a thought for their family? How dreadful for them to have spent all this time not knowing. That isn't right. We really must report it.'

'Believe me,' Katie replied, 'if the parents of the boy up there are still alive, they won't want to know how their son died. You see ... that guy didn't die because he fell into the glacier and didn't have any friends to pull him back out.'

Chris held up his hands. 'Okay. I know, I'm an asshole. A villain for saving my own skin. But ... '

'Let Katie finish,' Julia said.

'The boy up there,' Katie leaned forwards, 'was murdered.'

There was an icy silence.

The sound of laughter and applause floated up from the lakeside to the balcony. A white sail cut across the blue sky.

'Murdered?' Julia whispered, glancing at Robert. Katie would have loved to have known what that look meant.

'So how do you know?' asked Chris.

Katie took a deep breath. 'There was an ice-pick in his back. Or, to be more precise, between his shoulder blades. I had to pull it out so I could cut the rope.'

The silence was almost unbearable.

'We can't not tell anyone,' David finally said. 'Not if we're talking about a murder.' He looked sharply at Katie. 'You weren't going to tell us, were you? What made you change your mind?'

'Because I want to know what really happened up there. And because the police will close the case as quickly as anything.'

'What makes you think that?'

'Because that's what they did thirty years ago. Eight students vanished? That's a lie. Just like the stone in the clearing by the boat house.'

'How do you know?'

'Believe me, I just know.'

'So what do you suggest we do?' asked Julia. Katie could tell from her expression that they were thinking the same.

'Collect evidence. We need to collect whatever evidence we can find.'

'Evidence?' asked Chris. 'And how are you proposing to do that?'

'We already have a fair bit. The polaroid photo that Benjamin found in the cabin. And the photo of the girl that we found in the swamp. Have you got the photos with you, Ben?'

'You bet. I'm guarding them with my life.' Benjamin pulled an envelope out of his pocket and laid the photos on the table in front of them. Debbie's fat fingers immediately reached for the photo from the cabin.

'You can't see anything at all in this one,' she whined.

Katie didn't agree. If you knew the people in the picture, you could recognise them perfectly well. Mi Su – her mother – was third from the right, standing next to a girl with long blonde hair. But which one was the boy she'd found in the crevasse? 'I found something else,' she said slowly. 'Down in the crevasse. In the dead boy's rucksack. I haven't opened it yet.'

Katie took out the tattered money bag, unzipped it, and pulled out the contents.

An American passport.

She opened it and stared at the photo.

It was like travelling back in time. The photo of a young man staring earnestly at the camera. Passport photos might not be photographic masterpieces, but his clothes, his shoulder-length hair and his chilled-out expression told them that it had been taken decades ago.

Then she saw the name.

Katie couldn't breathe. Everything started to swirl around her.

'Katie, what's the matter?'

She shook her head and pushed the passport away.

Her head was pounding.

'What's going on?' she heard Julia asking. 'I just don't get anything any more.'

'Hey, what's up? Let me have a look!' Benjamin jumped off his chair and grabbed the passport. 'Oh my God. I think I'm in the wrong film. Paul Forster. This passport belongs to Paul Forster.'